Watch for Me
by Moonlight

A Midnight Twins Novel

JACQUELYN MITCHARD

raz**O**r
bill

An Imprint of Penguin Group (USA) Inc.

Watch for Me by Moonlight

RAZORBILL
Published by the Penguin Group
Penguin Young Readers Group
345 Hudson Street, New York, New York 10014, U.S.A.
Penguin Group (USA) Inc., 375 Hudson Street, New York, New York 10014, U.S.A.
Penguin Group (Canada), 90 Eglinton Avenue East, Suite 700, Toronto, Ontario, Canada M4P 2Y3
(a division of Pearson Penguin Canada Inc.)
Penguin Books Ltd, 80 Strand, London WC2R 0RL, England
Penguin Ireland, 25 St Stephen's Green, Dublin 2, Ireland (a division of Penguin Books Ltd)
Penguin Group (Australia), 250 Camberwell Road, Camberwell, Victoria 3124, Australia
(a division of Pearson Australia Group Pty Ltd)
Penguin Books India Pvt Ltd, 11 Community Centre, Panchsheel Park, New Delhi – 110 017, India
Penguin Group (NZ), 67 Apollo Drive, Mairangi Bay, Auckland 1311, New Zealand
(a division of Pearson New Zealand Ltd)
Penguin Books (South Africa) (Pty) Ltd, 24 Sturdee Avenue, Rosebank, Johannesburg 2196, South Africa
Penguin Books Ltd, Registered Offices: 80 Strand, London WC2R 0RL, England

For Yvette, Marta, and Aunt Anna

THE LAST SWEET TIME

THE LAST SWEET TIME

"You need to listen, Drew. My house is full of strangers," Mallory Brynn told her boyfriend, Drew Vaughn, who was hoping for a few minutes to kiss his girl instead of a nice stressful little chat. He thought, you know, the world might be better off if a girl never again said the words: "We have to talk." Nothing ever came of it but more talk and far less making out. The thing to do was to nip it in the bud.

"I know," Drew said, pulling Mallory closer. "It must stink."

But she wasn't having any.

"Drew listen! Everywhere I turn I bump into somebody else. Grandma on Saturday and Monday, not that she's a stranger, but you can't act like yourself around her. You have to be nicer. Big Carla on Fridays and Wednesdays. Sasha two mornings a week and . . . and now Luna! Luna is going to put me over the edge."

"Luna . . . Luna Verdgris? She's a semi-nice person, Brynn.

Aren't you being kind of judgmental?" Drew knew that Mallory, who had only recently given up wearing Drew's old T-shirts as ordinary clothing and started dressing like a girl, hated it when people judged anyone on their appearance. So he drew his hole card. "What, are you bent out of shape because she wears black? Well, black over black with black accessories?"

"Of course not! It's not that. She's a *psychic*! Can you imagine that part?" Mally asked. "For me?"

Drew gently framed Mallory's face with his hands and turned her chin up to his lips. They were standing in a foot of snow, bundled in parkas, Mallory in sheepskin boots up to her knees, Drew in brown Wellingtons. But they didn't feel the cold. Not only were they together and tucked out of the wind, but, despite it being home and therefore boring by its very nature, it was hard to ignore the clean winter beauty all around them. The caps and runnels of snow that decorated the hills of upstate New York made the tiny town of Ridgeline feel like being in the center of a frosted funnel cake.

However, the romantic setting was not on Drew's side.

Mally's next shove nearly knocked him over. It came at him packed with every bit of oomph that thirty guy pushups a day could give a ninety-pound girl. She said, "Just leave it! I'm talking! My house is like a train station. And everyone there annoys the hell out of me except Grandma and Sasha."

"Sasha's pretty," Drew said. "Really pretty."

"So go and lick her face!" Mallory snapped. "You won't pay any civilized attention to me. We used to talk all the time before we were going out."

"That's because talking was the extent of it," Drew told her reasonably. "Now we have better things to do."

"Well, you can go do those better things with someone else," Mallory said. "I need a friend right now . . . not a . . . goldfish who keeps globbing his lips at me!"

"That's harsh!" Drew said, pulling his knitted headband down over his eyebrows.

"I'm sorry," Mallory said, giving him a hug. "I'm really sorry. I'm just disturbed. I mean stirred up, not mentally disturbed. Although . . . I probably am mentally disturbed."

"You can say that again," Drew muttered.

"Today particularly. I'm edgy," Mally said. She turned her back but leaned into Drew's arms, looking up at the strong wooden walls of her ninety-year-old house. "I don't know why," she said. "I should feel lucky. Great guy. Great friends. No scholastic hell. Only sixteen fun-filled weeks until school ends."

Winter in Ridgeline was about to give up its last gust and surrender to spring. There had been a big snowfall, and the runnels in the storm drains from a brief January thaw had not yet done much to make a dent in the drifts, still dusted with sugar. A month after Christmas, the town's lighted stars and spangled snowflakes were still shining on down from the lampposts onto unblemished snow. There hadn't been time to get them taken down during the two warm days, and townspeople rather liked the warm, non-denominational glow from the street corners. For Mallory and Drew, it was a beauty that they had to remind themselves to appreciate. But for other people, it was a novelty—a little place lifted out of time.

Ridgeline was becoming more popular by the year. Until the past several years, no one had ever moved to a tiny place like Ridgeline, population 2,000. But as cities became increasingly expensive and difficult for families, towns like Ridgeline, only an hour or so from New York City, became big-time destinations. Each year, a dozen or so new families moved to Ridgeline, to the huge new housing developments of mini-mansions built on old farmland beyond Mountain Rest Cemetery or into one of the old original Victorians or Foursquares arrayed along lanes that rose like streets and trees in a model-train village. The houses sat along pavement that unfurled like a Mobius strip from the little town square, from the huge bronze statue of one of the pioneer wives from England or Wales—the first residents of the town.

The twins, Mallory and Meredith, lived in one of the oldest houses on Pilgrim Street, where four generations of their family had grown up. The Brynns' great-great-grandfather had been one of the first settlers of Ridgeline and was among the men who built the first five houses, of which theirs was one. It had been a mining town then, home to rough-handed men and their patient wives. Now, mining was a dreamy history, and newcomers cooed over Ridgeline as though it were a puppy. They loved the stationery shop and the Mountain Beanery Coffee Shop and the fact that the old flower shop, Bloomers, and the new funeral parlor sat amicably side by side.

All those "transplants" were, as the twins' grandfather, Arthur Brynn said, "running away from the lives they wanted in the first place." Little towns such as Ridgeline were getting to be what Grandpa referred to as "boutique" communities for urban refugees.

"You can walk downtown and see a dozen people you've never even met these days!" he complained.

Better than anyone except the police, the twins knew that although Ridgeline might look like a storybook hometown, it wasn't. Not always. To them, Ridgeline had become an invisible veil, through which they could see the secrets of people all around them. And they'd known most of those people all their lives. Drew brought up that very fact now.

"You'd think you'd be happy to have something normal to worry about," Drew pointed out, irritated that they were wasting the only time they could touch each other all day—the school's policy on "PDA-beyond-hand-holding" made by people who had either never been in love or were too old to remember it. "No insult intended, life at your house fits into a pretty broad definition of what regular people would call 'normal.'"

Mallory couldn't disagree.

Although no one except Drew knew it, Mally and her sister Meredith weren't the typical girls next door—and the fact that they were identical mirror-image twins wasn't the half of it.

While reading each other's thoughts and speaking in their own language were second nature for them, two years earlier, when they turned thirteen, everything changed. After a fire that nearly killed both of them, their "twin" telepathy became total telepathy—dark, scary, and tuned in to whatever evil dwelt at the roots of Ridgeline. In daydreams and nightmares, they saw bits of things and had to fit them together to make any sense of them at all. What they found out turned their relatively happy lives inside out—like the first time, when they learned that David Jellico, the older brother of Merry's best friend Kim, was actually a budding psychopath hunting for a girl to torture.

As they soon realized, they had the same power in two different flavors.

Meredith was born a minute before midnight on New Year's Eve, and Mallory born a minute after.

Merry could only see the past—from the recent past to long ago.

Mallory could only see the future, what would or what might happen—although she had no idea when.

What was clear from the first minute was that they were meant to try to stop whoever—or whatever—was doing wrong. But the lines of the battle were never clear. In visions, they received pieces of a puzzle, never a whole map. And the very search caused them as much frustration and fear as whatever they found at the end.

Even when the twins found what they were seeking, they weren't always successful. Just last year, the twins learned that Mallory's best friend, Eden, an older girl on Mally's soccer team, was the embodiment of an ancient Cree Indian legend. A shape-shifter, Eden was her tribe's medicine woman, destined to live her life alone, partly as a great, buff-colored mountain lion. When she rebelled and tried to run from her destiny, even the twins' combined knowledge couldn't save her.

For Mally and Merry, while "the gift" was nothing freaky (scary, yes, but spooky, no) and was as natural to them as Mally being a lefty and Meredith right-handed, they would have willingly given it up in exchange for a bad case of acne any day of the week.

But after "the gift" first emerged in all its awful glory, their grandmother Gwenny told them the truth about it. They would be this way not for a while but forever. All the female twins on their father's side of the family (and there were no male twins) back as far as anyone knew had the second sight.

Mallory and Merry's great-great-grandmother and her mother had written hints of it in spidery entries in their family bibles. In letters and diaries now vanished, events that described "the sight" probably showed up much further back than that. Their great-grandmother could virtually "see," with her mind, through the walls of houses. Even as a tiny child, she knew who was happy and safe. Their great-aunt was the other side of that coin: She could "see" through the walls of people who acted very pious and pure but actually had sad and violent secrets.

Mallory and Merry's own grandmother could foresee healthy babies before their birth and recovery from illness; but her twin sister, Vera, who died as a child, could foresee only stillbirths and death. Mally and Merry's power was the distilled essence of all those generations before them. None but they had such a powerful sight, with the ability to intervene in destiny instead of just perceive it. Mallory could perceive things before they happened; Merry could confirm that those things had happened. Together they could try to prevent them from happening again or getting worse. Grandma Gwenny—whose own gift meant only that she could see who would live and be healthy while her sister, Vera, saw only who would die—tried her best to convince the girls that their power was a force for good.

For Merry and Mallory, though, the only good thing that had happened over time was that slowly, they seemed to be learning how to turn the power on when they needed it—although they could never completely turn it off.

That winter day, Drew was about to point out that nothing had called "the gift" out in nearly a year. It was almost a month since the twins had turned fifteen. For them, a birthday was a renewal. A new year. A new age. A kind of pencil-sharpening time for the future.

"And you're complaining," he told Mallory.

"It's just that . . . since my mother went to medical school . . . it's like a home invasion. I don't even know these people. At first it was just Grandma Gwenny and Big Carla. . . ."

"Big Carla?"

"That nurse's aide from the hospital who helps take care of Adam and Owen," said Mallory. "Like everyone else in town does now! You'd know that if you paid attention to anything about me for the past four months!"

Adam and Owen were Mallory and Meredith's younger brothers. At twelve, Adam was able to take care of himself most of the time—especially in Ridgeline, where crimes were about as rare as unicorns. But Owen was still a baby, barely able to stand. It still amazed the twins that their mother, Campbell—at forty-four years old!—had picked last fall to start medical school, as if being head nurse of the ER at Ridgeline Memorial Hospital weren't enough. Either she should have had the baby or the new career, but not both! "You've met Carla. She moved here a couple of years ago? She's this big woman with red hair, not fat, but she's got to be a body-builder or something. She looks like a wrestler? She named her daughter Carla, too. . . ."

"I can't say I've had the pleasure of meeting her. And her daughter is Carla Two, like *Carla Two*, the movie?"

"Carla also, I meant," Mallory said and threw up her hands. "Oh, Drew! Why bother? You're just going to make a joke out of it!"

"I'm not," Drew said softly. He stroked Mally's hair and kissed the top of her head. "You smell like spring even in the middle of winter." Mallory relaxed a bit. Soon, it *would* be spring. Things were quiet and peaceful—at least on the psychic front if not the home front. Mally was making much out of nothing: She did need to settle down.

"You know, Drew, it's not that my mother shouldn't do what she wants. But these people have disrupted our whole lives! We quit choir this year 'for the family,' but even that wasn't enough. It's like you need a flow chart to know who's going to be there when you walk into the kitchen in your T-shirt and boxers to get peanut butter toast."

"I wouldn't mind seeing that," Drew said.

"I didn't used to mind you seeing me dressed like that before we were together," Mallory said.

"Weird that you mind now."

"Yeah," Mallory said and reached up to kiss Drew. However, mid-kiss, she was suddenly limp in his arms, clinging to his neck. Drew knew what this meant. In a few moments, Mally's eyes would snap back to their customary river-gray brightness, and she would either tell him or not tell him that she'd had a "vision" about something. It would be something crazy that was either going to happen or which she was going to try to stop from happening—that either would or would not involve Drew's boss at Pizza Papa yelling at him in Italian for being late to work because Mallory needed a ride to interrupt some kind of nuts mayhem no one but she and Drew and her twin sister would ever know about.

He sighed and held her close.

Mallory saw girls, six or seven girls, under a canopy of trees in new leaf. Spring. The future. Around a fire, they danced with six or seven other girls. And they were . . . well, they were wearing capes or long tunics made of gauzy black or silver stuff that left nothing to the imagination. Mallory could see right through, and there were no clothes underneath. And then, leaning forward with her open hands, one of them began to drop tiny, blond curls into the fire . . . one by one, as the other nudies raised their arms in some kind of celebration. A few of the other girls whirled and dipped closer to the fire. The girl holding the hair—who was it?—she was familiar in some way. She had a slim, pretty body, but some of the others should have invested in Spandex body stockings. . . .

"I just saw girls naked in the grove!" Mallory told Drew. "I mean, they will be naked in the grove in the spring. There were leaves on the trees."

"Well, uh, how about that," Drew said. "That's a real shocker. Whoever they were, they wouldn't be the first. Ow!" Mallory punched him again. The grove, near Mountain Home Cemetery, had been a make-out spot for generations.

"But . . . none of them was with a guy! And one of them was . . .

like . . . What were they doing? They were, like, dancing," Mally said. "One of them put some . . . hair in the fire. And I could tell it was a baby's hair, not someone with tight curls. It was silky blond baby hair. And then when it started to burn, they danced faster."

"With each other?"

"Yes, but not like dancing regular people do. And they weren't naked-naked, but they had on these things you could see right through. And there were other girls, too, with really big . . ."

"Describe it in detail," Drew said. "Leave nothing out."

"Rear ends," said Mallory. "That's what I was going to say. I hate myself when I tell you anything serious."

"That's why I opt for kissing rather than talking. Be reasonable," Drew said. Mallory kissed Drew again. And then, again, her eyes rolled back. Drew gasped. A double-header! This was unprecedented. "Mallory! Mallory? Brynn, come on. What's wrong?"

Just seconds later, Mallory said softly, "It's Owen. Something's wrong with Owen."

"What? What could be wrong? He's in the house with the sitter. It is Carla today, right?" Drew said.

"Carla? She creeps me out, anyhow. What if she slapped him or left him alone or something?"

Suddenly, both Drew and Mally heard the whoop of the fire engine. Pilgrim Street was one of the four roads that extended out from the downtown square like spokes of a wheel. It was only four miles to the ends of the roads—except the one that led out to Deptford and the mall. It was only four miles from the fire station.

Closer, they could hear it come. And closer.

Then the huge red truck flashed past, followed by an ambulance, lurching to a stop in front of Mallory's house. Mally took off at a run without a backward glance. "Let it not be anything bad! I take back everything I said about my house."

Mallory burst through the door just after the paramedics.

Big Carla hunched in the rocking chair while a paramedic worked over Owen, who lay on his back on a blanket on the floor. Even before she got inside, Mallory could hear her twin, Meredith, crying, as well as one side of a telephone conversation that Carla was apparently having on her cell phone with the twins' mother, who was working at the hospital.

"Campbell, I don't think he had a fever when I got here," Carla said. "Sasha said he was just fine all morning when he was with her."

Mallory looked down at Owen's little face with its tiny clefted chin. He was pale, nearly gray, and while he was breathing, it was in small gasps, the way he did when he finished his bottle and drifted off to sleep. His eyes were open only a slit, revealing the whites, like a cracked hard-boiled egg. "He didn't feel hot or even warm. He simply began to vomit," Carla added. "Oh, Jesus help him. Oh, merciful Lord! He looks like Ellie did. So closed and blue . . ." To the twins' surprise, tears began to course down Big Carla's rough-hewn face and her shoulders shook. "I didn't mean to hurt him."

"You didn't mean to hurt him?" Mallory said sharply. "What happened?"

"I mean, I didn't mean for him to get sick. . . . I should have protected him. I should have protected Ellie." Carla seemed to be on the verge of collapse, but suddenly, and with a big effort, she got control of herself.

She wiped away the tears and spoke calmly to the medics.

"He was sick all day," Merry whispered to Mallory. She added the words for "she's silly," in ancient twin language, "Folamish due, 'Ster. He just passed out a few minutes ago. I freaked out when I couldn't see anything after that and cut out of practice. Sasha brought me home."

Sasha Avery, one of the other sitters, was a transfer student to Ridgeline, starting over at a new school senior year—which was hard on anyone. She was from Texas and had joined the work-study program. Merry knew her better than Mallory did because she'd also been an immediate sensation on the cheerleading squad, elevated to varsity in week one with a special tryout. But no one knew very much about Sasha. She didn't talk about it, but her parents had apparently died pretty recently. And her older sister was in college. According to the older girls on the squad, she lived part of the time with an aunt over in Deptford and part of the time with another family she worked for. That made Merry feel sorry for Sasha, who was so nice that Meredith, even though she was fiercely protective of her role on the team, didn't mind Sasha being the star for a while.

Sasha had had a sad life.

And, Merry reasoned, worse come to worst, Sasha was not going to dominate anyone on the squad for long: She was going to graduate in a few months anyhow and that would be that.

Sasha had started working for the Brynns in August when Campbell began medical school, caring for Owen two mornings a week for her Child Development credit and working two mornings with Campbell at the hospital, for her Professional Experience segment.

At practice that day, when Merry said her brother was ill, Sasha was so concerned about Owen that she had driven Merry home from practice in her little beat-up car, the one she'd driven all the way from Texas to Ridgeline, New York. Even though Sasha had to run to get to her evening job, she made Meredith promise to call her the minute they knew what was up with the baby she called "Little Fella."

As he did with everyone, Owen had stolen Sasha's heart in just a few months. Sasha hadn't asked any questions about how Merry knew Owen was sick, a lucky thing to Merry's way of thinking. The twins never stopped worrying that "the gift" would be found out.

Kneeling in the kitchen, Merry still wore her cheerleading warm-ups and her letter jacket. She hustled on hands and knees over to the place where the medics were starting an intravenous line of what both girls knew was basically sugar water, in case they had to give Owen medicine through a vein later. Owen's arm was so little, like a doll's, his skin so soft and translucent that the twins and Drew, who had crowded into the kitchen, were glad he probably couldn't feel the paramedic prodding for one of his threadlike little veins. "I saw him throwing up all day in school," Meredith said a second time.

Neither had to explain to the other how it was that Merry could have seen her infant brother throw up six hours earlier. But she could not have seen what would come next. Only Mally could see the future, the emergency, and one contradictory complication of "the gift" was that if the person in trouble was someone super close to the twins, such as Owen, Mally was somehow prevented from seeing the urgency until the last moment—if at all. The visions weren't like home movies, in which every movement was clear. They were more like those blurry slide shows that biology students were forced to watch.

Suddenly, Mallory slumped down beside her sister.

Drew started toward her, recognizing the tiny trance that usually accompanied a daytime vision. But Mallory was already awakening. No one else had seen.

"Siow," Mallory told Merry in twin language, their word for "hurt" or "worry." She had seen a hand wiping baby Owen's chin as he vomited so profusely that he finally lost consciousness. For some reason, the sensation that accompanied this gentle gesture felt sinister.

On top of it, Owen's vomiting spell had *already* happened!

Mallory's vision was telling her it was going to happen *again*.

She was about to confide more about it to Merry when the female paramedic spoke up.

"He's coming around," the paramedic said quietly. "We're going to take him in."

Merry and Mally exchanged looks.

Each of them could hear an echo from her sister's thoughts. Each was wondering if Owen's faint meant that he had some horrible legacy from them. Worse, did he just have a touch of flu, this little baby who came along so late in their mother's life that they expected to feel like his aunts instead of his sisters? Or did he have some grotesque disease that would take him away forever? Neither the twins nor Adam had expected to love Owen with such a total love it was almost crazy. But Owen was a heart-stealer, and every one of them competed to be his favorite.

"I'll come too," said Carla, pulling on her orange jacket from Alley Cats Bowlerama over in Deptford. She sniffed at the sleeve. "Darn it!

Smells like smoke. Wish the girls at work who smoke would hang their coats somewhere else after they go outside and light up." Mally took a long breath of relief. At least Carla wasn't smoking around their house, unless she was trying to cover it up. Both of them had believed they smelled cigarette smoke on her before and wondered if she left Owen alone to sneak outside for a butt.

"Wait up!" Merry said as Carla found her purse and prepared to leave with the paramedics. "He's *my* brother."

"But what can you do?" Carla asked reasonably, all professional now. "You weren't here when he got sick. You can't describe for your mother or the doctors how it was. And are you going to leave Adam here alone?"

"I guess not," Mallory said. "You're right."

"I just feel it should be one of us," Merry said.

"One person can come," said the lead medic, as they covered Owen up and lifted him gently on a flat blue plastic board with straps that bound him at the chest and hips.

"Sisssa!" he cried, now fully awake and spotting the girls. It was his interchangeable name for them. Owen sobbed, but no tears came. He struggled to sit up.

"Go 'bye bye to see Mama, Owen," Merry said. "Go 'bye bye with Carla in the car to Mama."

"So he's that dehydrated?" Carla asked the paramedic. "So much he can't cry?"

"I do think he is, and that he'll probably have to be on IV fluids overnight," the medic said softly.

"I wondered why he didn't wet his diaper," Carla said. "Huh."

"You wondered?" Merry asked. "Didn't you know?"

"You don't go jumping to conclusions over everything with a sick baby. They can be fine one minute and terribly sick the next. You watch. That's what you do. I noticed, and I kept track of how many diapers he wet. But there were no other obvious signs of dehydration. I am trained!" Carla said bluntly.

"Well, sorry," Merry said. "I didn't mean it that way."

"Carla," Mallory said. "Will you call us?"

"I guess," Carla said. "Well. Maybe your mom better do that. She said he'd probably be okay."

"That's a comfort . . . probably," Mallory said. Carla was about as with it as a snail.

Now, looking like some kind of trucker in her big buckle boots and orange coat, Carla shrugged. "There are no guarantees with little kids. They get better from things that should kill them, and things that they should live through take them away." She sighed and looked down at a charm on her keychain that seemed to enclose a picture neither of the girls could see plainly. "Life goes on."

"Sayso nay," Merry said, twin language for "what's she talking about?"

"What about your car?" Mally said.

"I took the bus over. No reason to waste gas. I'll just take it home too from the hospital." And they watched as the paramedics gently loaded Owen into the ambulance and Carla clambered in behind him, without so much as a goodbye to them or Adam. Through the window of the ambulance, the girls could see Carla stroking Owen's head. It looked like she was crying again.

"Do you think there's any chance that Carla did something wrong?" Merry asked. "What did she mean with all that stuff?"

"Who's Ellie?" Drew asked, breaking his silence for the first time since the crisis had begun.

"No idea," Mallory said. "Maybe her . . . no, her daughter's named after her."

Merry said, "Well, I guess whoever Ellie is, what Carla says is actually good news. If even Mom thinks he's going to be fine, he will be. You know how she is."

Mallory's stress slipped down a few degrees. She had to agree that their mother was the most overprotective woman, if not the most overprotective *human being*, in the galaxy. When Merry and Mallory began to have the tiny fainting spells, tied to their visions—they were now adept at concealing them by lying down or sitting—Campbell had them screened for everything from Lyme disease to epilepsy. And when nothing showed up, their mother seemed almost disappointed—or so the twins thought.

A moment later, before the truck was even out of sight, Meredith's phone rang.

"It's Luna Verdgris," said a soft voice from the other end of the phone. "I sense an atmosphere of trouble. I'm getting bad vibes."

"Slow night on the police band?" asked Merry.

The twins knew how Luna "sensed" most things in Ridgeline.

Her mother, Bettina, spent her days in a dark room reading tarot cards for locals and tourists—or monitoring her state-of-the-art police-band radio. Luna had heard from her mom that the ambulance was called to the Brynns' house. Bettina used the radio in other ways. She was able to tell her wealthy clients that the son who'd gotten four speeding tickets in a row was "basically good" and would "straighten himself out."

It was harder for Luna to be an individual given how . . . individualistic her mother was. She tried hard to look as weird as possible, dressing entirely in black with at least six scarves draped around her neck at all times. She described herself as a "wiccan." She was also a top-notch babysitter who had a job every night of the week (because she was pure magic with kids) and a Sunday school teacher at the Good Shepherd Lutheran Church. Luna (whose real name, the twins learned from Luna's little sister, was Laura) probably wouldn't have been so annoying if she hadn't insisted on grabbing the twins' left palms, which were identical but opposite— Merry's right hand was still scarred from the fire—and "reading" their futures once or twice a week.

She had predicted that Meredith would become involved with a young, brown-haired guy, which described half the guys in New York state.

She had "predicted" that Mally would find happiness with a red-haired thin boy, which described 100 percent of the boys who lived next door to the Brynns.

"Owen's sick," Merry admitted.

"Was he rushed to the hospital?" Luna asked. "Was that who went?"

"Yes," Merry said.

"Mer, I'm really sorry. I hope he's okay. Can I help you guys any way?"

"No, Luna. We're steady here."

"Let me know, huh?" Luna asked.

"You bet," Merry said.

"Let me talk to her for a minute," Mallory said. Merry handed her twin the telephone. "Luna, this is going to sound weird. But do you ever have, like, a meeting . . . in the grove?"

"I know how you heard this," Luna said in disgust. "And it sucks the tailpipe. It's Corey Gilbertson. Her mother made her quit even though Wicca is totally a nature religion. She said we were Satanists. And it's not naked, it's called 'sky clad,' and it's not a sex thing and I'm not gay. . . ."

"Whoa!" Mally said. "That's way more information than I need. I never thought you were a Satanist. Are you?" Drew, about to leave, made a throat-cutting motion with his hand. Mallory could be way too blunt, which she admitted every time she realized she'd been way too blunt.

"Are you nuts? I'm a Lutheran!" Luna said. "It's just interesting, is all. Ridgeline! You might as well wear a T-shirt that says everything you do to save people the trouble of finding out! We only did it twice, last year at the fall and spring . . . whatever . . . the equinox. Mallory. It's an interesting thing. So-called witches are always persecuted. They've been persecuted since the beginning of time. Anyone with any healing ability or visions is always persecuted and called evil."

"I totally agree," Mallory said.

"You totally agree?"

"Yeah," Mallory said.

"I'm . . . I'm going to put a spell on Corey Gilbertson. Don't worry. I can't do really bad spells. But maybe something in an itch . . ."

"Oh leave her be, Luna," Mally said. "She didn't tell me."

"Then who did?"

"I saw it in a vision."

"Don't make fun of me, Mallory!" Luna said.

"I'm not."

"I just wanted to know about Owen. Geez!" Luna hung up.

"What was *that* about?" Merry asked.

"Luna was dancing naked in the grove with some other witches," Mallory said.

"Oh," Merry said. "Here I was thinking that it was something weird."

Just then, Mallory's cell phone rang. It was Grandma Gwenny, calling from her yoga class. She was out of breath because the whole class had been struggling with their cobras.

"I want you girls to know that Owen will be just fine!" Grandma Gwenny said. "He just needs fluids."

"How did you know? Did Dad call?" Mally asked.

"Well, actually he didn't," Grandma said.

"It's bad enough for us to be like this," Mally said, trying to joke with a thin will for it. "Having a nutty adult in the family is too much."

"Of course, you don't mean me!" Grandma exclaimed with a dry little laugh. "I know you're worried, so I'm coming over to drive you and Adam to the hospital. In fact, I'm already heading for the car." She wondered aloud what people at the hospital would make of an "old gal" such as herself in her bright yellow tie-dyed yoga duds.

"You're something else, Grandma," Mallory said.

"I'm a hip chick," Grandma Gwenny said, and Mallory smiled for the first time all day.

Drew had to get to work, so he gave Merry a shoulder hug and kissed Mallory on the nose.

"You know where I am if you need me," he said.

They did know. Except for Papa himself, Drew held the lifelong continuous work record at Pizza Papa, where he'd thrown his first pie (on the floor) at fourteen. He'd been fired twice (both times for Brynn-related issues, as he often reminded the twins) and rehired when Papa Ernie couldn't make it without him. He now made about thirteen dollars an hour, executive wages for a kid in Ridgeline. Drew loped to the door, late as he so often was, ducking the auburn mop that topped off his six feet under the door frame of the old house.

Merry pulled her brother Adam from the corner of the kitchen, where he was standing gnawing on his thumbnail. "Come on, Ant. Grandma's coming. We'll go over and see the Big O. But you have to stop looking so scared. He's fine. Babies are very resourceful."

"You mean resilient," Mallory said with a sigh.

"I know what I meant, word goddess," Merry protested.

Mallory's cell toned with two bells. A text. "Dad's on his way to the hospital, too," she said. For the first time, she really noticed her other younger brother and how freaked out he still was. "Adam, do you want some fish sticks or something? Owen's going to be fine, good as new, just like our sister, the genius, just said. Grandma thinks so, too."

"I know," said Adam, not appearing convinced.

"Major truth. He's totally already better than when I came in," Merry said. "C'mon. How about I make you a grilled cheese all burny like you like, okay?"

"I can't eat," Adam said.

"You can't eat?" Merry pantomimed a heart attack. "What next? You eat like a marathoner."

"'Ster," Adam said, using the baby name he used for both twins— and which they used for each other—"Owen threw up blood."

Mallory stared at her brother. She'd "seen" someone in her vision-dream trying to *help* Owen. And she knew Luna was acting weird, just a step above her normal-weird, really—except for the little-kid hair burning.

Why did both dreams make goose bumps stand up on her arms?

CALM BEFORE THE STORM
CALM BEFORE THE STORM

No more than a week later, Owen was fully back to his usual, comic, voracious elf of a self, laughing hysterically when the twins pretended to bite his nose, pulling himself up on their beds every morning. When Merry and Mally came down for school, Owen would be lying on the kitchen floor, using his feet to stack up the gigantic cardboard blocks he got for Christmas and then kicking them over. And he had his appetite back. He ate Cheerios and cooked peas with both fists and literally drank down as much of Grandma Gwenny's home-jarred applesauce as he could from his plastic cup.

The crisis was over, and the girls barely had a week to go shopping for the Valentines' Day dance. The Val Dee was a formal at school that, for some reason, everyone treated as a bigger deal than Homecoming. The twins felt free to enjoy it now. For a few days after the hospital emergency, Owen had been a little quiet and sad, Campbell said, sleeping in Sasha's arms in the morning instead of running around. The girls usually left early to catch a ride in with Drew, who played pickup basketball before school now that the cross-country season was over, so they rarely crossed paths with Sasha. But now, Owen was all two-toothed grins.

In fact, Campbell thought it was possible that he had simply over-reacted to new teeth.

This Sunday morning, Mallory had even taken off work at their dad's store so she could buy a dress. She worked every Sunday and had since she was twelve. Meredith could only imagine how much her sister, who was a renowned tightwad, had stashed away. The girls were geared up to head for the mall in Deptford when their mother stopped them and told them to sit down for breakfast first.

Meredith sighed. Her friends and fellow cheerleaders Neely, Kim, and Erika were going to meet them in front of Latte Java in an hour. Now, there would have to be a mass of texting and squiggling schedules.

"I wanted to tell you girls that I have to add just one more sitter," Campbell told them as they took their coats off and set them on the chair by the front door. "If I take another course next semester, I can probably compress this whole thing to eighteen months."

"Mom!" Mallory objected. "Five sitters?"

"Grandma Gwenny is, well, elderly, Mallory. And she happens to have a life of her own. Sasha has two jobs and school. So does Mrs. Quinn, Carla. She's trying to get her RN degree."

"Why don't you hire just one person, then?" Mally asked. "Do you think this is good for Owen? He never knows who's coming over next!"

"I tried to hire one person. The going rate for one person was twenty dollars an hour!" Campbell said.

"It would be better," Mallory said, thinking of the vision of the slender hand wiping Owen's mouth that still gave her the willies for no good reason.

"Would you rather have him in a daycare center?" Campbell said, her hands on her hips.

"At least there wouldn't be twenty-seven people taking care of him at a daycare center," Mallory said. She sat down at the table and laid her head on her arms, trying to let her "sight" come forward. But it wouldn't come. What was bothering her? Why did she have such a big thing on about this? Owen was fine!

"And it's fine that they're germ pits, right? At least the one in Kitticoe is. They let the babies sit in playpens all day! It's my personal feeling that children can't have too many loving people in their lives," Campbell said. "Or in their homes. Now, if you want to give up indoor soccer on Saturdays and working with Dad at the store on Sundays, I won't need Melissa Hardesty. She's a college student, and her mom is a doctor at the clinic. So I know her. It's not like I'm inviting everyone off the street to take care of my baby."

"You didn't know Sasha!" Meredith objected. "You hired her after, like, a ten-minute interview."

"I did a background check on her. She'd never even had a speeding ticket!"

"Sasha's nice though," Meredith interrupted. "What about Luna?"

Campbell turned back to the pancakes she was about to flip. Seeing their mother cook was always a rare event—rarer since she became a student and had a new baby. So once they got over having to put off leaving, the twins were actually glad to take advantage of homemade brunch.

"Why am I discussing this with you?" their mother asked the stove, clearly not expecting an answer from her daughters. "Luna is a perfectly good girl. She's unusual. Her mom's unusual. But Luna's just trying to find herself. She gets good grades. She's not a drug addict. If being weird were a crime, you'd be in jail, my darling daughters. You still speak in tongues the way you did when you were five even though you're fifteen."

"Mallory does have a point," Meredith said then. "It's your life, Mom, but it's our home. Our privacy."

Campbell placidly flipped a pancake and just as quickly lost her temper. Campbell's temper was a family legend. "Why Meredith!" she said. "You're right. I'd forgotten that your privacy was my top priority! Here I was concentrating on working fifty hours a week and going to school twenty hours a week, raising four kids I hope to at least help put through college and not having had a date with my husband since July! Silly me!"

"She doesn't mean it that way," Mallory said. "It's Owen we're thinking of. Look what happened!"

"Mallory Arness Brynn," Campbell said sternly. "I thank heaven that Carla Quinn was here and that she had medical training when Owen got sick! And yes, I know you call her Big Carla behind her back, and she may not have the most sparkling personality in the world. But she's a hard worker and a good nurse's aide. You're just . . . spoiled because you're used to your mom working two weeks and then having ten days off to be your . . . servant." Campbell had formerly worked straight through two weekends and then had ten days off.

"Fine, Mom," Mallory said. "I apologize." The twins finished their pancakes in silence.

"Apology accepted," Campbell said finally. "Now, on the red bus, try to make it a point to talk to all the creepy-looking people you see and accept rides home from them."

"We're fifteen, Mom, not six," said Merry.

"Laybite," Mallory warned her, using the twin word for "stop talking." Getting their mother angry, especially twice, was never a great idea.

"I forgot. Fifteen-year-old girls are never the objects of assault," Campbell said. "For real, have a nice day, girls. I'll see you at dinner."

"She's in a fine mood," said Mally, as they ran for the red bus.

The red bus, which was called ByWay, was a godsend for the twins, who were younger than most of the other people in the sophomore class and, besides Drew and their father, didn't have many friends with access to cars.

Fortunately, the previous year, the town had gotten a mini-bus system.

Two red buses went out to the four corners of Ridgeline and beyond, to the technical college and the Deptford Mall to the north and out to Kitticoe to the west, where there was a huge bargain store that took up three city blocks. For a dollar, a person could ride around all day, and some of the elderly people in town did just that, making stops at the library and church luncheons and resale shops to their hearts' delight. Even Grandpa Brynn had to admit that the new money in town had some advantages.

For younger high school kids, who wanted to grab a ride to the multiplex cinema or the mall without the indignity of having their father hug them when they got out of the car, it was pretty terrific as well. The only thing the red bus didn't have was a back seat or a trunk, so Mally and Merry had rolled their mother's tiny Green-Shop reusable grocery bags into their purses for the bargains they intended to find.

As they rode, Mallory glanced up at Crying Woman Ridge, the place David Jellico had fallen to his death two years ago after the twins "saw" the cemetery up there where he buried the animals he killed—where Mallory dreamed that a girl would lie next. It was also where the Brynns' old family cabin camp was, where all the Brynn aunts and uncles and cousins gathered for two weeks every July. Up there, except for the evergreens, all the trees had the appearance of the block prints children make by dipping raw potatoes in paint—stark, still, branches against hills like a brown series of lower-case letter m's. Looking down was depressing. Just in time for Christmas, the snow had melted into pools of gray slop.

"I'm hopeless," Meredith said suddenly.

"I agree," Mally teased her.

"No, I mean I am without hope. I've flirted with Sam Lido and Carter Roskov until I'm limp and they just pat me on the head.

All Sam can see is Allie, and Carter's either gay or dating a college girl."

"I know it's bizarre to you, Meredith, but there are straight guys on Earth who don't immediately want to fall at your feet," her twin said.

"Since when?" Merry asked honestly. "We're shopping for a formal for you. What's that about? A year ago, you wouldn't wear a dress, and nobody wanted you to!"

"I don't want to buy one, actually," Mallory said. "But I don't feel right borrowing one. It's Drew's last school dance except prom. And I'll probably need one for next year."

"Aren't you going to be true to him when he's in college?"

"Please," Mallory laughed. "He's going to be in Arizona! And Drew just wants me because of the convenience factor."

"You don't believe that," Merry said. "You really care."

"Yeah, I really do. I really do. But long-distance stuff, it never works out. I don't want to get hurt," Mallory said in a rare burst of vulnerability. "Plus, at his school, they probably have pretty, older girls there stacked up like firewood. There're about twenty pretty girls in Ridgeline—and I'm not one of them."

In fact, neither Mallory or Meredith was pretty, but both had the kind of strong features—thick, shiny black hair, high cheekbones, and lips red as plush—that would one day make them beautiful women. If anyone had asked about the Brynn twins, people would describe their small, straight-backed bodies, always in motion, alike as little mustangs, their freckles and their rainwater gray eyes. Because all twins are "cute," people called them that.

"Come on. He's loved you since you were ten. But I have to admit that it's a weird thought to kiss somebody you used to eat sand with in the sand box," Merry said to her sister. "I thought you were destined to marry the boy next door, like in the old movies."

"No, I'm definitely in the open options program next year," Mally said. "So the dress will come in handy."

"You're such a liar."

"Maybe I am. Maybe not. But I don't want him to be the one who breaks up with me," Mally said. "Let me think about now."

In the now, Mally was suffering about the dent that a dress would make in the money she'd hoarded for years, working Sundays with her dad. Merry was borrowing a dress from Neely Chaplin, her friend who, if not rich, was the closest thing Ridgeline had to rich. She lived in Haven Hills, a mushrooming development that was formerly a huge old farm and was now filled with gigantic new mansions and a golf course. The designer clothes Neely had came from real designers, although Neely's mother CeCe got a break on them since she owned a boutique hat, handbag, and jewelry design business that had some pretty upscale clients. Neely and Merry were going with their cheerleading gang—all of them joined at the hip in boyfriend-less-ness ("And we're the most popular sophomores!" Merry lamented. "How can this be real life?"). Despite this, borrowing instead of buying new was a sign of near-psychotic thrift for Merry, who could not keep twenty-four dollars in her pocket for more than twenty-four hours. But why spend good money, Merry reasoned aloud, on old worn-out guys like Will Brent?

"I know it's not for you, and shopping without buying must be like being allergic to cocoa and locked in a chocolate factory. But I'm actually glad you're with me," Mallory said. "I have no idea what looks good on me. I have no idea what looks good, period."

"The same sister who used to make puking noises whenever I got dressed up?" asked Merry, who never even went for a jog without lip-gloss and mascara. "You bought all those clothes last spring."

"Not dance clothes," Mally said briefly. Mallory's last shopping spree had been with her now-vanished friend Eden. "I humble myself to you, the patron saint of malls."

At that moment, Neely, Kim, and Erika came running up to greet them.

"Mallory's buying a dress for the formal," Merry said, in case anyone missed it.

"Mal, you could have used one of mine," Neely said.

"I think it's time for me to step into semi-demi adulthood," Mally said. "Kicking and screaming. At least, I have Wonder Shopper here to be my coach."

Kim was also shopping for a dress but wanted to go to the Little Luxie boutique instead of Hardwicke's. Neely wanted a questionnaire book and the notes for *Romeo and Juliet*, and Erika had serious skincare shopping to do. Mallory was silently grateful that no one but her sister would see her trying to get something to look sexy on a body that was basically shaped like a very tall and slender fire hydrant or a very short lamp post.

The dress the twins found did the trick.

It was black and hung straight to a few inches above Mallory's knees. It was spangled in a way that looked lush instead of trashy—

flexible and free, almost like something from nature. It showed off
her strong shoulders instead of her nearly nonexistent boobs. The
girls each had one pearl earring they could make into a pair (each
twin had three piercings in her ears, the first one made at birth so
their parents could tell one from the other). Then Merry insisted
that her twin buy silver pumps with three-inch heels.

"It's a dance!" Mallory complained, after she got the pumps on
her feet. They fit, but she had to grasp the row of chair backs in La
Bou and struggle to a mirror. "The specific purpose is to dance. If I
try to dance in these, I'll end up with a broken ankle."

"You're such a deef," Merry said. "You have a week to practice.
Lean on the balls of the foot. Yes. That's right. Push down and step.
Push down and step. . . ."

"Wow, Mallory! You look like a runway picture," said a soft,
sweetly accented voice, and both girls looked up to see Babysitter
Number Two, Sasha Avery. "Is Owen okay? You never called me
the other night, Miss Merry. I had to call your mom!"

"I'm sorry, Sasha," Merry said. "We were so freaked out that
night."

"Never mind," Sasha said. "Those are truly fabulous shoes, I have
to admit. And not too matchy-matchy with the dress you had on."

"Oh thanks! Oh help! Yikes! I'm so bad at this. I thought I could
get out of here without anyone seeing me," Mallory told her. "I feel
like a complete idiot, and these things already kill my calves."

"Heels take getting used to," Sasha said. "At my old job . . . at my
old school, girls wore them all the time with everything. Even jeans.
You got so used to it, it was like wearing flip-flops for me. Now I've

gotta find something that will work with the kind of dress we wore in Dallas, as in with two crinolines and a corset."

"What's a crinoline?" Merry asked.

"It's a big puffy skirt that goes under your dress. Yeah, I know, right, it is kind of dumb," she held up her hand to wave off a protest. "But it gets you noticed. It's a big gigantic slip, so the dress stands out like a Cinderella dress. Like in the Civil War? Girls didn't wear those little shift thingies down there, though I have to get one. They are really cute! Then again, my big rear end would be a liability. Doesn't show under a puffy skirt. When you had to go to a dance or a cotillion . . ."

"What's a cotillion?" Merry asked.

"Well, they're parties that parents had for girls my age to present them to, you know, society. To present them to the right kind of boys," Sasha said. "Whatever that is. I had friends who had them, and I went. But my parents weren't really in that social class. Cute guys though. Stuck up but real cute."

"I don't think you missed much, Sasha. It sounds like parading all the princesses in front of the prince so he could wave yes at one and no at the next?" Mallory asked. "I thought that kind of ended in medieval times."

"Kind of," Sasha said cheerfully. "When I was little, though, I thought that was the thing. I used to wrap my mama's robe around me and pretend I was at my cotillion. All the little girls did."

"Did your . . . uh . . . mama have one?" Mally asked.

"Well, yeah. Her daddy had money 'til he drank it all up. Mama got married three times and every time to a richer guy," said Sasha.

"None of 'em had any use for me though. Or my sister." A shadow that struck Mallory's heart passed over Sasha's pretty face. Then she was all toothpaste smiles again. "Keep working on that walk. To be beautiful, y'all gotta suffer! That's still true! But you guys are so naturally skinny you don't have to worry about every bite ending up on your butt, but y'all still gotta walk like a swan!" Sasha mimed a pageant-girl glide.

"Untrue!" Mallory said with a laugh. "About the calories. I eat like a draft horse, yeah, but I run it all off on the soccer field, and Meredith . . . I guess you could say she's an athlete."

"She's a terrific athlete. You guys should switch some time, and y'all try cheerleading, Mally. You'd be worn out!"

"I should, but I've promised to shoot myself first," Mallory said. Merry didn't blink. She was accustomed to her twin's cheer chauvinism.

"Who's your date for the formal?" Merry asked. "This dress is for the formal, right?"

"I asked Sawyer Brownlee. Do you know him? What a sweetie. He's like a gentleman, kind of. Almost like back home." Sawyer Brownlee was a neighbor of Merry's friend, Neely. *He'd probably taken lessons to waltz and used the right fork at dinner*, Mallory thought, *unlike Drew, who should put on a raincoat before he ever lifted a fork to his mouth*. "I'll see you guys tomorrow morning when I come to take care of that little pumpkin! I'm so glad Owen's all better!"

Just then, all three girls noticed Carla Quinn just a few feet away near a free-standing display of Valentine's Day teddy bears and little trucks with chocolate hearts inside.

"Hi Carla," Sasha said. "Doing some shopping?"

"Well, my daughter just wants gourmet chocolate now," Carla said sourly. "And clothes, clothes, clothes. These remind me of my little boy."

"How old is he?" Merry asked. "I never knew you . . ."

"I have to run," Carla said and stalked away.

Sasha looked at Mally and Merry. Sasha asked, "Carla is completely hostile! Why does your mom like her so much?"

"She's a good nurse, my mom says," Mallory answered. "Owen likes her."

"Personally, I think she's weird," Sasha said. "But your mom knows best. "Well, I have to find something or other here! See y'all later."

As Sasha walked away, running her fingertips experimentally over the shoe styles, Mallory stepped out of the pair she'd tried on.

"You win, 'Ster," she said to Merry. "I stood there all that time, and I didn't fall out of them. I'll practice ball first, step, ball first, step. I'm suddenly very tired of all these choices. Let's go eat. Please?"

"One more stop," Merry said. "You can't be all decked out without a smoky eye or something."

At the makeup counter, Merry used the deft skill of a surgeon to swiftly select exactly the right combinations of creams and gels and tints for her twin. "Let's get a free makeover!" Merry suggested.

"Enough, Mer," Mallory said. "I have product fatigue."

"Oh, fine. Who gets tired after less than an hour of shopping? It's like being on a date with a dead person."

"You should know," said her twin. "I've never seen one. At

least, walking around." Meredith rolled her eyes. Because she saw deep into the past, she had, at various points in her life, seen people whom she described to her sister as "technically dead." Mallory never understood the qualifier "technically," but Merry never really wanted to talk about it. It raised questions about religion that Merry told Mally she wasn't sure she could answer to a certainty, at least at this time in her life.

"I wish you could see ghosts," Meredith said thoughtfully, as she went on subtly dabbing different shades onto her sister's cheeks, giving the impression to passersby that there were two identical people, one of whom was mute. Mallory stood like a mannequin but widened her eyes in mock horror. "It's not like you think. They're interesting. I've been seeing ghosts even more lately. Keech innis," she continued, switching into their own language as a sales associate passed by and raised both eyebrows. When Mallory heard what her twin was saying, which translated to "in our house," her eyes widened in alarm.

Mallory asked, "Can I move my lips now?" Merry nodded, satisfied.

"In our house? You're seeing ghosts more in our house?" Mally asked. "More ghosts or more often?"

"Not just our house," Meredith went on calmly. "I see them other places too. I must say, you look nice. People wouldn't know it was you. I do have a gift. You can barely tell you have makeup on."

"So I'm paying fifty-six dollars for something people can't tell I have on," Mallory said. "We were talking about ghosts, Mer. Where in our house and where else?"

"Well, obviously, I see them in cemeteries, when we pass a cemetery," Merry said.

"At night?" Mally asked.

"Don't be a twit. As if ghosts care if they come out in the daytime or at night," Merry said. The sales girl was openly listening now, but Merry was beginning to enjoy both the salesgirl's and Mally's discomfort. Their history meant that Mallory usually "saw" the harrowing things—the acts of cruelty and danger that lay ahead. And though Merry was not in the least afraid of ghosts, she knew other people were, if only because the unknown was always more ominous than anything someone could think up.

"What are they doing?" Mallory asked then. "In the cemeteries?"

"In cemeteries, what do you think? Just sitting around talking. On the street, the same thing we are, except obviously they're looking for something we don't see. I saw a man once last year looking down into the little lake thing at the golf course by Grandma's house and then up at the sky, and I realized he must have been looking for a house that used to be there before. . . . I don't know how long before. And I saw a woman come down from the ridge, in her nightgown, in bare feet, in the snow, but not walking on the path."

"Do . . . do you want some, uh, samples?" said the salesperson.

"You bet," Meredith said, as the girl, who was probably in her twenties, stuffed a bag chock-full of moisturizers and little cologne sprays. "Thanks and bye now." The girl rushed away in the storage area.

"She just wanted us to leave," Mallory said. "What if she tells someone?"

Meredith smiled. "I used to worry about that but . . . imagine what they'd think of what she said."

"I guess," Mallory said, smiling too. "But I want to hear more about this, Mer."

"Fine. I just don't want to talk about immortality because I don't know if ghosts are memory impressions or really souls."

"Well, I'm curious about the ones in our house but for now, lead me out of this temptation and deliver me to pizza, Meredith," she said. "I feel faint." As they walked, Mallory said, "There's Sasha again." Sasha was still in the shoe department, with at least fifteen boxes lined up and pyramided beside her stockinged feet. "What she said was funny. Like she wants to be a nurse and a professional and get scholarships, but you can tell she wants to marry a rich guy, too."

"Being a nurse is a very good path to that," Merry said, waving to Allie and Erika, who were headed toward them down the mall. "Nurses marry doctors."

"What about Mom? She married a soccer player with bad knees who had a degree in *American literature*! If Dad were a doctor, we wouldn't be giving up our mother seventy hours a week!"

"Then Dad is the one who got lucky. Of course, by the time she's rich, we'll be out of college. We'll have to survive on our own, without our mother's help. I'm going to have to marry a rich man on mah own, y'all," Merry said, mimicking Sasha. "Don't you think I'm charming enough to be the fairest in the land?"

"You're so deep, Meredith," Mallory said. "What's a vixen like you doing without a date for the formal?"

They passed the mall fountain and could detect the steamy, awful-wonderful smell that issued from the collision of Latta Java and Pizza Papa on the far end of the mall.

"You know, we should stop quick and get Dad a birthday present while we're here," Merry said. Tim's birthday was in April and so was Adam's. Adam was easy. He'd gotten an iPod for Christmas, and the girls went in together on a fifty dollar card for him to fill it with songs. They drifted over to the CVS store and debated on buying Tim an electric toothbrush, reading on the package that it was good for "aging gums." They agreed it was kind of a cold present, which reminded them of the time that Tim had given Campbell a Crock-Pot slow cooker for their anniversary—in which she had, the next day, planted a cactus. Their father hadn't even dared to bring it up.

They began to run to meet up with Allie and Erika and, an hour later, had demolished a Monza Four Cheese pizza bought on discount from Drew. By the time they finished, the mall was about to close. Allie's mother was there to take her and Erika to the gym class they'd enrolled in on Sunday nights to improve their tumbling. Merry often said—in a pretty conceited way—she was glad to have learned her tumbling when she was six. The twins waved through the window of Pizza Papa to Drew and then jumped on the red bus that was just pulling up to the stop.

As they put their packages into the rack and settled into seats, Meredith suddenly punched her sister hard on the bicep.

"What was that for?" Mally demanded.

"For telling me I'm a loser because I don't have a date for the formal! 'I'm not defined by that'—that's what you'd say," Merry said.

"You could have fooled me," said Mallory. "Anyhow, I'm sorry. . . . Speaking of that, what are you going to wear for a coat if you wear something sleeveless? With our luck, there'll be a foot of snow that night. You'll look great in Stella McCartney with a parka."

"You can wear Mom's old opera cape. Grandma can take it up a few inches. Neely's lace dress is long-sleeved," Merry began, and then stopped in the middle of her sentence. She had only ever seen pictures of old movie stars like James Dean, but the boy standing under the streetlight at the gates of the Deptford Mall looked like all those pictures. His hair was cut short on the sides and fell forward in a long blond twirl onto his forehead. His hands jammed into the pockets of a beat-up brown leather jacket, he slouched against the light post, next to where flowers bloomed in the spring. When the bus rolled past, he looked up, and Merry thought she had seen the face of an angel. He wasn't big, maybe only six or seven inches taller than Merry, but she could see how his shoulders filled out the jacket. It was, however, his eyes, blue as seawater even in the half-darkness, and the unendurable loneliness in a single look that made Merry dizzy. They had just begun the forced march through *Romeo and Juliet* that every sophomore class did, along with comparisons between Shakespeare and writers such as Christopher Marlowe. Meredith had decided she would name one of her five kids Christopher Marlowe and call him "Kit," as Shakespeare had called his friend. Now she murmured, "Whoever loved that loved not at first sight?"

"What? Why are you suddenly repeating song lyrics?"

"Poetry. Look at that boy, Mallory. Isn't he the hottest boy you've ever seen, counting Drew, counting anybody?"

"What boy?" Mallory stared from the bus window. It was past dusk, now truly dark. Mally had trouble seeing anything through the window, which had evidently been an easel for a little kid with sticky handprints.

"Are you blind? Right there, under the big old-fashioned light," Merry said. "Look, right back there. Don't stare. Just look."

"It doesn't matter if I stare or if I don't," Mallory said, glancing at her sister. "There's nobody there."

"Now he's gone! I told you to look. Didn't you see the boy in the leather jacket, Mal? He was so gorgeous. He even walked sexy."

"I'm sure that's true," Mallory said. "Except you're hallucinating. The only person in the whole parking lot except us is old Mr. Highland, that guy who lives down the street from Aunt Kate. I think it's Mr. Highland. The one carrying the big black garment bag? Oh, the tedium of living in a small town. I'm going to college in . . . London or . . . Indiana or someplace where I'll never see the same person twice."

"I'd see this guy twice. I'd see this guy twice a day. I have to find out who he is," Meredith said. She flipped open her phone. "This is a job for Neely Chaplin."

That was a bulls-eye, Mallory thought. Although only a year ago, Neely had been one of those uprooted urban blossoms, no one had put down roots more quickly. Neely had a kind of knack for social activism: She had cultivated the network of her and Merry's friends to unearth and spread gossip so quickly, she was like a twenty-four-hour news service. And although all the girls routinely got in trouble for rampant over-texting, it was Mallory's opinion that Neely had opposable thumbs that had evolved even beyond the ordinary video-game-playing teenager. As she told her twin, if there were a text-typing competition, Neely would medal in every event.

That was what Merry was counting on.

THE BOY IN THE BROWN LEATHER JACKET

D on't talk to me," Neely told Meredith as they leaped down, grinning like fools, from their respective pyramids.

"What did I do?" Merry asked Neely through closed teeth, as she dipped her shoulder and flipped her hair forward in the first steps of the last quarter of the half-time cheer dance they were practicing after school. It was four days after Merry and Mally's shopping trip.

"You ruined my perfect record of finding out everything about any cute boy anywhere anytime if he's within a five-mile radius," said Neely. "At least I failed so far."

"So you don't know who he is," Meredith said, dropping into a split and madly waving her hands above her head.

"Are you sure he didn't just come through on a bus and leave?" Neely asked, as the two of them jumped up and retreated to a corner to wait for the music to signal their final tumbling run.

"No, he lives here. I'm sure," Merry said. "Neels, I'm shocked. This is your . . . your art. Your gift."

"The problem is not me or my lack of talent. It's that I don't have enough information. I need vital statistics. Height, weight, hair color, preferred method of dress," Neely said. "Not he's just so hot and cute and wears a jacket."

"Okay, well, he's got blond hair . . . long," Merry said. "Really long in front, like almost as if it would cover his eyes if it were wet."

A sharp note sounded on the whistle. "I'm very sorry to interrupt your chat, girls," Coach Everson said. "But I was hoping we'd actually finish this practice tonight. Let's take it from the last sixteen bars. Please."

After practice, Neely ran off to study with her tutor for her Latin final and was then gone after lunch on Friday taking the test at the private school in Kitticoe where her parents had arranged for her to study three afternoons a week. Ridgeline offered only Spanish and German. Convinced that Neely would be a doctor—or a lawyer like her father—the Chaplins had insisted she study Latin since eighth grade.

So Meredith had to content herself that she wouldn't be able to share more about the boy with Kim, who was staying over at Neely's along with Meredith after the dance on Saturday.

Forty hours. It wasn't really that she truly wanted her best friends to start a text campaign about him, Merry realized. She knew she would see him again. All she had to do was wait and be. But waiting was nearly impossible. Meredith just wanted to talk about him and not, for some reason she didn't understand, with Mallory.

All those hours.

Meredith thought she would count every one of them by the hands on the clock.

As she dressed for the dance, Meredith didn't know how short the time would really be. And she didn't know how short a time it would be until she wouldn't need—or even want—anyone's help when it came to the mystery boy.

STRANGER AT THE DANCE

STRANGER AT THE DANCE

"Look at all my beautiful girls," Campbell said on the night of the formal.

Campbell included Sasha, putting an arm around her shoulders, and the twins didn't mind. After all, Sasha had worked that very morning, taking care of Owen (Luna, who disdained any school function, would come later when Campbell left for her night shift). Their father was still at the store and would be until nearly midnight because of the After-Christmas Crazy Sale at Domino Sporting Goods—which lasted until about March 1, when the town workers finally got around to taking down the lighted snowflakes and signs that read PEACE.

Because she basically had no family, Sasha had no one to make a fuss about her formal or take her pictures. She hadn't complained, but her predicament went to Campbell's heart. Sasha seemed so touched by the attention that she showed up early. She went up to the twins' room, where she stood in her crinolines, and with a few twists put Meredith's stick-straight hair up into a froth of loopy curls. The crinolines were almost as wide as the twins' attic bedroom, but Meredith couldn't believe how beautiful her hair looked.

"How'd you learn to do this?" she asked Sasha.

"Oh, just fooling around," Sasha said.

Then she slipped her pale, jonquil-yellow strapless gown over her head, and she really did look like something from some old-time movie the twins' mother forced them to watch at the Belles Artes Theatre to make sure they didn't grow up "uncultured." She looked, in fact, like Cinderella, right down to shoes with Lucite heels, each of which had a yellow rose in it.

"Where did you find those shoes? Not in Ridgeline," said Meredith.

"I got them second-hand online. The lady at the other place I work just got a new laptop, and she lets me use it. She's really nice and she's not really that old. She used to garden and do all these things, but she got sick the last few months."

"That's too bad," Mally said. "At least she's not crabby."

"No, she's getting weaker every day," Sasha said softly. "I don't think she'll live very long. It makes me sad."

"Come down here, you guys!" Campbell yelled.

As each of them descended the stairs, Campbell and Mrs. Vaughn from next door started snapping pictures. There had to be pictures of the twins together, then the twins with Sasha, and then of Mallory and Drew, as well as Neely and Meredith, who were riding to, but not from, the dance with Drew and Mallory. ("I'm staying at Neely's. Her dad will pick us up at the school, or send the driver," Merry said.)

After forty or so photos, Drew finally yelled, "Stop! I'm losing sight in my right eye!"

Finally, Campbell took a picture with her telephone and sent it to Tim at the store. He texted back and said, "I HATE WORK MAKING ME MISS THIS. I'LL DROP BY THE DANCE." Although they loved their dad, both girls devoutly hoped their father, who was best friends with every coach at school, wouldn't make good on the offer.

Just then Luna made her entrance, in black combat boots and a floor-length lace dress that looked like someone's hammock.

"Stylin', Luna," Drew said.

"This is so juvenile," she answered. "I wouldn't go to a Ridgeline High School function willingly if somebody paid me. I can't believe I even show up there every day."

"You have all honors classes," Merry said.

"Not willingly," Luna said. "Merry, did you know your aura is orange? That's healing and love. But yours is dark," she said to Sasha and Mallory. "Troubled."

"Who decides this?" Mallory asked Luna. "Is there an aura color wheel?"

"Nothing like that. You just know. You know if you know," Luna said.

"I guess you'd know, with all that sky dancing," Mallory said.

"If you say one more word about that, I'll make you have dreams about things that will make your hair stand up like that all the time," Luna said. Mallory thought, *If you only knew.* . . .

Then, bright in his new penguin footed pajamas, Owen came running into the room, making noises like a truck. Luna's whole face changed. "Hi, big guy!" she said, scooping him up. "Wanna party?"

"Luna," Merry whispered. "Do you know that your mother's father stands at the end of her bed every night and that he's pissed? He knows about the stamps she sold before he died when she thought he was in a coma."

Luna stared hard at Meredith, who was, in fact, telling the truth. Then her face converted to its usual mask of vaguely bored superiority. "Don't be foolish," she said.

"Watch out," Merry warned her. "That noise in the attic isn't mice. It's Gramps looking for those stamps."

Having heard nothing, Campbell hugged the girls and then Sasha. "I wish your mom could be here to see you," she said.

"It's okay," Sasha said. "I got over being a little girl a long time ago. But I sure am glad you let me be part of your family for the night." She began to wave her hand and held her head back so tears wouldn't run down. "Look, now what a slob I am. I can't get all sad at times like these. It doesn't change anything. My sister's in college, and I'll live with her when I get finished."

Mallory said, "That's very courageous. I can't imagine having lost everyone at my age."

"Not everyone is as lucky as you are, Mallory," Campbell said. "Not everybody can grow up surrounded by a healthy family. Aunts and uncles. All but one of your grandparents is still alive." Campbell's mother had died in an accident when the twins were young, and her father lived in Virginia and Florida. He visited three or four times a year.

"Your mama has been very kind to me," said Sasha. "I'm very grateful. Y'all can get lonely."

Drew said, "Let's get going! Your grandma's going to be mad. You know how she is about manners." Grandma Gwenny had offered to cook dinner for the twins and their friends, as much simply to see them in their finery as to save them the cost of a restaurant meal—which, she assured them, would not be half as good as what she would produce. About the only thing that could bring out the vanity in Grandma was her homemade this or her family recipe for that.

"You're right!" Merry almost shouted. It was a relief to break the moment, which was stretched thin as elastic wrap.

Slipping Campbell's opera cape around her shoulders, Drew told Mally, "Your coach awaits!"

Drew's Toyota, the Green Beast, still kicking at 185,000 miles, had once been silver but now was painted perhaps the ugliest color anyone had ever seen on anything that wasn't in a test tube or a horror movie. But Drew treated it with pride and care—and more than once, it had been a welcome sight for the twins in one of their life-and-death spots when there seemed to be no hope left.

It all seems so long ago, thought Mallory.

The night was glorious. The stars were out, and although she could see her breath, it wasn't frigid. They sang with the radio all the way to Bell Fields, where Grandma and Grandpa Brynn owned a spacious ranch, not at all like the deluxe mansion-ettes that multiplied in size the farther up and out you went into the concentric half-moons of the more upscale Haven Hills. One was Neely's house on Pinnacle Way, sprawling like a cream-colored castle at the very top, overlooking the whole town and the hills that surrounded it.

It was for the acre of land that their grandparents bought the new house. Their old house, where Mally and Merry lived, with four bedrooms and two-and-a-half stories, was just too much for them. They'd sold it to Tim after he and Campbell had the twins.

The twins knew they could count on their grandfather to point out at least three times that everything except the shrimp and the flour came from his and Grandma's own gardens—yep, they would practically be self-sustaining if they had a cow. ("And a pipeline to Alaska," Mallory sometimes whispered when Grandpa Brynn got all wound up.) He did, but tonight it was comforting instead of annoying.

Whenever they were around Grandma, Mallory got nostalgic. She thought about things she never thought about otherwise.

Grandpa and Grandma were getting older.

Mally and Merry might go to different colleges, although that was basically unthinkable.

Owen would soon be talking in sentences. Adam was already as tall as his sisters.

As Grandma brought out strawberry shortcake, she leaned over and whispered to Mallory, "Hush now. Every girl feels that way. Like your mom says, it's just biology. By the way, will you tell your mother I'm not about to keel over? I don't know what her problem is. Actually, I do know what her problem is. Campbell's always had a mind of her own. I think she's afraid I'll alphabetize the canned goods. I can watch Owen every day for a year or more if need be. Tell her to forget about adding that Melissa Hardesty."

"Melissa Hardesty isn't just one sitter too many. It's all of them," Mally said.

Grandma went on, "Tell you the truth, I have to agree, Mallory, and I'm not one to put an honest person down. I don't like a whole bunch of people taking care of my grandson, especially now that he's feeling a little poorly. I'm not that cool with it."

"You're not that cool with it?" Mally asked, trying not to laugh.

"No. Plus, I'm a lot cheaper. I'll do it for nothing. I swear Campbell treats me like an old woman. Dr. Hardesty is my doctor, and I happen to know that Melissa Hardesty smokes—and not just cigarettes. Wacky tobaccy too."

"Grandma!" Mallory said, losing the battle to keep her laughter inside.

"You didn't think our generation knew about anything but elderberry wine, huh?" Grandma put her hands on her hips and mimed holding a long cigarette holder and pushing an invisible hat brim down over her eyes.

"That's not it. But I'll tell Mom. I'm relieved. Merry will be, too. It's not just everyone prying into our lives. It's Owen. Like you said." Mallory followed her grandmother into the kitchen, carrying some of the serving plates. "I don't want so many strangers around him either."

"Exactly," Grandma Gwenny said. "Someone who smokes has heavy metal residue in their hair and clothing even if they don't do it around the child. Bad enough Carla Quinn does. I know she doesn't smoke. But her friends do and that's all over her. I'm not saying she's a bad person."

"But she's weird," Merry said. "She started crying over someone named Ellie when Owen first got sick."

"Oh, mercy. That was such a sad thing."

"You know about Ellie?"

"Well, yes, it happened just a couple of years ago, and she hasn't been right since. She used to go to our church, but she's part of this sort of Catholic cult now founded by a priest who left the church because it wasn't strict enough."

"Who's Ellie?"

"This isn't the time or the place," Grandma said. She seemed to have come back from someplace far off and noticed that the voices around the table were growing quiet as, one by one, the other kids started listening in on her conversation with Mallory. "The important thing is that I love my Owen, and I likely won't get to know him as well as I know you." Mallory's eyes suddenly glittered with unspilt tears. "Oh, Mallory. You act so much like the hard one. Your sister cries at the drop of a hat, and you put on a big act like you're so past all that."

"I can't imagine Owen not knowing you."

"Okay, I'll live to be a hundred. That suit you? I'll be an old pest and tell everyone what to do."

"Thanks Grandma," Mallory said. Gwenny put her arms around

Mallory and had a flash in her own mind of Mallory's children—
of what a strong woman and a good mother she would be. Mally
added, "I love you."

"You aren't so bad yourself," said Grandma Gwenny.

After dinner, Mallory was afraid her stomach would protrude
visibly, making all those beautiful shiny little fish scales stand on
end like quills— while she was trying to dance and remember to
press down on the ball of her foot and then step. Fortunately, the
mermaid-glisteny dress had a little welcome stretch in it.

"I feel like I gained ten pounds," said Sasha, feeling the strain in
her tight-waisted gown.

"I wonder why Brynn's grandparents don't weigh two hundred
pounds each with all that homemade pie and bread and stuff,"
Drew added, as Sasha left. They all watched the ritual of Sawyer
helping Sasha, who'd in fact eaten only about three bites of her
dinner, into the front of his car. Even with the passenger seat canted
far back, Sasha's dress still stuck up in front of her face like a huge,
diaphanous umbrella opened wide. They were both laughing,
though, so Sawyer obviously didn't mind. He was driving a Ford
Explorer. All the richies had gas guzzlers.

In the Green Beast, Drew thought, Sasha would have had to sit
in the trunk and dangle her feet.

"Grandma is always doing something, going a hundred miles
an hour," Merry said. "She's always bringing meals to what she
calls old people, even though she's like seventy-five."

"She's seventy-seven," Mally said.

"She looks ten years younger than that at least," said Drew. "Did she have a face lift?" Drew stopped to let Neely get into the car.

"Who got a face lift?" Neely asked.

"My grandmother," Merry said. "Except she didn't."

"Maybe she had, like, face work?" Neely continued. "Injectible wrinkle remover? My mom had it and she's not even forty."

"Crack me up," Merry said. "My grandmother would be as likely to climb Mount . . . Wait! Drew! There he is!"

They had just turned off Cambridge onto School Street when Merry saw the boy in the brown leather jacket walking along the side of the road. He was headed toward the school.

They passed him so quickly that when Merry turned to look back, the boy had vanished in the dark winter shadows.

"Neely, that was the new guy. He's the one! I told you! He's got blond hair cut like the guys in *Grease*? And he wears this old bomber jacket?"

"I missed him," Neely said. "I was lining my lips, which is hard in this car, I might add."

"Drewsky, do you know who I mean? Is he a senior?" Merry asked then.

"I don't know every senior guy, but I'd know if there was somebody new," Drew said.

"Weird," Merry said with a sigh. "Oh well."

They pulled up to school just as the Winter Princess, Angela DiJordano, was getting out of the car with her mom and dad. A surprise choice: Because she was in a wheelchair from an accident, Angela was one of those lucky picks—a girl who was both a sort of hero and one of those types who would look drab in the movie until she whipped off her glasses and morphed into a beauty. She couldn't feel anything below her thighs due to a spinal injury from falling when a dock collapsed at Sugar Moon Lake when she was nine or ten.

Merry said, "I wish I had slowed down to say hi to that guy."

"Why?" Mally demanded. "Just being cute doesn't make you a good person."

"I still would have liked to meet him and talk to him. There's something about him."

Drew said, "I'm so going to stop on a dark street so you can talk to some random hitchhiking killer. I can feel your dad's hands tightening around my windpipe."

The huge glass wall that formed the foyer had been decorated with mermaids and whales and starfish for an under-the-sea theme. Inside, hanging from the middle of the gym, where there normally would be a glass disco ball, was a red paper Chinese dragon at least ten feet long with streams of green and blue tulle radiating out from it likes waves. Twinkle lights swayed among the faux waves.

"How is *that* symbolic of sea life?" Mallory asked her twin, as Neely lined up with Pearson Ainsworth, who was assigned to escort her as one of the Winter Princesses on Angela's court.

Merry, who had gone so far as decorating the gym to snag a last-minute date, said, "You never know what's down there. It was cheap and it looks good."

Everyone began to applaud as the girls were presented.

"It's so unreal that I'm not even on the Rose Court," said Meredith. "Next year I'll be over the hill."

"Yep, I can already see fine lines," Drew said. "Silken Smooth can reduce the appearance of fine lines in just six weeks of continuous use, although side effects can include nausea, dizziness, seizures, muscle weakness, and a kind of liver tremor resulting in death."

"Shut up," Meredith told him.

Angela's parents were crying, and her little sisters were jumping up and down. A photographer from the *Ridgeline Reporter* snapped pictures as Angela beamed and twirled around with her real-life boyfriend, Danny Sutton.

The first song began to play, and Mallory was grateful, despite all her push-down-and-step practice, that Drew was tall enough to basically move her around like a life-sized chess piece. Gradually, Neely slipped into Pearson's arms with what looked like something other than an obligation. Kim and Allie and the others were gossiping happily at one of the net-draped tables.

The disc jockey played three slow songs in a row and, thankfully for the girls and guys who were there single, finally spun some old '90s music.

Mallory glanced around the gym. She had learned to put faith in her funny feelings.

Merry's posse was all present and accounted for, but where was Merry?

"Do you see my sister?" Mallory asked Drew.

"She has to be in the bathroom. We've been here a full half hour. I'm surprised she lasted this long."

"But she would never go to the bathroom without her gang of peeps," Mallory said. "They can't respirate alone."

"That's true enough. But look, Mallory, you're not your sister's keeper, and this is a dance, not the treacherous mountain path with a killer on the loose." Drew made claw motions with both hands and then slipped them back around Mally's waist. "She's a big girl. You're acting like your mother."

He figured that would shut her up.

He was right.

SNOWFLAKES AND MOONLIGHT

Through the glass wall of the atrium outside the gym—where Merry wandered alone, suddenly desperately thirsty for water—she could see the full moon embraced by clouds.

The sign on the concession stand said "Back in Five," which she knew meant back in fifteen or worse. Carefully holding back the tendrils that cascaded from her intentionally messy updo and opening her mouth wide to avoid ruining her elaborately lacquered mouth, she leaned over the water fountain just next to the door.

When Merry looked up, his face was a few inches from hers, watching her from outside.

Although normally Merry would have jumped a foot and run back into the gym screeching, for the sake of drama if nothing else, instead, she gave the boy a shy wave. His blond hair looked soft and clean in the moonlight, and his eyes shined with something forlorn but kind.

There's no reason to be afraid, Merry thought.

As if her legs had minds of their own, she moved toward the door to the foyer, which had been locked from the inside.

Then she stopped.

Her friend Kim's older brother had been as handsome as a model but was a hollow-hearted monster who might have killed dozens of girls if the twins hadn't risked their own lives to stop him. This boy was even more beautiful.

What if he pulled her out into the night and left her torn up and trampled in a ditch?

Meredith knew he wouldn't. She opened the door.

Instead of stepping toward her, the boy took a step back, away from the brightest lights.

"Hi," Merry said. "I saw you walking on the road."

"My old school," he said. "I just felt like seeing it."

"And the other day at the mall."

"I saw you, too. What's your name? I mean, if that's okay."

"It's okay. I'm Merry Brynn."

"Is your dad Kevin?"

"Tim," she said. "Kevin's my uncle. Why?"

"Just . . . I know lots of Brynns. My mom was a teacher here. She taught English."

Merry said, "So, you should come in. A lot of people who went here come to the dances. Did you transfer? Did you play football or anything?"

"No, I was too small for that. I ran cross country."

"My sister's boyfriend does that. Do you run cross-country in college? I mean, if you're in college."

"I'm not in college now," the boy said.

"Well, anyway, my *parents* used to go to school dances here until we got into ninth grade and forced them to stop. My mom didn't even go here, but my father has a morbid attachment to his youth. I'm sure you can come in."

"I'm not dressed for something like that. Just jeans and my old jacket. I just wanted to look."

"Are you from here?"

"Yep," said the boy.

"Where do you live?"

"Oh . . . outside town. On Pumpkin Hollow."

"My Uncle Kevin and my Aunt Kate live there! In the big Victorian house that's painted all different colors of green? Have you seen that house?" If this boy were from here, even if he were visiting family, he would have had to know about the fire at Uncle Kevin's and Aunt Kate's. Two years later, the gossip about who started the fire that nearly killed Mally and Merry was still something people brought up, especially on dark winter nights. No one had ever found out who threw fireworks up on the roof and ignited the blaze. Merry and Mally were sure it had been David Jellico.

"It was the house that set on fire, a couple of years ago?" Merry said.

"I've been away awhile," the boy said. It must have been a long while.

"Do you know the Aldridges?" They were a couple in their fifties who'd moved from Minnesota and had a small farm for awhile with their disabled son, a guy in his twenties who acted like a ten-year-old and was one of the nicest people in Ridgeline. They moved to Ridgeline to get their son away from the stares and pressures of the city.

"I don't know them," the boy said. "Not really."

"How about Mr. and Mrs. Highland? They're really old. They live way out just across from the . . ."

The boy's face brightened. "I know them. Do you?"

The only encounter Merry had ever had with Mrs. Highland was being screamed at from the porch for riding her bike over the edge of the Highlands' lawn. Merry was swerving to get out of the way of a car that nearly sideswiped her. At the time, Meredith thought, would Mrs. Highland have rather seen Merry get creamed in the road like a deer in hunting season? She decided Mrs. Highland would indeed have preferred that to wrecking one corner of her lawn. Like her grandparents, the Highlands treated their lawn, garden, and orchards like babies—or so Meredith recalled. Mrs. Highland yelled, "Don't you have any respect for other people's property?"

Later, Aunt Kate told her that Mrs. Highland wasn't really mean, just troubled, and that Merry shouldn't take it personally. Merry hardly remembered it now. It had been five years ago or more.

"I only know them a little," Meredith said.

"They don't go out a lot," said the boy. "They're nice though. My mom . . . is the one who used to teach English—remember I said that?"

What did that have to do with the Highlands? Merry thought. Was he saying he was related to them in some way? Talking to this boy seemed to raise more questions than it answered. Her dad had to know his family. Tim knew everyone and seemed to have tentacles with eyes that reached out and told him every move his daughters made. Just then, the DJ began to play one of the songs Merry's parents embarrassingly danced to in the living room—"Moon River," from one of Campbell's favorite old crazy black-and-white movies. The DJ said it was because there was a beautiful moon out that night over the newly fallen snow. The speakers piped the music out onto the lawn, where the flattened snow was decked out with soda cans and candy wrappers and the occasional fast-food container sat up like a little white coffin.

"I guess I should go back in," Meredith said. "It is a beautiful night though, like the DJ said. It seems warmer than when we got here. And the moon makes it as bright as daylight."

"Come outside for a moment," the boy said. "I'm Ben."

He put out his hand, and Meredith almost touched it, acutely aware of the electrical bolt that shot up her arms and spread like a small sun throughout her whole midsection. Now, she should have shut the door between them. Now, she should have been afraid. *Something* was weird.

What kind of boy would ask a girl, alone, to come outside into the darkness and the cold?

"Trust your guts," Campbell had often said to the girls. "They'll never lie to you."

Meredith's "guts" were saying this boy was only shy, not evil. But how wrong had she been before about David Jellico?

The boy called Ben said suddenly, "I know you're thinking I'm

probably some kind of creep and I want to hurt you. I don't want
to hurt you. And look behind you. There are like six people buying
water and Coke and stuff. I'm not going to pull you out to my car. I
haven't even got a car. I won't even touch you. It's just been a really
long time since I stood next to a beautiful girl."

As much because she was embarrassed as because she was
enthralled—and she was enthralled, her breath coming in little
gasps as she tried to control it—Meredith stepped outside.

"I remember this song," said Ben. "Do you want to dance?"

"Of course," Meredith said and almost added, *I love you. I've
always loved you.* How could she think something so crazy? But
Romeo and Juliet had. Whoever loved that loved not at first sight?
Their whole deal lasted, like, three days, and Shakespeare wrote
a play about it that had lasted five hundred years and inspired a
bunch of movies and *West Side Story*, too.

Ben was a stranger, but Merry felt as though she had known
him all her life. He didn't quite touch her, even when they danced.
She couldn't feel the pressure of his hand against her back, as they
moved together in gentle patterns and hesitations. He didn't dance
like other boys. Most guys just shifted from foot to foot and tried
to get their hands around the front of the girl from the back or
squeeze her until they could feel her whole body without having
to ask. Ben didn't even clutch Merry against him. Merry wanted
him to. The door closed and locked behind her. She didn't care.
His chest looked taut and muscled under a clean white T-shirt,
and his skin, when he leaned down, smelled like pine needles and
soap and something else—nutmeg maybe or another spice. *Kiss*

me, Meredith thought. *Kiss me before I have to turn back into a pumpkin.*

"My mom taught me to dance," Ben said. "Back when I was about your age. How old are you?"

"Fifteen," Meredith said and then shook her head. "I turned fifteen on New Year's Eve. How about you?"

"I'll be eighteen in May."

So he wasn't too old. Two little years.

"Meredith!" came a shout. "What are you doing?" Drew and Mallory stood in the doorway. Drew held the door as Meredith rushed toward her sister. "You're spinning around out here like . . . like you're bewitched."

Merry spun around again to make them mad.

Ben had, of course, taken off. Mallory would scare wild beasts.

"It's thirty degrees out here. Your hands are white," Mally called.

"I don't feel cold."

"Are you crazy?" Mallory asked.

Meredith said, "Absolutely." She took one last spin in Neely's gently draped dress as a drift of lazy, lacy flakes of snow began to fall.

DREAM SPACE

DREAM SPACE

I t was snowing in earnest by the time Meredith and Neely got into Neely's house, driven home by Stuart, the driver who took Neely's dad into his New York office Monday through Saturday.

Freezing, they hurried up into Neely's room and shut the door behind them, quickly running over to warm themselves by the small peach-tinted marble fireplace, with gas logs that looked real and felt better than real logs. There was a fireplace big enough to roast an ox in Neely's parents' bedroom. In fact, there was a fireplace in every room except the downstairs bath and the workout room.

Soon Stuart's wife, Ludamila, the housekeeper and maid, knocked at Neely's bedroom door. She took both girls' dresses to be cleaned and left a pitcher of hot chocolate and a tray of cookies and miniature meringues with kiwi fruit in the middle. Meredith thought her mother would be as likely to serve this to the Brynn kids as deep-fried rattlesnake with ketchup. But the girls got into their flannel 'jama bottoms and sweatshirts and settled in happily.

"Do you need anything else, Neely?" Ludamila asked. She was sort of like an aunt to Neely because her own parents—a busy lawyer and a fashion designer—might be around at any given time or might not and Neely never knew which. *Gas fireplaces were great,* Merry thought, *but they didn't make up for parents you could lean on.* Then again, her parents had sort of moved over lately and let the kids semi-raise themselves. Meredith was fairly sure that Campbell was so exhausted and Tim so distracted that the girls could have sold pot out the kitchen window without their noticing.

"No Luda," Neely said now. "Thanks a million. Merry and I can chow down. No boys around."

Ludamila laughed. "Okay. Okay. Okay, nothing ever change, Okay. Okay. Okay," she said in her heavy Eastern European accent.

As soon as Ludamila left, Neely jumped up and stared out the window at the moon.

"How can we be sitting here? It's like . . . 10:30. What are we going to do for fun? Do you want to sneak out? Why didn't somebody have a party? Why didn't I?"

Meredith said, "Well, tonight it's best that you didn't."

Neely whirled around.

"Neels, I have to tell you something. I'm glad Kim had to go home this time after all instead of staying over. I don't want the whole world to know what I'm going to tell you," said Meredith.

Neely's eyes sparkled so maliciously it was almost endearing.

"Are you pregnant?" Neely asked.

"Huh?" Merry said with a gasp.

"Did you . . . do it?"

"What? It's nothing like that, Neely!"

"Well, whatever it is, you can count on me," Neely said. She moved her library books and took out her little liquor stash, pouring herself and Meredith small helpings of Bailey's Irish Crème in toothbrush cups. Merry smiled. It was totally unbelievable that Neely's parents knew she had liquor in the house and let her keep it because they supposedly felt that Neely needed to test her limits. Tim and Campbell would have had her or Mallory testing the limits of the size of their room for the same offense. Meredith had been delighted that she could count on Neely to spread the news about meeting the new boy with the speed of a forest fire in August.

Now, strangely, she wanted to keep everything about him to herself.

"You started to tell me something," Neely began.

"Well, yeah."

"So tell."

Weirdly, Merry felt that even saying some of what she felt would somehow disgrace what she felt about Ben. "He's just a cute guy. That's all."

"That wasn't what you said at practice. You said this was the guy. The guy you completely had the biggest crush on in your life on Earth."

"That was before," Merry said, getting up and taking her sponge bag into the bathroom. She began to wash off her makeup with Noxzema. There were about forty things better and newer than Noxzema for washing your face. But Campbell had used Noxzema on her face, and Meredith had to admit that for someone that old, her mother didn't have as many wrinkles as her friends did. And Campbell was outside all the time, too—at least she used to be— running and biking and stuff.

Before medical school and Owen hit like twin tornadoes.

Merry sent up a silent apology to her favorite saint, the one who shared her confirmation name, Brigid, for comparing Owen to a tornado.

"Do you care if I shower for a minute?"

"No, but . . . as soon as you come out, I want the truth," Neely said, flipping on her flat screen.

In the shower, Meredith took her time, and not only because the six jets in Neely's shower made getting cleaned up like some kind of spa experience. She thought about what love meant and if she even knew that. Love, her mother said, was hoping the other person always got the best strawberries. She barely knew this boy. She had talked to him exactly once. But she knew and could not tell Neely or anyone, that what she felt was love in the worst degree. Yes, of course, she wanted Ben to be happy, but she wanted him to be happy with her, with Merry. If he found someone else, she could imagine herself forgetting to eat until she shriveled up like a seedpod in fall. A spot just below her ribcage still tingled where his hand had almost touched her waist, a glow that spread throughout her whole body and made her heart hammer. When she tried to think of anything else, Ben's face swam back before her eyes. They were eyes into which Merry could fall and drown. His gentle, slightly sad voice threaded through her ears, telling her not to be afraid.

Afraid?

Merry knew she would follow Ben into the darkest cave and be utterly confident, so long as he was beside her.

Was *this* love?

Desire?

Insanity?

As she began to wash her hair, Merry shut her eyes and actually swayed. She was dizzy. This is stupid, she thought. Maybe it was love. Maybe it was the flu. She had to use the shampoo twice. Sasha had done a brilliant job on Merry's hair, but unless she got all the gunk out, it would stay in those tendrils and whirls permanently. Sasha had used nearly a full can of firm hold spray to get Meredith's thick, mane-straight bobbed hair to look like a little curl castle. When Merry stepped out, she swathed herself in peach towels the size of kitchen rugs (everything was peach and black in Neely's room) and then slipped into her flannel sleep pants and one of the fluffy robes the Chaplins kept for Neely's guests. Maybe, she hoped, Neely would have changed her mind by this point and gone on to something else. Maybe she was engrossed in some horror movie on TV.

Fat chance.

As soon as Merry came back into the bedroom, Neely said, "So, how long have you been seeing him? When we were at practice, you hadn't even talked to him. That was fast work."

"Well, now that I have, it's different."

"Merry! You look weird. As in semi-conscious. I'm your best friend in the world except for Allie and Kimmie and Erika. You're sitting there like you've got a secret. We don't have secrets."

"It feels so new and different. It's just not something I want to gossip and laugh about. I saw him tonight at the dance and we talked."

Neely said, "Why didn't you bring him to meet us?"

"We talked outside the gym. And for maybe about two minutes."

"Sounds like a stable relationship," Neely said. It was weirdly something exactly like what Mallory would have said.

"You would understand if you had been there," Merry insisted. "Remember when I said I saw the guy on the road? The blond guy with the leather jacket?" Neely nodded, stuffing her mouth with the gourmet cookies, as if hypnotized by food and Merry's strange reluctance. "That was Ben. That was him. I met that same guy tonight hanging around in the dark outside the gym. He took off, probably because Drew and my sister came out yelling so loudly, he probably thought she was mentally ill. Mally has such a big mouth, and she says I'm the one who never shuts up. But he said his name was Ben and he's eighteen and he lives out on Pumpkin Hollow."

"By your aunt. Where the fire was," Neely ate two of the meringues at once and said, "It's a little creepy. Him doing that. Walking down the road in the dark and hanging around outside a dance."

"He doesn't have a car. He used to go to Ridgeline. I don't know why I never saw him. It's not that big a school. But maybe he was there when I was still in junior high. Well, sure he was. It's like another world. Basically, as far as people in high school, I only knew Drew back then. And Mally's friend Eden."

"Is he in college?" Neely asked. "Because if he is and he's just home for a break or something, that's why I couldn't find out the straight stuff on him. I can't be expected to cover all of New York state as well as college communities."

"He said no," Merry said. "He's not in college." For some reason, she was embarrassed by this. As if to compensate, she went on, "He said his mom was an English teacher at Ridgeline a long time ago. I think what he *really* said was that his mom used to be an English teacher at the high school and that her mom, his grandma, was old Mrs. Highland, and that she used to be an English teacher too." Meredith paused for a moment. "Actually, I have no idea if he said that. There was something about him knowing the Highlands... I couldn't stop staring at him. I was like an idiot. He looked like James Dean."

"Who . . . is James Dean?" Neely asked. "Not to be stupid."

"It's not stupid. No one our age knows who he is. He's like Elvis . . . only not. He's this old-time actor. He's dead. But he died while he was young and beautiful. He was probably only about twenty. You never heard about him because your parents are too nice to force you to go see movies from the Pleistocene period at the Belles Artes Theatre." Neely made a face. "But James Dean, I didn't mind. We saw this movie called *Rebel Without a Cause*. And the guy he played . . . was like a real person. His parents were always on his back and fighting."

"I couldn't bear that," said Neely. "Bad enough they're never around."

"Anyhow," Merry went on, "he was really a good actor, and he would still be cute now if he were alive. I mean, he wouldn't be cute now. He'd be old, like ninety. But if he were to be in movies now, people would still consider him amazing. He even made smoking look good. I think he died in a motorcycle wreck. Like, long ago. Before my parents were born."

"We could Google it," Neely suggested.

"No, that would just show you what Ben looks like *to me*," Merry told her. "Sort of." She let herself remember the sight of Ben's slight ripple of muscle under his plain, sparkling clean white T-shirt. Though he wasn't a big guy, or a pretty boy, he had this gentle loneliness in his smile that went straight to Merry's soul—or where she thought her soul must be, somewhere in the region of her stomach. And his eyes weren't sly or ready to laugh with the next joke directed at girls—their hair, their cell phones, their gossip. They seemed to hold Merry gently, a gaze only for her, a promise that Ben would always protect her. "He . . . he has really long hair. But it's soft and pretty. Not greasy or knotted up."

"Guys," Neely said, "so do not know how to manage long hair."

"Very true," said Meredith through a mouthful of cookies. "He does. He's different in other ways too."

"So he lives with his grandparents?" Neely said.

"Either that or . . . maybe his parents live in one of the new houses on that street."

"Are you really dating?" Neely asked.

"Uh, no," Meredith answered.

"So no harm, no foul if you ask your dad about him; he knows everybody."

"I guess. I just don't want my parents glomming all over this like they did when Mallory had a crush on Eden's brother. Cooper? Remember? I mean, my mother got in his face at our birthday party! I just want to figure out if I really do like him first."

"Makes sense. Why face the hassle?"

Meredith said, "See, Neels, I got the impression he couldn't really afford to go to college yet. Maybe he's working for a year."

"Well, it shouldn't be hard to find him. Aren't there only, like, five houses out there? We could take a walk."

The very thought was horrifying to Meredith. She didn't want the round of gossip to start: *He said this and she was like whatever and I was like no way. . . .* Ben was better than that. Startled, she realized that she might talk about him to, of all people, her sister. Or maybe someone older, like Sasha. But not to her friends. They were too silly. Hurriedly, she said, "Oh no. It wouldn't be that easy. That's the thing. Not anymore. There were only a few houses when we were in the fire. But there are way more houses out there now on Pumpkin Hollow than there were *then*, at the time of the fire. Last year, Mr. Aldridge started selling lots from the land where he used to have the part of his farm where he grew sod. And at least three houses went up like . . . like lettuce. There are some retired people in this pretty two-house thing and a couple of families with little kids and bigger kids too. There could be families with older kids at home. People I don't even know. Don't worry about it, Neels. When the time comes, he'll be there."

"That's bizarre," Neely said.

Merry couldn't explain. She just shrugged.

But through the night, from wherever he was now, she could literally feel Ben thinking of her. It wasn't as though Ben had actually held her against him, but she seemed to remember the heat and tenderness of his touch in her mind and in her body. It wasn't like the touch of the guys in school, who tried to glom all over your body even if they didn't know you— the kind that made you want to shower with bleach. She felt odd, almost as though Ben had blessed her. She could say that, so she said, "He was . . . so kind to me. Like a prince."

"I think you're like . . . on drugs," Neely said. "Hey! Want to go out and drive around? I only have my permit but we still can. I'm a very good driver."

"If we get caught, I'll be grounded for a month, and you'll be the same as you are right now," Meredith said, and both the girls flopped back on Neely's massive bed, laughing. Neely never got grounded. Her parents viewed whatever she did that was wrong as Neely's way of expressing her frustration with young adulthood. It was such a joke that Neely said it took all the fun out of rebellion.

But Neely was, by then, already sleepy and Meredith was as well. Neely curled up on her side of the bed, slipping her gel mask over her eyes and putting in her ear buds. Meredith knew what Neely listened to—an endless loop of crashing surf. She said it soothed her, but Merry would have gone around the bend.

Merry got up and glanced out the window again. As Thornton Wilder had written a hundred years ago (they'd read *Our Town* in ninth grade), the moonlight was terrible. She wanted to see Ben and . . . and what? Just to see him would be enough. Not seeing him made her feel like a belt was pulled tight around her ribs. Finally, because the snow thickened until it made smudges of the lights in the houses down the hill, and finally even the smudges disappeared, Merry lay down.

She dreamed of Ben.

They lay together in the sun, in a blooming big orchard where apple blossoms swayed over their heads. Merry wore a sundress and Ben his white T-shirt, and the sun beat down on them while the birds chorused madly. Ben held her close, so close she was almost trapped beneath his strong body. But there was no sense of pressure. Ben would never hurt her. Merry closed her eyes against the sun, with their lips about to touch, his love for her all around her like a bath of warmth in which she could never drown. He said to her, "Meredith. It's not so far. It's not so long. We're just that close. We can be together. Don't you see? Don't say no, Meredith."

She missed the first crystal ping of her cell phone that told her she had a text message. Dreaming as hard as she was, slowly waking, she imagined that the second ping was Ben, throwing a snowball at the window, asking her to step out onto the balcony off Neely's room and speak to him in sweet syllables.

The third ping actually opened Merry's eyes.

"No need to come now," her father had written. "Owen is back in the hospital but he's already better. Having tests. Don't worry. Love u, Pop."

Don't worry?

The warm bath of imagined love quickly went cold. Merry lay down again, but sleep was banished. When the window light was gray, before Neely awoke, Merry scribbled a note on Neely's stationery pad and ran downstairs in her sweats, asking Stuart to drive her to the hospital.

PREDATOR

PREDATOR

Meredith burst through the door of the emergency room entrance, and the first person to catch up with her was Kim Jellico's mother, Bonnie. Bonnie was Merry's own mother's closest friend.

"I hate it when people say, 'I know what you're going through,' but I know what you're going through," Bonnie said, hugging Merry tight. Not only had Bonnie and her husband Dave lost David, their eighteen-year-old son two years ago (in what everyone, except the twins of course, assumed was an accidental fall), just six months ago, they had also suffered through a surgery to correct a minor heart defect that Christian Loc Jellico, the baby boy they'd adopted from Vietnam, was born with. Christian was fine now, a healthy toddler instead of the big-eyed skinny little ghost he'd been. But the night of his surgery was the only time Meredith ever remembered both their parents asking the kids to pray.

"Bonnie, do you know how Owen is?"

"He's asleep finally," Bonnie said. "He had a tough time of it. Not as bad as last time. But he was on the edge of dehydration, and we couldn't stop him from vomiting. They gave him a little something to sedate him. It was the whole story all over again. First he chucked up his dinner, and then Luna gave him a bottle of formula. That's when he really started to heave. Luna just wrapped him in his snowsuit and a big towel and drove him right here. Good girl. She's in the waiting room now. The plan is to test Owen for allergies to milk-based products."

"Thanks Bonnie. Is my sister here?"

"Home with Adam. She says Adam's worse off than your parents. He's terrified."

"Okay. I'll go back to my mom now. Where is Owie?"

Bonnie led the way to the swinging doors—the twins treated the emergency room as though it were their mother's office—and pointed to a curtained section in the middle of the trauma rooms. "Let me check what's going on. I'll come right back and get you."

Before Meredith could turn around, however, someone tapped her shoulder. Luna had come out of the family waiting room.

"Luna! Have you been here all night?" Merry asked.

"I thought it was my responsibility," Luna said. "Would you have gone home?"

"Well, it's a hospital and my mother's with him, so yeah. Aren't your parents furious? It's almost six in the morning!"

"I'm sure my mother doesn't even know or care where I am, and my dad's still at work," Luna explained. "Merry, I felt something like

this coming the moment I stepped up on your porch. The first step."
Luna looked like the long-lost older sister in the Addams Family,
her pale face made whiter by her kinky choice of foundation, her
lipstick like a blackberry slash.

"If you felt it coming, Luna, why didn't you just call my dad and
tell him it was going to happen?" Meredith asked, more sad than
irritated.

"People don't believe you. He would have just thought I was
crazy." Merry both could identify and could not imagine what it
was like to be Luna. People did think she was crazy, if in a harmless
way, and, since the hunch Mallory had about the witches dancing in
the woods, Merry was among those who thought so.

Still, she asked, "What if it was a matter of life or death?"

"I would know if it was that," Luna said. "I knew Owen would
be fine. I can, you know, talk with the dead."

"Hmmm," Merry said. "What do they have to say?" Merry
already knew very well what they had to say. Her ancestors and the
few other ghosts to whom she had talked were generally—although
not always—sweet, yearning people who were worried about their
lost puppies or their rose gardens or, most often, the people left
behind who grieved so horribly that it kept them, well, around.

"They tell me who's next," said Luna.

"So who's next?" Merry asked, wishing Bonnie would come
back and free her from Luna's hungry eyes.

"I'm not really at liberty to talk about that, Merry. But it's not
always who you'd expect."

"Okay," Merry said.

"And if I did say anything, I'd be treated even more terribly out there than I already am," Luna said. "People are utterly intolerant."

That was the understatement of the millennium, but Meredith felt a fleeting wisp of real sympathy for old garden-variety wannabe psychic Luna. She wasn't doing anything but waiting in the hall, so she decided to indulge Luna, whose customary intensity seemed really torqued up to an almost eerie degree. So Merry asked, "So you really, really had some kind of . . . premonition that my brother would get sick? That's amazing."

"I absolutely did," said Luna, tapping the blond wood doorframe with one black dagger of a fingernail. "The moment I went into the kitchen, I had a flash of being here, right here, with him. It scares me to death to think what it would have been like if I hadn't been there."

"Me too," Meredith said. "But do you have these feelings often?"

"Yes. Well, I do know when a bad event is about to happen," said Luna.

"Thunderstorms? Losing your lunch card? Or just people stuff?"

"Anything."

"Can you do it at will?" Merry asked.

"I don't want you spreading this around school," Luna said, lowering her voice. "Not everyone is Miss All-American Apple Pie like you and Mallory. But yes, I can ask my voices anything and they will tell me. For example, right now they're telling me that Owen isn't really allergic to milk."

"Well, I'll let you know," Meredith said, turning to look for Bonnie, who was approaching and beckoning to her. Merry gave Luna's arm a squeeze. Luna's cologne lingered, a blend of something like vanilla and mustard. Meredith had to admit that it was pretty sweet of her to stay there all night. Then again, Luna's life with her nuts mom, Bettina, and her mostly absent dad, was probably a little short on genuine drama. As she went through the double doors, she glanced back at Luna, who was still standing in the hall, then nearly collided with her father.

"Merry heart," Tim said, giving Merry a hard hug. "Owen's asleep. I'm sorry. But I'm glad he is." Tim opened the door and propelled Meredith back outside the door of the emergency room. Luna watched Tim and Meredith with that craving look—a look that suddenly set off an alarm in Meredith's stomach, which began to knead back on itself as though she hadn't eaten in a long time (in fact, she hadn't). Maybe it was only hunger, but she had learned to trust physical sensations that had psychological strings attached. "We've been up all night, but Owen's so much better. The test for milk allergies was negative, so I'm going to run home now and get his formula, in case there's some contaminant of some kind. We have the super large-sized can, so we've been using it for a while."

"I used the last of it up," Luna said, striding across the room.

"There was a lot of powder left," Tim answered. "It was a monster can."

"Well, when I got there, I have to confess that the bottles smelled sort of peculiar, so I threw them out and made new ones. But he'd already gotten sick once by then," Luna said. She gave Meredith a significant look. It hadn't been "smell" at all, but one of Luna's alleged "feelings." Meredith found a chair in the hall and sat down.

"But the rest of it?" Tim asked.

"The rest of it spilled into the sink when I was making the new bottles," Luna said. "I didn't feel right about those either, so I washed them out too."

"So . . . there's nothing the doctors can analyze that might have made Owen sick?"

"Not at your house," Luna said. "I'm sorry. I know that stuff's expensive."

Tim pressed his lips together and turned back to the curtained-off space. As he did, several nurses, including Campbell, wheeled Owen out in a huge crib, like a lion's cage, heading up toward the Pediatric Intensive Care Unit, which at Ridgeline Memorial, amounted to two rooms.

"Luna said she threw out all the formula and made more and threw that out," Tim told the group. "Then she spilled the rest of the can."

"That's . . . crazy!" Campbell whispered explosively. "Luna! Why would you do that?"

"She said the formula smelled funny after she gave Owen his bottle," Tim said.

"So maybe we could know now what was wrong!" Campbell said. She was yelling, but in a whisper, so as not to disturb the baby. "But spilled the rest of the can of powder?"

"Do you think that's not true?" Tim whispered. But Luna heard him.

"You think I'm lying?" Luna asked. "I sat here all night with you guys and I'm lying? Thanks a lot."

Meredith got up from the chair and kissed her mom. "No," she said. "She's not lying."

"How do you know Meredith?" Campbell asked. "You just got here. Luna, I'm not trying to say anything that will offend you or accuse you, but this is the kind of situation where we have to consider that Owen might have been exposed to contaminated food."

"I understand that," Luna said formally. "But I'd look at the person who made the bottles instead of the one who tried to throw them out so they wouldn't hurt him! Namely me! Or at the manufacturer, disgruntled employees are always putting rat hairs and urine and . . ."

"Oh that's enough, thanks," Tim said.

Owen stirred slightly, and one of the other nurses said they'd go get him settled upstairs and wait for Campbell. The lights outside the curtained area were glaring, and Owen clearly was becoming restless. Meredith reached between the bars to touch one of his tiny, starfish hands and leaned down to kiss it. She turned back to her mother, and to Luna, who had her arms crossed tightly across her chest in its skull-embroidered sweater.

"I talked to Luna for a long time, Mom. You taught us to be able to tell when people are lying. I don't think she is. About this anyhow."

But the conversation in the waiting room wasn't the reason Meredith was so sure.

In a sudden vision, just moments before—the reason that Meredith sat down hard in the metal chair outside the ER assessment area—she'd seen the spilt formula in the sink and Luna's ever-so-unmistakable hands with their black nail polish cleaning up the mess. What confused her was that she also saw someone making bottles—someone with plain, unpainted shaped oval nails, like Campbell's. But the fingers didn't look like her mother's short, practical fingers. They were long and slim. Young hands. Not Grandma's. Sasha had made bottles for Owen earlier in the day, before the winter formal. But that was in the early morning. All those bottles would have been used up before they even left for the dance or poured down the sink later on . . . and Carla was younger than Campbell. She had plain hands, too.

But she hadn't worked that day.

Meredith needed to talk to Mallory.

What was really going on?

How badly did Luna need to prove that she was really a psychic? Was there something crazy about Luna, beyond the obvious?

Campbell turned to Bonnie and Dr. Staats, the doctor who'd delivered the twins, Adam, and Owen and who happened to be on call in the ER that night, since she—and every other doctor in Ridgeline—had stopped delivering babies. Campbell kept saying she was going to be the one brave enough to start doing it again, and Tim told her that she'd better start saving now for the million a year in insurance premiums it would cost her, since doctors who delivered babies got sued more than anyone else did.

Dr. Staats said that this meant they'd have to try to analyze Owen's stomach contents, but they'd already disposed of the junk he'd spewed in the ambulance. The only hope was to try to insert a tube. . . .

"I'm not putting him through that," Campbell said with a voice like a judge's gavel coming down. "It's fine to test him for other allergies and hope something will turn up. There are plenty of other things in formula besides milk and maybe there's something else. Maybe in his baby food. She didn't throw that down the sink too?"

Luna's face was expressionless, like a Halloween mask. She said, "The jar is right in the fridge in front. I put plastic wrap over the top and then the cap. He only ate half of his chicken noodle and half of his applesauce."

A moment later, Carla Quinn came through the swinging doors.

"Campbell," she said. "Owen sick again?"

"Yes, he is, Carla. How did you know?"

"Oh, you know," Big Carla said, "heard it through the grapevine. My neighbor works overnights. She called and told me."

"It's seven o'clock on a Sunday morning!" Campbell exclaimed.

Meredith stared, shocked silent. It was the invasion of the babysitters.

"News travels fast. Anyhow, if he's being admitted, you won't need me tomorrow right? Or will you?" Carla asked.

Campbell shook her head. "Carla, why did you come all the way in here to ask me that? Why didn't you just call? Call me at the desk? You're not on the schedule today are you?"

Carla shrugged. Today, she was dressed up in a Seven-Up green pantsuit over her black men's rubber buckle boots. "It's on the way to church."

"What church?" In Ridgeline, the Catholic Church that the Brynns attended, St. Thomas More, was on Church Street, as were the Methodist, Unitarian, and Congregational churches. Church Street was about as opposite from the hospital as someone could get. "I'm sorry for how that sounded," Campbell said. "I just . . . I'm stressed and it seemed strange."

"That's okay. We do a basement thing, in someone's rec room. I'm old Catholic," Carla said. "You know, we still have the mass in Latin and all? It's out in Deptford by the quarry. The priest—well, he used to be a priest—thought the church is too modern for him now. I started going after my husband and Ellie died. I feel closer to them there." Carla stepped forward and hugged one of Campbell's shoulders with her big hand. "We'll pray for him. I'll start a prayer chain. Poor baby. Not much older than Ellie. How much more can he take without giving up?" There were suddenly tears on Carla's big cheeks. She pulled out a man's oversized handkerchief. "I just hope he doesn't give up." Carla turned and clomped out toward the parking lot.

"I know Carla's husband died in a car accident," Campbell said. "Who's Ellie?" Campbell turned to Luna. "I'm grateful to you Luna for helping Owen. Please forgive us if we're over-reacting. He's just a little baby. And this has all happened so fast." Luna shrugged but finally nodded and slipped into her own coat. She refused the offer of a ride home.

"She's a witch," Merry said. "Maybe she has a broomstick."

"Merry, this is bad enough," Campbell said briefly.

"I'm sorry, Mom," Merry said. "I just can't bear how sad this is." Holding back tears, she hugged her mother. "Should I go home, Mom?"

"Go ahead. Dad needs to get those baby food jars anyhow, honey. I'll be in touch every minute, if anything happens. Adam has homework. He was up at 2 a.m., and I hope Mally got him to go back to sleep."

Merry didn't say a word on the way home; nor did her father. He didn't flip on the exasperating talk radio that seemed to be an extension of his right hand, either. Merry texted all her friends, who were eager to know the details of Owen's latest illness. For Allie and Erika and Neely and especially Kimmy—whose own younger brother, adopted from Vietnam, was only three—Owen was like a special little mascot. He had his own Ridgeline Rockets vest that he wore to games and competitions, sewn for him by Kim's mom, Bonnie, and his own pom poms. Every time they saw him, they made him wiggle his rear end and say, "So fine!"

When they got to the house, Tim simply put the two jars in a plastic ziplock bag and kissed Merry briefly on the head. Then he left without a word.

Meredith shivered. The house seemed to be freezing. Either Adam was up in his room on the ancient computer his parents had passed on to him or had gone back to sleep. Plainly, Meredith could see her sister passed out on the sofa, so deeply asleep she had obviously not even heard Tim and Merry come in. She was slipping one of the two thousand afghans Grandma had knitted for them over Mally's shoulders and checking the thermostat—it wasn't cold; only the usual freezer temp that Tim and Campbell said was good for a person, sixty-seven degrees—when she heard a knock at the door.

Dad had forgotten something. And the car was already running with his keys in it.

But when she got to the door and pulled back the curtains, there, in the gauzy sunshine stood Ben.

THOUGH HELL SHOULD BAR THE WAY

M erry forgot to breathe.

Ben had just lit a cigarette and was about to walk back down the steps when Meredith finally gathered enough presence of mind to open the door. She despised smoking. But for some reason, the cigarettes had no odor. And when she sat down next to Ben, he didn't have that rank, sickening smell.

"Hey," Ben said. "I missed you."

"Me too," said Merry.

Why do I feel so comfortable with a stranger?

"I feel like I've known you all my life," Ben said. "Is that strange?"

"If it is, I'm strange, too," Merry said.

Ben moved closer to her, so they were almost touching. Meredith felt a longing that spread up from her tummy, a combination of every fever she ever had in her childhood. Around Ben there seemed to be a kind of light. His seawater eyes were filled with nothing but Meredith and the longing she could tell he felt for her. Her concern for her little brothers—the one in the hospital and the one she assumed was upstairs asleep—was like a distant siren, alarming but far away, having to do with someone else. She only wanted to be with Ben, kissing Ben. She wanted to touch the muscles in Ben's back and his chest and the curve of his lips. Although it was cold, somehow Meredith didn't feel it, even though she wore nothing but sweats with the sleeves cut short. When she finally remembered to breathe, her gasps made clouds of smoke in the cold air. It was as though the two of them were enclosed in a bubble of light and heat.

"I was going to come to find you," she said.

"But I knew where you live," Ben said. To Merry's bemusement, he actually looked surprised. "This is the Brynns' house. You . . . you always lived here. Kevin and Tim and Karin and everyone . . ."

"Well, that was a long time ago. Those people are way older than we are, Ben, so . . ."

As though to turn her away from the subject, Ben said, "I wish I could kiss you. I want to. It's . . . I know it's too soon." Then he said, "Let lips do what hands do . . . like it says in your favorite play."

"It's hardly my favorite. But I'm liking it more these days. I kind of see the point of *Romeo and Juliet*," Merry said, holding her small palm up so that what she and Ben felt vibrated between them. "I don't mind if you kiss me," she added. "In fact, I really want that, more than I ever have with anyone. I can't believe I said that. But my little brother is in the hospital. I don't know why that matters. I'd just hate to be enjoying myself when he's sick, and I'd hate to be worrying about him the first time I kissed you." Ben's eyes melted with pity. "And my other little brother is upstairs scared out of his gourd."

"I thought you had a little sister."

"I have a twin sister," Meredith said. "Mallory is an identical twin to me. We have two little brothers."

"I didn't remember that," Ben said. *What could he mean*, Mally thought? Ben seemed to think he was talking about another family. Well, they had just met.

"So I have to go in," Merry finally said. "My little brother might want me. My sister's asleep. She was up all night."

Immediately, Ben sat up and smiled. "That's fine. I don't want your parents to think I'm corrupting you." He held out his cigarette. "Pretty disgusting." Meredith laughed.

"You are corrupting me. I'm not used to feeling like . . . this."

"You've never been in love?"

Love, Meredith thought. *LOVE?*

"Ben, I just met you! Love is something that grows."

"How do you know, if you've never been in love?" he asked. "But who am I to talk? I've never been in love, either." Meredith sat up and crossed her legs under her suddenly freezing butt. She'd been sitting on cold concrete, and it would take her hours to feel her rear end.

"I have no idea. But that's what they say. It takes time," Meredith told Ben. "I always thought it would be sudden, for me. But people tell me that's just attraction. It's not real. It doesn't last."

"Whoever loved that loved not at first sight?" Ben recited.

"How did you know that? And why did you say that? I said that the first time I saw you, through the bus window. We're studying *Romeo and Juliet* at school."

"My mom made us memorize and recite."

"We have to do that, too. It's good for you I guess. Trains the brain. But I can't see how I can memorize a long poem and then say it in front of people. I picked a short one."

Ben leaned back on his elbows. He asked, "What poem did you choose?"

"'Stopping by the Woods on a Snowy Evening' by Robert Frost. 'And miles to go before I sleep. And miles to go before I sleep.' It's like saying a dream."

"Because it's easy," Ben teased her.

"Because I love it. What about you, smart guy?"

"Watch for me by moonlight. Wait for me by moonlight. I'll come to thee by moonlight, though hell should bar the way."

"What is that?"

"Look it up," said Ben, pulling up the collar on his leather jacket with one finger and bending down to kiss Merry's nose. He didn't touch her, but again, she felt that glow, that strange, golden sense of being claimed and loved. The awkward, stiff-lipped, eighth-grade kisses from Will and Dane were nothing like this. Without laying a hand on her, Ben made her feel like a woman, a woman in blossom. "Will you be safe here? Do you want me to sit outside and watch out for you?"

She sighed and said, "No. I'm fine. Thanks, though. I'll see you later."

"You can bet on it," Ben said, sprinting down the steps. "I've got your glove. I found it on the porch! You must have dropped it coming in."

"Give that back," Merry said, half teasing.

"It smells like you," he said and took off down the street at a jog.

Meredith had to get inside and think.

As she stood, she was suddenly dizzy and her last thought was, *No . . . no, what was this?*

The land was like a park, but surrounded by twisting, broad-leafed, unfamiliar trees, hung with vines. The grass was worn away, but beautiful birds bounced on the branches of the trees. Wearing a helmet, his face smeared with grease and streaked with sweat, Ben was saying, "Come on, buddy. Just a few more feet. Just a few more feet." All around him in the dust, something struck like hail, sending up showers of dirt. "Come on," Ben said, throwing himself down on his face and covering the back of his head with his hands. It was a game, a sport of some kind. There was a goal everyone was headed for. Everyone needed a helmet. Everyone was filthy. The ground was wet and slick. And Ben looked frightened—frightened and terribly sad.

"Merry, are you coming in?" Adam said. "Are you okay, 'Ster?"—a word he used only when he was feeling especially tender or shaky. Merry guessed that he felt both.

"I'm fine, Adam Ant. I just was out here trying to get some air. I'm learning to . . . um . . . meditate. So I don't talk so much."

"Well, you looked like you got the hang of the trance thing.

And you got a lot of it. Air. I could hear you talking to someone under my window." Adam liked his room cold and always kept his window cracked open. Campbell went in and closed it before she went to bed, but she wasn't at home. Merry hadn't figured on him opening his window and eavesdropping.

"I don't really like being alone in the house right now," Adam said. For a twelve-year-old guy, this was a huge admission. Merry thought he really must have been scared.

"It's morning!" she said. "We're both here."

"Mallory's asleep like a dead person. And it's a creepy time of year."

"Winter?" Meredith said, incredulous. Adam loved winter— skiing, Christmas, snow days.

"When we were alone here last night, I heard things outside," Adam told his sister. "Okay? It creeps me out. I could hear . . . possums and bats and junk. And voices. After Luna left. Creepy voices."

"And bison, I bet," Meredith said, teasing. She prayed, *Don't let him be like Mallory and me.*

"Go ahead and laugh, Meredith. You're so never scared of anything. Like, just waking up screaming in the middle of the night."

"Once in my life," Merry said, referring to a dream she'd had the previous year.

"Merry, I'm so sorry, but that's crazy," Adam said angrily. "I'm not one of your stupid friends who think you two look oh-so-much alike that you're the same person. I heard both of you screaming a bunch of times. Mally, too. Like scream in your sleep the way you do in a nightmare. And you were just out there talking to yourself."

"I was repeating a poem," Merry said. "Med-i-ta-tion. It's peaceful."

"You're about as peaceful as a fire in a fireworks factory!"

"Let's go look it up. It's for school." Merry had to distract him.

She stood on Adam's knee to pull down Tim's dusty volume of *Treasures of British and American Poetry*. She didn't find the line Ben had repeated. Merry went to the computer and typed in, "Though hell should bar the way." Immediately, this poem, pages long, sprang up.

"This old poem, Ant. Listen. There are Web sites for it. People are just crazy about it. There are about a bazillion mentions," said Merry.

"Fascinating," said Adam.

"Listen," Merry said. She read to Adam about the poem. It was old, as old as . . . crazy old, like from before the turn of the century. And not 2001. It was about a girl watching out the window, waiting for her sweetheart, the highwayman. Her name was Bess, the landlord's black-eyed daughter, who tied a dark-red ribbon into her long black hair. After a brief visit and a single kiss, the highwayman set out to rob someone. Bess was captured by British soldiers who took over her father's . . . uh, hotel. They wanted to shoot her boyfriend, who, while being a highway robber, was evidently a good person in other ways, rather like Robin Hood. At least, Bess seemed to think so. The soldiers got drunk and tied Bess to a bed, with a gun under her stomach, so that she couldn't move. It grew dark, closer to night. Only she knew that her lover was coming up the road.

She heard the hoofbeats.

The soldiers heard the hoofbeats.

Then, Bess moved her finger and pulled the trigger. Excited, Merry read the poem aloud to Adam.

> *He turned; he spurred to the West; he did not know who stood*
> *Bowed, with her head o'er the musket, drenched with her own red blood!*
> *Not till the dawn he heard it, his face grew grey to hear*
> *How Bess, the landlord's daughter, the landlord's black-eyed daughter,*
> *Had watched for her love in the moonlight, and died in the darkness there.*

"Can we watch TV? Can we go shovel the walk?" Adam whined.

"It didn't snow," Merry told him.

"I know but I can't take anymore of this poem."

"Adam! Listen, this is the good part." She told her brother about how the highwayman found out about Bess and turned back. The British soldiers shot him down in the highway, "down like a dog" in the road, where he lay in his own blood.

Meredith began to cry. She could see Adam watching her

curiously but couldn't stop. The old poem, to him, must have seemed boring or creepy. It was the most beautiful thing that Merry had ever read. And when she got to the end, she thought she might cry herself sick.

"This is the end," she told Adam. "Just a few more lines."

"It better be," he said.

> *And still of a winter's night, they say, when the wind is in the trees,*
> *When the moon is a ghostly galleon tossed upon cloudy seas,*
> *When the road is a ribbon of moonlight over the purple moor,*
> *A highwayman comes riding*
> *Riding—riding—*
> *A highwayman comes riding, up to the old inn-door.*
> *Over the cobbles he clatters and clangs in the dark inn-yard;*
> *He taps with his whip on the shutters, but all is locked and barred;*
> *He whistles a tune to the window, and who should be waiting there*
> *But the landlord's black-eyed daughter,*
> *Bess, the landlord's daughter,*
> *Plaiting a dark red love-knot into her long black hair.*

"What's that all about?" Adam asked. "What's a love-knot?"

"I don't know," Merry said, gulping. "I think it's like a French braid."

"What's a French braid?"

"Nothing. Adam. It's about love outlasting death. They're ghosts. Did you get that? She shot herself to warn him but he was still shot down."

"That's terrific. Kind of a happy ending thing," Adam said with a sneer. He turned on the sports channel, standing on tiptoe to point the remote over Meredith's head.

"But they're still together. Isn't that the most romantic?"

"Sure. That took four pages?"

"I never heard it before. I'm going to copy it and keep it."

"Knock yourself out," said Adam.

SOMEBODY'S SON

SOMEBODY'S SON

Mallory woke on the couch and nearly jumped to her feet. She felt as though she'd slept for nine or ten hours. But when she glanced up at the exceptionally ugly clock Dad had won in a Chamber of Commerce raffle—a bas relief in wood of the Pioneer Woman statue on the square with the arm she pointed forward as the minute hand—she saw that it was barely eleven a.m. Still Sunday.

The dance had only been last night. It felt like a year ago.

She'd lain down at eight, perhaps eight-thirty, once she was sure that Adam was finally out like a light after she'd made him cinnamon toast and cocoa for which he was starving but too shaken to eat. Adam kept asking if Owen was going to die. Merry kept assuring him that he wasn't. By then, Mally was herself exhausted.

It had been a long, long night since she and Drew got the panicky call from Adam. Drew dropped Mallory off immediately. Although

Adam usually loved being left home alone, he acted weird, almost as though he were a little kid afraid of the dark instead of nearly a teenager. He followed Mallory from room to room until she finally got him to go to sleep.

Something was bugging Mally.

It wasn't like her to ever forget a moment from one of her dreams—the extraordinary kind of dream that she greeted with undeniable attraction and dread. But being up all night, sleeping on Sunday morning, alone in the house—all of it had Mallory turned around. So it was with a shock that she remembered, while brushing her teeth, what she'd "seen" during her nap.

There were a man and a woman, seated side by side on a generous, wide old wooden porch—the old man leaning forward to touch . . . his wife? Perhaps his wife . . . Mallory could hear them speaking in old, reedy voices she somehow knew were accustomed to soft reassurances of devotion, now raised in anger: *I'm taking them now, Helene. You can't go on like this forever. I'm taking them to the museum in White Plains. They got a real nice display there. It's finished now, darling. It's finished.*

Don't you touch them . . . or if you have to, only take the things they gave us. Not the toys or the pennants. Please leave me that. Please.

I won't give away . . . childhood things, Helene. Not to strangers. Just the part that happened over there. I'd like for some of the toys and such to go to the children. Perhaps they'd like to have them.

I don't want anyone to have them! At least, not all of them. Not now. Wait until I'm gone, too.

We got grandchildren now, Helene . You don't want to go looking to leave them. You said all you wanted was . . .

I know what I said.

It's true! You don't pay those girls and their brother any more mind than if they were puppies. It has to stop. I'm not ready to go live in a box. I feel just like you do.

You don't, no. You couldn't.

"Meredith?" Mally called out softly.

"I'm here, 'Ster."

"What were you doing?"

"I did some homework. Adam's okay. He's upstairs in Mom's room, watching TV. I saw Owen at the hospital. It was strange. Luna poured out all the formula? So they couldn't see if there was some contaminant in it. Not for that reason. She told me she had a premonition. But actually, I think it must have tasted funny or something."

"Luna was good to get him to the hospital," said Mallory. "I could eat my own leg. Is there food?"

Inspecting the fridge, Merry said, "Well, there's a hotdog. And some pickles. The pickles look a little iffy." Unless the twins pressed a list into his hand and insisted, Tim lagged over getting the groceries. Over the past few months, they'd had mac and cheese or cereal for dinner so many times that even Adam was begging for broccoli. One of Carla's jobs was supposed to be to cook something the Brynns could freeze. She'd done it once. A tuna casserole with peas and pearl onions and big clumps of cheese. After that, Campbell gently told Carla that she could skip the food-prep thing.

Merry said now, "There's a hotdog. And . . . mmmm . . . something in a pan. And a big jar of Gram's applesauce that hasn't been opened. And some gross leftovers in bags that look like they're from Thanksgiving."

Mallory stood on a chair to take down the huge box of oatmeal. She hated oatmeal but it did stick to a person's ribs. "Aren't you hungry?"

Merry said, "No, I . . . no. I'm just not." And then she blushed.

"What's up with you?" Mally sensed something else in the room— something wild and a little dangerous but also as seductive as a sprinkler on a summer lawn.

"Ben was here. Ben came to see me."

"Who's Ben?"

Meredith fell silent, remembering the nearly tearful look Ben gave her when he had to leave. Then she said, "He's that boy I saw last week. At the mall. And walking along the road. That beautiful guy. He . . . I don't know how but he knew we lived here and he came to see me."

"He *stalked* you?" Mallory asked, horrified.

"Please Mallory. We're in the book, and he said he knew our family and stuff. It's not like he had to be a private investor."

"Investigator. My sister, with the brain of a jellyfish . . . Why didn't you let him in? Like you went outside the gym last night?"

"Whatever," Merry said.

"He knew Dad? How did he know Dad?" Mallory asked. It occurred to Merry that Mallory was far too upset over what was basically nothing at all.

"I don't know. Maybe he was on a team Dad coached when Ben was little."

"Ben must have been a girl at that time then," Mally said. "The only team Dad ever even helped coach when we were little was my soccer team." She paused, stirring the glop of oatmeal congealing in the pan. "Did you do anything? Like *do* anything?"

"Just talked," Meredith said. "I wanted to do more, but I guess it's too soon to be making out. I barely know him. I think he's the one, though."

"The one? Please. You've known this guy a total of about an hour, Merry. That's nuts even for you. What's his story?" Mallory asked. Meredith didn't answer, except with a shrug. That silent dismissal told Mallory that nothing she said would matter. Merry turned away.

Then, suddenly, she threw open the refrigerator door and grabbed the wizened hotdog, tossing it into a plastic bag with all the rest of the dead leftovers and dropping it into the trash. She rinsed the pan of what looked like applesauce but was all runny and gross. She scraped dishes that were in the sink and stack them in the dishwasher. She then dumped out leftovers and rinsed and stacked those pans and bowls and opened a new box of baking soda for the refrigerator. Merry got out the broom and the counter and sink cleaner and a fistful of old washcloths they used as rags.

This alone was enough to make Mallory want to take her twin's temperature. She waited until Meredith had finished wiping down the countertop and sweeping the floor before she asked again, "Who is he, Merry? We don't even know anybody who knows him."

Merry didn't answer. "Okay! Listen to this. So, why am I dreaming about . . . him? Or, at least I think I am."

Why am I? Merry thought. But she got angry.

"Because you're crazy? Too stanap," Merry said—twin language for "This is stupid," in case Adam was listening. "Did you hear me? His family knows our family. Maybe he just came back to town! We'd have been in seventh grade when he went to Ridgeline. We didn't know anyone in high school but Drew and his sister." She looked around her for something else to clean but there was nothing left: The kitchen was as immaculate as an operating room.

Mallory, who had not lifted a finger to help, tried to start the conversation again. "Meredith, this guy. It's not like he dropped out of a cloud, though. People would know things. Your cheerleader friends, the older girls . . . if he's as hot as you say, why didn't anybody ever mention him?" Privately, Mallory was wondering: *If my dream of those voices is about Ben, what does that mean? Ben was the only new thing on the horizon, except for Owen's strange illness. It had to be about Ben; they had to be talking about Ben. But how could it be?* Mally said, "Let me tell you about my dream at least. When I was napping."

"No," Merry said. "Don't tell me about it. Just pretend you did. I'm going to go upstairs and read until Mom calls."

"It's not some killer or weird being thing. It was just some lady telling her husband or her father or whatever that she didn't want to get rid of some old toys."

"What does that have to do with Ben or anything?" Merry asked, relieved. "You're on someone else's radar."

"Nothing. Or nothing I know about. But it's going to happen. I don't know why I should know. But I'm afraid I'll have to find out. About Ben . . ."

"Why do you care so much? Why are you all over this? You have a boyfriend. It's not like I'm a freak because I met a new guy," Merry said. "If you want more information, ask Luna. She can really see the future!" In fact, Merry wanted to talk about Ben endlessly—especially to Mally, who, for all their bickering, was the other half of her heart. Yet, at the same time, she didn't want to mention him at all. It felt as though jabbering about him the way she would an ordinary guy would . . . break the spell. So she told her sister about her encounter with Luna in the ER, followed by Big Carla's odd visitation and her prayer chain.

"Mom sure can pick 'em," Mallory said.

"I'm with you on that. Thank goodness for Grandma and Sasha. And that Grandma talked Mom out of the next candidate."

"And I'm sorry. I have no idea why I'm all over this. I really don't, 'Ster. But I am and there's a reason."

"I have to lie down for a while," Merry said.

"Okay," said Mallory.

There was definitely a full moon, Merry thought. Owen throwing up, Ben showing up, Luna thinking she was clairvoyant, Big Carla acting like she actually was clairvoyant, and Mallory having random visions. Her head felt like a sack of pebbles brushed about by the sweep of seawater. With the volume of poems in which she'd found "The Highwayman" clutched to her chest, Merry lay down on her bed and began to drift off to sleep.

Suddenly, Mallory was in the doorway. "Mer? Did I tell you the other thing about Luna dancing naked in the woods? It's been bugging me."

"I don't know," Merry answered.

Mallory bit her lips. She seemed to be debating whether she should speak. "In that big bonfire. They were burning hair."

"Their own hair? That's not a crime. I assume they weren't setting it on fire while it was still on their heads," Merry said.

"No, it was little curls. Infant hair. From a baby. Blond curly silky baby hair."

Neither of them had to say who had curls that looked just like that.

EVIL WORK

EVIL WORK

At four on that endless day, Merry awoke to a commotion downstairs. She sprinted for the stairs, expecting to see her father and mother with Owen. In fact, it was only Drew, whom Mallory could see outside on the porch, banging on the door as a rising wind with a skein of snow in it pulled at his hat and the armload of white paper packages he was bringing to the Brynns.

When Merry got down into the kitchen, shivering and trailing the comforter around her shoulders, Mallory told her that their father had called to tell them tests on Baby Owen were only beginning in earnest. They would be home alone that night. Outside, it was darker than murder. Drew had worn a light jacket to work at Pizza Papa's but said his fingers nearly turned to kindling in the time it took Mallory to answer the door. The sun had fallen behind Crying Woman Ridge, and the nip of the wind reminded them that winter would take its sweet time on the way out and for the residents of Ridgeline not to get giddy and store their parkas in the cedar closet.

"Wait a minute," Mallory said as Drew inspected the thermostat and stuck his hands inside his own sweater. "Why were you out there banging on the door? You don't knock on the door. Nobody does."

"It was locked," Drew said. "You were sacked out on the couch. You wouldn't know. The door was locked."

"It was not," Merry and Mallory said simultaneously.

Mallory admitted being out of it. She and Adam had both fallen asleep downstairs to some dreadful old movie, sleeping away the hours the way people do when life is tense and nothing can be done for it. "Did you lock the door?" she asked Merry.

"I just said I didn't! I was asleep too."

"Then, who did?"

Nobody in Ridgeline locked their doors, except possibly in Haven Hills, where every room had the equivalent of an electronics store in gadgets and every wall was hung with art. In the Brynns' house, there was nothing of value to steal. The gigantic boat-shaped dining-room table was an antique, given to them when Grandpa and Grandma Brynn moved out of the house, but Tim often said he thought the house had been built around the table because no door was wide enough to carry it through. The art in the Brynn household could look like abstracts from a distance but were in fact matted and framed geometric shapes and finger paintings that Adam and the twins had brought home proudly over the years, never imagining they'd still be forced to confront it years later.

Whenever their mother said that their blots and shapes looked like half the stuff in the Museum of Modern Art—and she was careful to say this when there were people around—Mallory wanted to deflate like a helium balloon.

Adam came up out of the den, rubbing his eyes. "I passed out," he said.

"Did you lock the door, Adam Ant?" Merry asked. "Drew couldn't get in."

"I didn't lock the door," said Adam. He looked suddenly panicked.

"Laybite," Mallory warned her twin in their language. She didn't want Adam getting spooked. "Let's forget it. It probably happened by accident. It blew shut. Somebody turn on some heat."

"Even if it did blow shut, it wouldn't have locked," Merry went on. She glanced out into the darkness. "You need a key to lock that door. That's why Dad's getting a deadbolt, like we have on the back door. If there was a fire, you'd have to be trying to find the key to get out."

"Scarik hum vis wers," Mallory told her twin, more forcibly this time. It was twin language for "stop saying things like that." Adam's eyes were widening. But it was too late. Meredith was on a roll.

"It creeps me out. We were just there sleeping, and somebody came into the house and locked the door?"

"That's unusual in the annals of crime," Drew said. "A door-locking prowler."

"It's not funny," Mallory said. "What if someone's in here with us?"

"Let's split up and look around," Merry said. "I'll take our room, and Adam, you go down and look in the basement."

"Meredith! That's so juvenile. That's what they do in horror movies. Everybody splits up and goes around the house, and the psycho pulls out a fuse and picks them off one by one."

"I'm calling the police," Adam said. There was a ring of white around his mouth, and his eyes were like twin moons.

"What are you going to say?" Merry asked. "We want to report a locked door?" She paused and gazed out into the dark, where snow was now sparkling in gusts of confetti under the porch light. "We'll look around. I'm not scared."

"Neither would I be if I had picked our *bedroom* to check," Mallory said. "Although that's inevitably where they are. He probably walked out of a closet behind you."

"I thought we were trying to avoid scaring Adam?" Merry said. "Stop being an ass, Mal. Think. So who besides us has a key? Grandma, Mrs. Vaughn? Maybe. Nobody else as far as I know."

"I don't think even Sasha or Carla has a key to our house. They come to work while Mom's still here," Mallory said. "Mom is uber security conscious. Grandma has one. But Grandma would have called out to us."

"It was probably my mother," Drew said. "She's a compulsive door-locker. Does anyone want some pizza? Because I have like, six pizzas here, and the price is right."

"Drew," Mallory said. "Come on, let's look around."

Armed with Tim's twenty-watt floating flashlight, which was the size of a small cat, and the heavy tool from the kitchen that

Campbell used to sharpen knives, the four of them began in Tim's tiny basement office and checked every corner of the two and a half upper floors, opening every closet with Merry's involuntary gasp and Mallory's equally involuntary reprimand. Tightly squeezed next to Drew, Adam carried his aluminum ball bat.

"Why are we whispering?" Drew whispered. "If there's a mad killer in the house, is it less likely that he'll get us if we talk quietly?"

"I don't know. I feel like we're in some British mystery," Mallory said.

"I feel like we're in *Scooby Doo*," said Drew.

Soon, every light in the Brynns' house was on. It would have looked, from the outside, as though the family were hosting a party. But there was no one in the house but the people who lived there and Drew. And all those *ghosts*, Mallory kept thinking.

They all jumped when the telephone screeched. Fumbling to grab it, Merry said hello to Sasha, who said she had been called in unexpectedly to her other job or she would have come over to see if she could help. She was going to drop by the hospital on the way to the house of the elderly woman she cared for.

Sasha said, "I was just thinking. On Friday, he was playing with his blocks and jumping on the sofa like the happiest little boy in the world. And suddenly, just like before, down he went. I'll make something special for him when he comes home, like some pudding, the poor thing. I hope he didn't eat spoiled or contaminated food."

"I cleaned the whole refrigerator and threw everything out."

"Oh," said Sasha. "That's good. And now, I have to run. Sorry, Merry." Sasha was usually chatty, unlike Carla or Luna. But before Merry could say another word, she hung up.

"Who cleaned out the fridge?" Adam, who had been eavesdropping, asked.

"I did," Merry said.

"Did you scrape that apple gunk out of the pan? Not Grandma's applesauce, that reeky stuff?" he asked. Merry only dimly remembered, but the small saucepan she'd scrubbed was still in the dish drainer. "Did you make it at school or something?" Adam went on. "I looked at it before you got home because I was starving— which I also am right now by the way— and I wanted to barf. Who put it in there?"

"I thought you did," Merry said to Mallory. "You know I can't cook a hard-boiled egg. Maybe Grandma or Dad made something this morning. But no one was home except Adam and you."

"That's true," Mallory said softly. "But what's really strange is that's not our pan. I've never seen it before."

CLOSING IN
CLOSING IN

The pizzas had not improved with time spent searching the house.

Hunger won out.

It was well past the ordinary time for dinner when the four of them sat down around the table. Before they could open the boxes, Campbell called to ask if they would be okay without Grandma. Mallory said, "Of course we will. We love you, too. Kiss the baby for us. Yes, Drew will be leaving shortly. Yes, I am aware that it is Sunday night. Yes, I know Merry has practice for the conference tournament. Neely's picking her up early." Mallory paused, rolling her eyes, and then said, "Um, Mom? Did you lock the door to the house? Okay. Well, no. No biggie. I don't know an Ellie." Mallory directed a shrug at her twin. "I'll ask Merry."

"You know, Big Carla brought that name up when Owen first got sick? And then she brought it up again at the hospital," Merry said. "Mom didn't know what she meant but Grandma does. I have to make a note to ask Grandma."

"Whatever," Mallory said. "I have to eat or die."

The pizzas were unfortunate.

Drew explained.

Last night had been the night of a dance to which not everyone was invited.

So Pizza Papa received about double the usual number of orders for prank pizzas. Ernie had given Drew the inevitable pies with yucky toppings that were returned by the recipients. Prank pizzas, along with pit bulls that their owners treated like bunny rabbits—yelling at the delivery driver rather than the dog with the slobbering fangs—were the bane of the pizza business. Ernie lost money on the batches of super-large pies sent from untraceable phones to boys by girls who were crushing, or who'd been dumped, or who were alone watching reruns of *Friends* while everyone else was at the formal.

Of those, the largest was the worst—triple cheese, peppers and anchovies. The anchovies, Mallory said, were gone but not forgotten even after they all diligently picked them off.

"What's this?" Merry asked, lifting a thumb-shaped orange disc from an otherwise normal mushroom-and-cheese pie.

"Apricot," Drew said. "Usually served with shrimp and avocado but sometimes combined with mushrooms on a revenge pizza. I tell Ernie not to even make them. I know some of the people's voices. They're repeat offenders. But he says it's bad business."

"It's bad all right. Ugh," Merry said, tossing the fruit onto the slush pile of anchovies, green olives, bacon slices, and Chinese chestnuts.

"Not as ghastly as the meatball and salami stuffed with gorgonzola you brought that one time," Mallory said. "I like meat, but cats were following me for weeks."

"I provide sustenance at a price all can afford," Drew said. "At considerable cost to my dignity. I drive halfway to Deptford to save you from the worry of cooking."

"Well, we do have other worries," Meredith told him. "They're going to test Owen for being . . . well, sort of like a bubble boy. One of those kids who has to be in a wheat-free, peanut-free, whatever-free classroom. Which would be horrible."

"You're exaggerating, Meredith. It's not at that point yet. But it's scary. It wasn't like this when Mom was nursing him," said Mallory. "Before she went full-time to school and work. Babies aren't supposed to have formula so their moms can study to become doctors who tell mothers not to give their babies formula."

"I'm sorry," Drew said. "I always think a little levity will be welcome but the timing is always bad."

"Do we have anything else?" Adam asked plaintively. "Like more toast?"

"Adam," Merry said. "Eat. Just scrape everything off the pizza and eat it. Don't whine about it."

"I'll puke," Adam said.

"That's it," Mallory said. "I'm taking money from the swearing jar to get eggs and bread and junk. Drew, will you drive me? What homework do you have, Ant? Get it done now, and you have the rest of the night off. It's liberating."

"I did it all," Adam said. "I feel liberated already."

"You're lying."

"History," Adam admitted miserably. "The Civil War."

"Sixth and seventh grade," Drew mused. "You never get past Reconstruction. I had no idea there was a twentieth century until last year." Mallory punched him and grabbed twenty dollars out of the jar into which Campbell and Tim put a dollar every time they swore.

"I'll help you with homework," Meredith told Adam. "You help me clear up here."

They decorated one big leftover pizza with half of all the despised toppings, leaving it for their father, who would eat anything. Then they spent an hour at the kitchen table discussing the day that Abraham Lincoln was shot.

"He actually lived all night," Merry told Adam. "He was so tall no beds were built to fit him. So, in the bed at the house across from the theater, where they took him, his feet hung over the end. People watched him all night, but he was so badly wounded that there was no chance he would live. He just had a very strong body. He wasn't that old. He was only fifty-six. A lot younger than Grandpa Brynn. Not even ten years older than Dad."

"What *date* was it?" Adam asked. "When he died?"

"Why do they torture you with that?" Merry asked. "It was just after the war ended, so I think it was April 13 or 14. But the interesting part was that a guy with him used modern paramedic type things to resuscitate him. And Lincoln's wife? She was a husband-beater. She pulled out his hair and hit him with a broom and scratched his face."

"Get out," Adam said, interested despite himself.

"She had depression," Merry said. "Or worse."

"Like the old lady who lives down the road from Alex," Adam said, referring to his cousin, Uncle Kevin and Aunt Kate's son, who was exactly the same age.

"I guess. I think she did more than yell at kids who ran on her lawn. That was a long time ago. You're talking about Mrs. Highland." The thought of Ben's face, smiling and yet somehow crossed with the greatest sadness, flickered across Merry's mind. Tears nearly burst into her eyes.

"She yells even when nobody's there. Alex and me watch her. She just stands out there and yells at her apple trees." Merry put her head down on the table.

She saw a young woman—not young, really, but younger than Merry's own mother—wandering in an orchard, stopping to hug every tree and sobbing as she stared up into the branches. Her beautiful long blond hair swung loose about her shoulders, and she wore an old oversized white man's dress shirt with the shoulders rolled up and the front knotted, over ancient ripped jeans. In her arms, she held a jacket like Ben's. As she sank to the ground, sobbing like a child, so hard she was shaking, she held the jacket to her. She was forming a name with her lips, but Merry couldn't hear it. . . .

"Mer?" Adam said. "What's up? Did you fall asleep?"

"I . . . I'm tired. You think you'll do okay?"

"I'm going to go lay on Mom and Dad's bed. I feel like I did when I was little," Adam said. "I have the jits." His cinnamon freckles stood out against his nearly translucent skin . . . so like Owen's.

Merry messed up his hair. "'Kay," she said. She put her head back down on the table. She slept but no dreams came.

VISIONS AND BAD PIZZA

Across town at the Quick Save, it was Mallory who had her head propped on the dashboard of Drew's truck, Mallory the one whose mind was drifting. Gallantly, Drew had offered to run in for a few groceries. Mallory listened to four or five Annie Lennox songs, irritated by Drew's obsession with hundred-year-old music. During the song "Sweet Dreams," her mind began the inevitable twirl that she could never resist. . . .

There was a park. Flat, level and beautiful, more beautiful than a golf course lawn, with stone benches and shade trees just beginning to bloom. She could see only one person. But she knew that another one was there, approaching. She could feel the person. She knew it was a girl.

The place was not a farm, not a ball field, not a golf course, but its carefully tended center reminded Mallory of all those things.

In the center stood a single tall spire. She had seen it before. Where? Where?

In the dream Mallory moved closer to the person on the ground, whose back was turned. A light rain was falling. New grass had sprung up.

It was Ben. Mallory had never seen Ben, but she knew beyond a doubt that it was he.

Ben was there, sitting down on his heels near the spire, wearing plain green cloth pants and . . . Mallory felt, rather than saw, the steady approach of someone else, the girl.

Ben smiled, and his smile made the cloudy day glorious. As Merry said, he was beautiful. Ben's was a wide white grin that transformed his sad, sweet, solemn face, and when he stood up, his blond hair fell forward, curly and unruly as a little child's. Still, something was off. He was like a radio signal on a mountain road—one second clear, the next wavering.

"Hi," he said to the person whose shadow lay across the snow. "I missed you so much. Come with me, Merry. Please. It won't hurt. You won't be hurt. I love you."

Mallory tried to shout, but her lips would not move. She made a sound, a tiny cat's cry. She saw her sister step forward into the sunlight, near the mound where new grass had grown.

"Wake up Brynn," Drew said, placing three gallons of milk on the roof of the Green Beast. "I'd ask you why you're drooling on my dashboard, but if you were dreaming and not really asleep, please don't tell me because I don't want to know."

"Don't worry. I'm not feeling very talkative."

"What's up?"

"I saw that boy, that boy Merry has a crush on."

"You saw him at the Quick Save? Or you saw him in the woo-woo way? Okay, I can see by your face that he wasn't in there buying peanut butter," Drew said. "And so, yeah, let's change the subject."

"There's something funny about him. I don't mean funny bad; I mean funny weird," Mallory said.

"What did you fail to understand about the words *don't tell me*?" Drew asked.

They drove back to the house in silence. When she spotted them, Merry turned and fled up the stairs.

"She's been like this all day," Mallory said, struggling in with two paper bags of groceries. "When I tried to talk to her, she started *cleaning the kitchen*. It's either love or a virus. Meredith hasn't been on the phone with one of her friends in more than eight hours. We're talking serious illness."

While Merry finished helping Adam in the living room, Drew and Mallory put the groceries away. It felt strange. It felt like what they would do if they were ten years older and together. Mally and Merry's parents were spending the night at the hospital. It was an odd feeling. For the first time, Mallory and Merry were on their own overnight without a grandparent or some other relative "looking in."

Before Drew stepped across the yard to go home, he told Mallory, "You know, I don't have to leave, Brynn. I could stay here and guard you from door-lockers." He held her against him, adjusting the clefts and curves of her small body to his own. "I'd sleep on the couch."

"But would I?" Mallory asked. "This is the part where you being three years older gets in the way. The next step is . . . too serious. You can't go back."

Drew's chin jutted forward as he glared at Mallory. "Do you even think I'd try to get you to do something that you didn't want to do? Or that I'd even want you to do more than make out with me at your age?"

"What if it wasn't you who wanted to? We're so comfortable together it would be easy to slip past the blinking yellow light," Mally said. "I don't have my learner's permit yet, and I'm not talking about driving."

Drew kissed the top of Mallory's head, wondering whom she'd be with when she did see the blinking yellow light turn green. He wondered if he would be the one or if he would be happy for her if he wasn't or if his heart would fall out of his chest. He took a long breath.

"Do you really have to stick around all night? Couldn't just disappear for forty minutes or so?" Mallory knew where he intended to go. They'd steam up the windows down on the dark road broken by bulldozers. But as nice as that prospect seemed, somehow Mally didn't want to leave her house.

"Don't hate me," she told Drew. "I know my parents aren't here, and I'm going against everything a person my age is supposed to do. But Meredith is obviously not paying any attention to Adam. We're all on edge, and she is the big hero in her own drama, too. Now

Adam's probably watching *Slasher Beach* or something right now."

"Is this all about Merry and the invisible hitchhiker?" Drew asked.

"He got visible this morning, and now Meredith thinks she's the Juliet of the twenty-first century. Plus, I want to be home if my parents call. You can come in and hang out for a while, if you want."

"You're paying as much attention to me as Merry is to Adam. And your brain is at the hospital with Owen. I know when I'm being dumped." Drew pretended to pout.

"You're not being dumped. I just have this feeling. I don't know what I'd do if I weren't here and anything happened to Owen. It's not like they went out of town to stay overnight in New York or something. They're with my baby brother."

"Hey, I get it honey," Drew said. "I wouldn't like you so much if you didn't love the little kids the way you do. I'm going bowling. I have a rare Sunday night off. Bowling is very underrated. And since I started hanging around with you, my bachelor friends are getting disgusted."

"Can't have that," Mallory told him. She hugged him around the middle. "Drewsky, you're so sweet. But you're still also my best friend."

"Not an easy job," Drew remarked,

A few hours later, Mallory lay down to try to sleep.

It was a lost cause.

She tossed side to side until she finally gave up and got out of bed. Sitting on the window seat, she looked out their little round attic window at the road, where a few porch lights cast a bell of yellow glow on the snow. It still looked like Christmas. Mallory felt herself slipping. *No, not twice in one night. . . .*

An older woman, weeping, leaned on the arm of a younger woman near the mound of what was clearly a new grave, surrounded by a dusting of snow. But, there were other people there, at least a couple of dozen, and when one of the women turned to speak to another . . . it was Mallory's mother! Her dad and Aunt Karin. Her uncle Kevin. What? The old lady stepped forward unsteadily and leaned down to place a small tree, sweetly decorated with hearts and bells, beside the grave. Her solemn face was beautiful in grief. She wasn't that old, but terribly weak. Mallory knew her. She almost knew her. Her blond hair was streaked through with gray, but still long.

She woke to the chimes that told her that she had a text message on her phone, which lay on her night table in its charger. The clock face read one a.m. Great. Drew would be a whiz in CP Physics tomorrow.

The text from Drew read, "U wouldn't go so I went to the grove w/o U. Ha ha. Went with the guys."

Beer, Mallory thought. *Great again.*

A second text arrived a minute later. "Kito drove. D/N Worry. Saw Sasha walk out of the house DTRd fr yr aunt. In a uniform? Y?"

Y indeed? Mallory thought. *What house?*

More importantly, why were her family gathered at Mountain

Rest Cemetery? Why were they going to be there . . . well, soon, judging from that little funeral Valentine tree? Mally shook her head to clear her thoughts.

No!

Why would the Brynns, not just her parents but an aunt and uncle too, those at least, be going to Mountain Rest Cemetery? What other reason could there be other than a death in the family?

Oh, God, Mallory prayed. *Help Owen. If you help Owen, I'll serve You wherever this gift takes me, I promise. I'll never even hate it again, no matter how scared I am or how sick it makes me. I'm going to say this on Meredith's behalf too. I know she won't mind.*

REAL OR FATE?

REAL OR FATE?

Grandma Gwenny was in the kitchen, quietly scrambling eggs, when Mallory and Meredith hit the bottom step, dressed for school.

"Sheesh!" Meredith gasped. "You nearly gave me a heart attack, Grandma. I never expected you to be here. When did you come in?"

Just a half second behind her twin, Mallory wanted to fall on her knees in gratitude that she hadn't given in and let Drew sleep over—even on the couch—after all.

"The shower was on, so I guess about a half hour ago," she said. "Eat something, now that you're up. I was going to put these in a warmer. Is Adam awake? I'll drive him in. They won't be home with Owen until late this afternoon at the earliest." Her grandmother heaped Meredith's plate with cheesy eggs and toast made from her homemade bread. Breakfast was difficult for Merry at the best of times, unless it was Sunday and she could curl up like a python and digest it. Now, she proceeded to push the eggs around on the plate and break the toast up into small bits.

Grandma Gwenny settled into her usual friendly silence. She never started a conversation, preferring to let others take the lead. Today was the exception. Taking Merry by surprise, Grandma said, "Meredith Brynn, I've never heard you abstain from talking for this long in my life. The silence in here is deafening."

"How can you hear someone not talking?" Merry asked. They both smiled.

"I can hear that you have a hornet's nest buzzing around in your head. Is this about Owen? I see that Owen will be well, although I'm not sure he'll get over this right now. At least he's well now. Are you ill? Worried? Constipated? In love?" Meredith glanced up. Her grandmother said, "I guess that was the bingo."

"I can't talk about it," said Merry. "I don't know why."

"I'm sure you have a good reason," said her grandmother.

"Let me just ask you this. Is it possible to feel as though you've known someone all your life when you've just met?"

Grandma Gwenny got up to open the oven and pull out a tray of muffins she'd set to heat. "I suppose that's true of everyone who falls in love, at least in the best of all possible worlds." She added, "It doesn't mean that you shouldn't get to know him in real life though, despite how you feel."

"I don't know how I feel. This is all new," Merry said, and Grandma Gwenny hugged her. Then Adam rolled into the room, his four or five cowlicks standing at attention on his head, his jeans and T-shirt clearly left over from the previous night. As soon as Drew left, Mallory had checked on Adam, who was asleep crossways on their parents' bed, having taped all the windows of his and their room with drawings of skulls and writings of "POISON" in red marker, for no reason Mally could discern. Adam hadn't done anything so childish in years.

"I'm saved!" Adam exclaimed. "Somebody's finally here who knows how to make real food!"

"Not only that," said Grandma Gwenny, "let's get this place cleaned up for your parents."

"Grandma!" Adam complained, mouth full. "I have fifteen minutes before I catch the bus."

"But I'm driving you, so you have an hour. Go up and jump in the shower, and I'll give this place a shake. Your parents are going to be busy. Owen is coming home today. Your mom has school tomorrow. And Wednesday, there's a small funeral service at Mountain Rest Cemetery. I guess Sasha will stay with Owen." She paused and tried to change the subject. "Why does your father still have Christmas lights up outside?"

"We usually leave those up until Easter," Mallory said.

"A funeral?" Merry said. "Who died?"

Grandma sat down at the table with her cup of tea. "It's no one you know. But it's a very sad story. It's someone I used to have babysit your father, actually all the kids. This boy died a long time ago. Actually in the Vietnam War. But he was MIA—do you know what that means?"

"Missing in action," Merry murmured.

"Yes and it is only now that they have found enough of his things . . . that is . . . his remains to identify him and to bring him home to be buried. Nearly forty years later. It's so very sad. Helene Highland suffered and hoped all this time that Ben would be found in prison, alive."

Mallory glanced at Merry. She looked like a much younger kid, Adam's age and scared of the dark. Mally asked, "Were there any other kids in the family?"

"Of course there was David, his older brother. I'm not sure if there were any children younger than Ben. His parents weren't social friends of ours. I do know that someone named a son after Ben."

"That's it!" Merry cried, leaping out of her seat and executing an impromptu Herkie. "He must be a relative, here for the funeral! That's why he's here!"

"Who's here?" Grandma Gwenny asked. "Why so much joy over someone's child being buried?"

Meredith scraped her dishes and ran from the room, dropping a kiss on Grandma Gwenny's head.

"Grandma," Mallory said, as Gwenny began wiping down the countertops, "you mentioned that person named Ellie the other night."

"Yes."

"Well, you said you knew who that was."

"One of my old people is disabled, and Carla takes her to church. They're very, very conservative Catholics. My friend told me that Carla hopes somehow to get in touch with Ellie somehow in a vision or through prayer."

"Ellie is . . .?"

"Elliott, her baby son. Carla's husband was killed in a car accident just after they moved here from New Jersey a couple of years ago. Elliott was hurt badly. He was at a children's special care hospital in New York City. And they were just about to bring him home, or so I gather, when he suddenly got an infection," Grandma said. She went on, opening the door to set a few bags of trash in the lidded cans outside the back steps. From beneath the sink, which was kept baby-proofed, she took a roll of towels and some glass cleaner. She explained how Carla was at the hospital day and night and was in fact holding her little boy when he suddenly stopped breathing. There was even, according to Grandma, a horrible rumor that Carla had some role in Elliott's death because she didn't want to raise a baby who would have had very special needs because of an injury to his brain. "No one really thought that. But my friend says she lost her reason for awhile and had to be hospitalized herself."

"So Carla is crazy?" Mallory gasped.

"Mallory Brynn. Grief that overwhelming and a period of depression are hardly crazy. I've met her once or twice, and she seems like a very devoted mother to her daughter. She still grieves for her baby. It hasn't been that long. And she's just not like most people. If that were against the law, I know people who'd be in trouble," Grandma Gwenny said with a measuring look at Mallory. "What's with your sister and her reaction to the Highlands' son being buried?"

"It's a long story," Mallory said with a sigh. "And I think it's going to get longer."

TWICE IN A LIFETIME

T he next afternoon, when her second practice of the day ended, an exhausted Merry met Mallory, who was waiting for her at the door of the house.

"Let's go upstairs," Mallory said. Her tone was commanding, serious.

"I want to see Owen," Merry told her. "Hi Ant."

Adam was in the kitchen, just a few feet away from the girls, elaborately spreading peanut butter on bread. He was spreading it so slowly that he might have been applying the final touches to the *Mona Lisa*. Merry could almost see his ears lengthening as he strained to hear his sisters' conversation. Mally caught Meredith's glance. This discussion, which she had blown a math test to plan, was nothing for Adam's ears. And she knew that he could tell that simply from their tone of voice.

"Mom and Dad won't be home for another hour at least. So . . . renow itsap," Mally said in twin language. "Renow itsap renow." Meredith, her pointed chin stuck straight up in the air, did hurry up, as Mally instructed in twin talk, flouncing up the stairs. By the time Mallory had Adam set up with his long division, Merry was supine on the bed in a quite good pantomime of actual sleep.

"That might work for some people," Mally said. "Not me." No answer. "Sit up and tell, Mer." Meredith reluctantly unrolled herself from her bed.

"So, this is the answer. Your Ben is the son or the grandson of the guy who died in Vietnam. Okay. Why am I dreaming about him? I don't have those *dreams* about just anyone. Unless that person is a threat to someone. But I don't feel like he's a threat." Meredith didn't open her eyes. "Explain. Tell me. I'm on your side." Mallory decided to go to the point. Since she saw the future, she had very little experience with ghosts; Merry, however, saw them all the time—had since she was little, happily watching their Brynn ancestors bustling around the house and through the walls. So she asked, "What does a ghost look like, Meredith?"

"Where did that come from?"

Mallory lay down on her own bed. "I just want to know."

"Like anybody else," Meredith said. "They don't float or wear sheets. Some of them wear, you know, what they wore when they were buried, long white dresses."

"Are they scary?"

"Not so much."

"Even when you were little?"

"I didn't see them so much when I was really little. I just barely felt them, and I wasn't scared."

"What about now? What about since we got older?"

"There were a couple who scared me," Merry said thoughtfully. "There was a man in the garage when Dad was doing the addition. I don't know who he was, but he had on a long black coat and a black hat, and he said, "Go away from here, people!" He had a thick, funny accent, like an English accent but garbled up. But it was like I heard his voice later and just saw his lips move first. And he looked kind of like a slow movie. Very strange. I was probably Adam's age. I was so scared I wasn't scared, you know? I just told him to get out of our house, that this was the Brynn house. And he said a funny thing."

"What?"

"He said this: 'Where is my Mary? I don't know these Brynns.' Then he just vanished, bit by bit."

"Like the Cheshire cat?"

"No, idiot . . . like fading, just getting more and more see-through, like a little at a time."

"Oh," Mallory said. "Tell me about the other time."

Meredith carefully got up and knelt by the window. "I don't talk about the other one."

"To me?"

"Even to you."

"Merry, please. I think I saw a ghost. I think I know who it is. I have to know what makes a person sure it's a ghost. The only person I ever knew who saw ghosts is you."

"I don't want to talk about her."

"It's a her."

"Yes." Merry turned back. "She lived here."

"In Ridgeline?" Mallory asked, pulling her quilt around her shoulders.

"In this house. In this room. It wasn't a room, though, then because it was the attic." Instinctively, Mallory pulled her feet up off the floor.

"In our *room?*"

"I came up here one night, and this was really a long time ago, looking for my school pictures from when I was in kindergarten for Spirit Day. I saw her sitting by the window. Sitting on a little stool. She wasn't more than sixteen, and she had long, blond hair, longer than Sasha, down to the ground almost. She was drinking something out of a little cup. Medicine. But then she fainted or fell. And I knew she was dead."

"She killed herself? In our room?"

"Mallory, I don't think that she meant to. I don't know how I knew. But she took more than she was supposed to. I don't know what it was. I was scared because I was seeing a dead person die. But mostly, just sad. I could see the letter she had."

"A letter?"

"Yes. I walked toward her, but I couldn't get close enough."

"You didn't run?"

"No, I'm used to this. I walked slowly toward her and it said . . . someone was writing about coming home. But not to you. I have the deepest respect . . . and something or other. And then I heard her say, 'Oh, please no.'"

Mallory got up. "She was dumped. I bet she did it on purpose."

"I would know, I think. I like to believe she was just trying to put it out of her mind."

"Was she on your side or my side of the room?"

"Yours," Merry said, and Mallory sprang up off the bed as though she was blocking a shot on goal at soccer.

"She's nothing to be scared of. I've seen lots of ghosts. Grandma's Gwenny's twin, Vera. I've seen her ten times at least. She loves us. I've seen Grandma's mother. Twenty others at least. Those were the only ones I was ever scared of. And I was scared about them, not *of* them."

"Describe Ben," Mallory said as she brushed out her hair and got into her pajamas. Merry described the boy with the curly blond hair and big shoulders, the boy who, Mallory now realized, had been in Mountain Home Cemetery, near where she and Drew often made out. "I saw him tonight Merry. I saw him when I passed out for a second. Mer, I think maybe he's the boy who died. I just think that. I don't know when. He died a long time ago, I think."

"That's crazy," Meredith said. "He's here because of what Grandma said."

"Oh? Are you sure?"

"Mallory, I knew you were going to say something like this. First, I don't believe it here." She pointed to her heart. "He didn't talk like those other ones. It wasn't like he was under water or something. And second, it wouldn't matter. I would love him anyway. That's all there is to it."

"Meredith! Let's at least check it out. Let's find out who Ben is."

"I don't care who he is," Meredith said firmly.

"Let's go to the funeral."

"NO. I went to my last funeral when David Jellico . . ."

"Then you don't really believe he's real."

Merry rolled over and pushed her face into the pillow. "Fine," she said. "Fine, fine, fine."

THE SECRET OF BEN

L ater that same day, they all spoiled Owen when he got home. His little arms were scored with the tracks of welts where doctors had tested him for life-threatening allergies, to things such as peanuts and shellfish. Next week Dad was taking him to St. Therese's Research Hospital in New York for a second round. The doctors in Ridgeline confessed that he needed a specialist. One of them told Campbell that allergies were "specific and unusual" and that anything in the air or sky could be affecting Owen. The doctor also admitted that the vomiting symptoms weren't usually provoked by allergens, although again, in rare cases, it was possible.

Tuesday was a teacher's in-service, so the girls were home. Sasha was there when Mallory woke up, as Campbell had to set out for class at seven. Mally had planned to take Adam for some practice soccer drills, but it was cold, so she took the lazy route, dressing in black flannel velvet pants and a roll-neck sweater and carrying a book downstairs. That night at school was the All County Tournament, the last basketball game of the year. Campbell had only school today, no work, so she would be able to see Sasha and Merry cheer. There had been three practices in the past two days, and there was an early practice today as well. The All County was a big deal.

But Sasha didn't have to work out with the squad, as Meredith did. She told Mallory, "I've practiced that last tumbling run until I could do it in my sleep." The tumbling run looked like something out of the Olympics. It was a round off to a full front flip and an immediate back flip, ending in a split. When she did it, the other girls watched as though Sasha were one step from the medal stand. Now, she picked Owen up, hugged him, and then set him down on the floor as she told Meredith, "I *have* to go by my other job for awhile today too. They have a funeral tomorrow, the poor things."

"Is it the Highland funeral?"

Sasha paused a moment and then said, "Why . . . yes."

"We're going to that," Merry said. "The Highlands were friends of the family I guess. I hate funerals, although I've only been to one."

"Part of life, I reckon," Sasha said, prying a small tack out of Owen's chubby fist. "I don't think we want to play with thumbtacks, slugger." Owen began to scream and cartwheel in a circle, his little face puffed and red. Quickly, Meredith bent down to pick him up.

"Don't do that, Mer," Sasha said. "He's not hurting. He's just mad." Sasha urged Merry further to tell everyone not to make such a fuss. "He'll just start to have real tantrums. Y'all will have to stop treating him like the sick kid. Please. He's such a sweet happy little guy."

But even Sasha wasn't immune to spoiling Owen a little. She had brought Owen a red bus in honor of his first big word, which was "kitty bus." By saying this, he correctly identified the ByWay bus in his own language, meaning "city bus." Sasha had found a hard plastic model of a London bus, which was at least the same color, and Owen ran it all over the walls and the floor making engine noises. Sasha sat down and played with him and patiently let him run the truck up and down her arms while she changed him. Then she took him upstairs to give him his bath. About half an hour later, she came back down with Owen in his duck towel.

"Where's that pan of mine?" Sasha asked them. "With the apple crisp?"

"I ate a lot of it," Adam said, coming into the kitchen and handing Sasha the saucepan. *So it was hers*, Merry thought. Was Sasha the one who locked the door? Adam lied, "It was really good. There was a semi-desperate food situation this weekend."

Sasha laughed and began pouring organic soymilk into sterile bottles. Campbell had switched over from formula to soy because Owen still liked milk bottles in the morning and at naptime. Campbell said it was dumb that doctors said babies had to be off the bottle by exactly one year or before.

"Are you going to try out for cheerleading squad in college?" Merry asked Sasha.

"Sure. Along with nursing," said Sasha. "Everything I can do to help me get a scholarship."

"Do you know where you're going to college yet?" Merry asked.

"I don't know. Probably Texas A&M. They're big into cheering, and I am still a resident there. I didn't try for early acceptance because I might have to work a year after graduation. Your mama says she'll help me get a full-time job at the hospital if I start off with a few classes at the tech college. She even said I could live here without paying rent if I help with Owen. She's so sweet."

"We could squeeze you in somewhere! I'll take Owen. You have to go, don't you?"

"I really do. I know Mallory wanted to take Adam out."

"It's okay. He's sleeping late anyhow," Meredith said. "He's almost a teenager."

Sasha said, "I'm so glad you guys are here because I absolutely must get on to my other job. I usually never have to go during the day, but the lady I help is in a bad way."

Owen jumped into Sasha's arms like a bear cub. She gave him a smacky kiss. "Get all better, okay Shm-owen? You hear me, little fella?"

Owen said, "K."

The two girls clapped. Merry went upstairs and Mallory came down. As Sasha slipped out with a quick wave, Mally sat down next to Owen on the floor and let him run his truck over her stomach.

The door opened and Neely Chaplin came in.

"Sasha's like a force of nature. Where's she going now? She gets to skip practice. Coach Everson lets her. I guess because I have to admit, Mer, she's so much better than all of us. Her toe touch is a full horizontal split in the air."

"Ouch," Mallory said. "That must hurt. And I'm Mallory, Neely. Merry's upstairs. Did Merry forget to tell you? She's not going to the practice either." She spoke in a lowered voice, hoping Neely would leave before Merry had a chance to make it down, so that she could talk just a little more with her twin about Ben.

"I heard that Mallory! I am too going to practice!"

"My mistake," Mally said.

"That's the first time I've ever mixed you two up," Neely said. There was a bounce and a clatter from upstairs. Merry's timing was all off. She'd dropped her gear and would have to pick it all up. Neely went on, "Maybe it's because you're wearing normal clothes."

"Well, yeah. Thanks. What I meant is, that toe touch must hurt."

"It does. I work on it every week with my private coach. My thighs feel like somebody barbecued them afterward."

Mallory looked up at the heavens for guidance as Owen began banging a spoon, his sign for food. She sat him in the high chair and opened a jar of pears, taking out the cooked carrots Sasha had left covered in the fridge. She gave him some of the carrots and a biscuit, along with a tiny cube of melon. Taking aim, Owen threw the melon straight at Mallory's forehead. Sasha was right. He could end up being a little tyrant. But she had to smile anyhow. "I meant about the splits, Neely. I meant that it must hurt your feelings that Sasha can do it, and nobody else can."

"Of course, that, too," Neely said. "I'm used to being the best."

"No doubt about it," Mallory replied, listening to the sounds of her sister bounding down the stairs. "Sasha's definitely the all-around human. Say, Neely, does anyone know what she does at her other job?"

"I do, of course," Neely said.

Mallory let Neely savor the power of the information broker and then asked, "Well, tell. What does she do at night?"

"Oh, you know that old lady she lives with? She's off her rocker and her husband can't handle her. Plus she's got something wrong with her too . . . not just in the head. She has, like, seizures or something."

"I thought that she lived with her aunt," Mally said softly.

"No, she has a room and food and a small salary. Trista Novak told me. It's out . . ."

". . . on Pumpkin Hollow," Mally finished.

"Why'd you ask me if you knew?"

"Lucky guess," said Mally, gently lifting her little brother out of his high chair and softly inhaling the intoxicating scent of his clean ringlets. *Oh, Owen, she thought. I could bottle you.*

"Neels?" Merry called. "You ready?"

"I've *been*," Neely said, tapping her foot. "The car's waiting." Mallory smiled. She loved it when Neely behaved like the heiress queen.

Merry glanced in the hall mirror and put the finishing touches on her makeup, the merest touch of gold-not-quite-glitter high on her cheekbones and a vertical slash of raspberry in the middle of her lower lip. The All-County was the last of the basketball tournaments at school. Seven teams played to double elimination, with Ridgeline traditionally losing just when everyone in town gave up their cynicism and dared to hope. More importantly for Merry, it was an informal display of chops for cheer teams from Deptford, Kitticoe, Warfield, Melton, and a couple of other little towns. Deptford Consolidated, with the rugged sons of miners and machinists tromping the guys from Ridgeline into the paint every time.

But the cheerleaders took the opportunity to bring it on.

Merry would do her scorpion on top of the pyramid tonight and then front flip to the four stalwart mounts who would catch her. Campbell said that seeing it made her want to throw up every time. And then to the last moments of the cheer called "Heat," Sasha would do her tumbling run, landing in front of the rest of the squad, who'd be in V stance.

For kicks and grins, and since Campbell was going to be home that night along with everyone else, Drew and Mallory were going to the game, too. Unlike Merry, Mally didn't have to contort and starve herself beforehand to look cheer-a-licious, so she was looking forward to a rare treat—her mother's eggplant parmigiana.

That evening, Campbell sat down with a sigh, pleased to be with her family, hollows of exhaustion at the inner corners of her eyes. She looked at Mallory with abundant love and weariness. Campbell was not in a good mood, but then, she rarely was anymore. The girls wished that their mother could love them more by laughing, less by worrying.

"I do too much, baby," Campbell said tonight with a long look at her daughter. "I feel guilty. I'm missing the best years of your life."

"Mom," Mallory said softly. "We complain and moan. But although I really hate to say this, I'm proud of you."

"Really?" Campbell asked.

"Really," Mallory said.

"Campbell. Here's what to do. Find a way to do less," Tim said then. "Make a list of things you could do without."

"What if you were at the top?" Campbell asked.

"Did you know that Sasha doesn't live with her aunt?" Mally asked, stepping into the beginnings of a squall between the parents.

"Yes," Campbell said.

"You knew that? Why'd she say so then?"

"I'm sure the reason that she doesn't talk about having to board out is because it's something she's ashamed of," Campbell said. "Do you want to make her more ashamed? She's one of the kindest people I've ever known."

"Is there any way we can help more?" Tim said.

"I've tried to drop little hints about winter coats and such because that old camel-hair thing she wears is too thin," said Campbell.

"I'll get a ski parka from the store. She can at least wear it to school. We'll tell her it's got a flaw, so I'm getting rid of it anyway."

"Would you Tim? I already asked Kate for anything she might have she could spare. She's so slender and tall like Sasha, and she has such beautiful things."

"Kate will be happy to help," their dad said. "So would Karin. I'll ask tomorrow when we go to the service." Owen aimed and threw his carrots at Tim's chin. He then applauded himself. Adam joined in.

"We want to come to the service," Mallory said.

"Why?" Tim asked.

"We're studying Vietnam," Mally said. "I don't mean that to sound disrespectful, but there's a whole generation of people who were missing in action."

"We're aware of that," Tim said with a smile. "They were my cousin Wyatt's age. Wyatt would have gone, too. But he got a high number. He was right at the tail end of the draft."

"What do you mean, a high number?" Mally asked.

"It wasn't a popular war," Tim said. "You know that. In fact, it was basically pressure and demonstrations from generations older than me that put a stop to it, and the last straw was finding out that President Nixon . . ."

Mallory bit her tongue. Asking her dad one question opened the way to forty answers. Tim asked for another helping of eggplant and cut a bite, complimenting Campbell on what he called the first home-cooked meal he'd had in months. And then he continued, "So, nobody wanted to go. I remember the adults talking about it. They started a draft and used a lottery system for every day in the year. They sent out the numbers one New Year's Eve. I can remember my parents and Kevin watching. He was home from college. His number was, like, 299. But other people he knew . . . they got number 9 or 19. And they knew that was it for them."

"And then they had to go no matter what else they wanted to do with their lives? Or if they were in college? Or had a family?" asked Mallory.

"*Now* it doesn't matter if you have a family," Tim said.

"Tim," Campbell said. "Save the speech."

"Anyhow, my cousin Wyatt got a high number. David Highland did, too, but he went anyway. Big hero for the town. And so Ben, who was just a couple of years younger than David and idolized his big brother, dropped out and enlisted before he even graduated. David came back, but Ben didn't. He was never found, so their parents kept hoping. There were these stories about Viet Cong soldiers up in these caves who didn't know the war was over and still had prisoners."

"But now they found him," Adam said, wide-eyed.

"What was left of him. A few bones, some teeth, his senior ring . . ." Tim said.

Campbell said, "Tim!" She glanced significantly at Adam.

"Campbell, he's not a baby."

"A few bones? Some teeth?"

"Hey, Campbell," said Tim, using their mother's favorite phrase against her. "It's just biology!"

Campbell let it pass. She was half-asleep with her cheek pillowed on her hand. Mallory wondered if her mother could last until halftime to see Merry cheer. Big Carla was coming to put Owen to bed and look after Adam so their parents could go, but Campbell looked like someone should tuck her in too. *Adam should be able to get Owen to sleep*, Mallory thought. But her brother refused to stay alone with Owen since he'd gotten sick. Mally turned back to her father. "Dad. Now David, the brother who went to war and lived . . ."

"He's out in California. He has a bunch of kids. Four or five at least. Of course, he'll be here. He's already here. At least some of the kids were here too."

"Since when is four kids a bunch?" Campbell asked sleepily. "You were the one who . . ."

Tim stared his wife down. "At least four or five, from Adam's age to college, I think. And he named one of those kids after his kid brother."

"Are they all coming? The kids?" Mally asked. Drew would be here any moment to take her to the game. She wanted to get as much out of Tim as she could. She thought of texting Drew to wait up a few moments. But then they all heard the asthmatic honk of Drew's truck in the driveway.

Campbell roused herself and began picking up plates. "Tell Drew he can come in here."

"Mom?" Mally said. "Why?"

After instructing Adam to cover the baking dish with plastic, Campbell told Mallory, "That honking junk bugs me. He was all nice as pie until I broke down and let you go out with him a year before you were supposed to go out with anybody, and now he honks for you like you're his servant."

"Adam, do the dishes. Bye, Mom. Bye, Dad," Mallory said.

The telephone rang and Campbell rapped on the counter with her knuckles before Mallory could flee out the front door. Rolling her eyes, Mallory stepped back inside and closed the door.

"Wait up," Campbell said. "Carla Quinn needs a ride over. Her car won't start. So you two pick her up first please? And then go on to the game."

"Mom!" Mallory pleaded.

"You can stand to miss fifteen minutes," Campbell said in a

tone that didn't invite an argument. "I'm not going to get her. I'm getting dressed. People in town don't recognize me anymore unless I'm wearing a white coat."

Big Carla's house was small and as green as prussic acid. Mallory had no idea what prussic acid was, but when Drew said it, it sounded good. A limp Charley-Brown-type Christmas tree lay in the yard, with ears of cooked corn and cranberries and suet balls all over it. "It's for the birds," Drew told Mallory.

"It sure is," she said.

"The tree is! People use dead Christmas trees to feed birds, nimble brain!"

"Oh, stuff a sock in it, Drew," said Mallory. Tentatively, she went up to the door and knocked.

The kid Mallory recognized from the sporting goods store, where she'd come to buy soccer shoes, was Carla Quinn, the one everyone called Little Carla. She smiled and said, "You're Adam's sister."

"Yes, I'm Mally."

"He's cute," said the little girl, who had dark blue eyes and long red hair. She was only little in age, Mally realized. In fact, she was taller than Mallory and probably had a good two inches on Adam. Mally almost laughed. She had never thought of her brother as being old enough for a girl to think he was "cute." But hey, he was in seventh grade. Meredith was "going out" with Will Brent in sixth grade.

For about six days.

"I'm here to pick your mom up to take care of Owen," Mallory said.

"Please come in," Carla said. "She's just getting out of the shower. I'm waiting for my girlfriend's dad to take us to the game. Your sister is the best, best cheer girl. I want to do that someday. I practice all the time. Mommy . . . my mother . . . says I can have lessons tumbling when she gets her degree and we have some more money. You don't think it's too late for me, do you?"

"Why?"

"Your sister started when she was six. That's what Adam says."

They were walking down a long narrow hall. The Quinns' house was what Grandpa Arness, Campbell's dad, called a "shotgun" house: If you stood in the front door, you could fire a gun right out the back door. All the rooms went off that one hall. "Our kitchen and our living room are at the back," Carla said. "Come and sit down."

"You know, Carla," Mally said, her heart softening, "there's a program at the high school where the cheerleaders take a little sister cheerleader and let her practice with the team and help her out."

"There is?" Little Carla cried.

There is now, Mallory thought. *For at least one cheerleader.*

"Let's sit in my mom's sewing room," Carla said. "It's sort of our library too. Mom reads a lot." She glanced at Mally. What's wrong? My mom is just out of the shower. She'll just be one minute. Please have a seat. I'm sorry she's late."

Mally said, "Sewing room?"

The room was filled with sewing projects and bolts of material. A pair of brown pants, probably capris, were still draped over the sewing machine. Different sizes of bookshelves lined the walls.

But there was a baby rocking horse and a huge teddy bear, and the border around the top was a circus border.

Carla looked down at the toes of her shoes. "That used to be my little brother's. Elliot's. Ellie died two years ago. It wasn't my dad's fault. It was a drunk driver."

"Oh, I'm so sorry! You must miss him so much. My little brother's been sick, and I can't imagine what you're going through."

"It was when we just moved here from New Jersey. Dad was so happy. It was his first house with a backyard. I like to remember him being happy. Daddy . . . I mean Dad, that is. My little brother was only nine months old. It's been a long time. But sure, I miss Ellie. I'll never forget him. Sometimes, before I wake up, it's like he's still here. I'm glad Mom's getting stronger though. Mom just doesn't want to give up these couple of things."

Mallory thought, *Poor Big Carla. Why would she want to give these little things up? But maybe those were the voices I heard in that vision!* Maybe the woman arguing with the man about getting rid of old things that had belonged to someone else was Big Carla. But Carla had no husband. Those people were older, judging by their voices. And Big Carla was younger than Mallory's own mother. And whom was she talking with about it? Little Carla's grandfather? Her own father? And Helene . . . who was Helene? And even if all that fit, if Mallory had dreamed it, it hadn't happened yet.

Just then, Big Carla came bustling into the room.

"Mallory, I got busy with a pair of summer pants I'm making for Carly and lost track of time. Honey, here's your five dollars and the extra phone. Don't use it except for an emergency, and be sure that Mickey's Dad drops you off by ten. Mr. Brynn promised he'd be home by 9:30 because he's only doing inventory at the store, so I'll probably be here before you are. Be a good girl."

Mallory said, "I'll ask my sister about that program. And I'll tell Adam you like him."

"Oh no," said the younger girl. "I mean yes about the program but please no about Adam. I'd just die."

Big Carla rushed out with Mallory and Drew got them back to the Brynns' in record time. Carla got out and slammed the door without even bothering to thank them. Drew shrugged. "Was the kid nice?" he asked.

"Real nice," said Mally.

"Hmmmm," Drew said. "Maybe Carla's just the quiet yet obnoxious type."

STEAL AWAY HOME

By the time Drew and Mallory arrived at the end of the second quarter, Ridgeline was up by eight points. The gym was buzzing, thick with the atmosphere of wet wool, popcorn and excitement. Everyone in town seemed to be there. Even practical people, like Grandpa Brynn, had their faces in their hands, wondering when the big fall was going to come. It was pretty pitiful, Drew said. Ridgeline fans were so conditioned to failure that when Mike Corrigan scored a three-pointer, they hardly dared to cheer.

Mally and Drew found their seats. Just as they settled in, making pillows for their backs out of their coats, Mallory saw her parents arrive with Uncle Kevin and another man she didn't recognize. They all found seats higher up in the stands near Mallory's grandparents.

Out on the floor, Meredith was on her knees on the sidelines, pounding the floor with her pom poms. "We're the best! Forget the rest! We're the best! Go, go! Go west!" the girls shouted. Kitticoe High School was west of Ridgeline.

When halftime came and Ridgeline was up by eleven, people were acting as though it were New Year's Eve.

The cheerleaders ran out onto the floor. The cheer was called "Heat."

We have the heart and we have the heat

And we have the beat for . . .

Victory!

We have the goal and we have the soul

And we're on a roll for . . .

Victory!

It was when Merry was perfectly balanced in her Lib on top of the pyramid that she looked into the audience and zeroed in on Ben.

She didn't lose her composure—which could have led to a broken vertebra—but she made a soft kissing motion that no one except Mallory saw. He grinned. And when Meredith and Neely hit the floor, while Sasha whirled past them in a flurry of green and white, Merry whispered, "Tenth row up, twelve from the left. That's him! That's him!"

"The guy?" Neely asked, as they rushed off the floor to the crowd's applause.

"What guy?" Kim asked. "Oh, that guy! Where?"

"Right there in front of your face!" Merry said. "The guy wearing the white T-shirt and the beat-up leather jacket." Covertly, she waved to Ben, who lifted his palm.

Behind her back, Kim and Neely exchanged looks.

There was no one in the seat tenth row up, twelfth from the left.

The only people in that row were old people, no cute boys.

When Mallory saw her sister's intense gaze, she, too, glanced over at the spot. For an instant, she believed she saw something, a shimmer in the air. But then nothing. Her head dropped forward and she leaned against Drew.

Hands held Owen over the kitchen sink as he choked, then wiped and rinsed his mouth. Owen tried to smile. It wasn't like before. He seemed to be okay except for the throw up. He clung to the arm that held him and gently began to pull off his onesie.

"We have to go home," Mallory said. "Owen's going to get sick again."

Both of them ran for the gym doors, and Drew set the land speed record on the back roads getting back to Pilgrim Street.

Just as they walked into the kitchen, Big Carla was lifting Owen out of his high chair as he began to gag. Carla looked all concerned, even frightened, and when Mallory and Drew burst into the door, she seemed to try to hide Owen behind her.

"It's not how it looks," she said.

"It doesn't look any way," Mallory said. "Why do you say that?"

"I mean," Carla said, her face cast down with shame, "I wasn't just letting him lie there and throw up. I wouldn't neglect him." Mallory didn't answer. Carla held Owen over the sink and gently wiped his lips with a little cloth, just as Merry had seen. Then she drew herself up and glared at Mallory. "What are you staring at? Why'd you come sneaking in here? You come running in here like you think I'm sticking him with pins. It's not my fault. I can't help it he's sickly!" She set Owen in his play yard and he began to cry. When he did, Carla took a deep breath. She seemed to get a grip on herself. Her face changed and Mally could see traces of the loving mother her daughter saw and the young woman she might have been before the tragedy. "He's okay, I think," Carla said. "He's sure not dehydrated, and it was only this one incident of nausea. I'm going to let your mom know, but I call it okay. I'm sorry I yelled at you. I guess I just got scared. There you go, big boy. That's a big boy." Carla sat down in the big rocker and held Owen against her chest, softly rocking him back and forth, back and forth, stroking his hair as Owen's tense little body first wriggled and fought, then finally relaxed. Carla held him closer, and the look she gave Mallory was one of pure sadness.

Mallory thought Owen probably reminded Carla of her own baby.

• • •

Later that night, when Owen was peacefully asleep in bed with their father, Mallory said to her twin, "It's frustrating. I don't know why I can't see who's with Owen when he gets sick. I see him. I see hands. That's it! At least it wasn't bad this time. I was the last one who fed him. Maybe he's allergic to something in our house."

"That would be awful," Merry said, yawning.

"Why aren't you over at Neely's?" Mally asked.

"Tired," Merry said.

"Why don't you have your night shirt on?"

"Too tired."

"Who were you making kissy faces at while you were cheering?" Meredith didn't answer. "We have to go to that service tomorrow." Merry said nothing. "Dad gave me this whole talk about Vietnam and how the brothers both went, both of old Mr. and Mrs. Highland's sons, and one died." She waited for Meredith to react. "One part, you were right about. The older brother did name one of his kids Ben after his brother." Mallory paused. "Merry! Answer me. I'm the one who ignores you!"

"I'm not ignoring you."

"You're not telling me something."

There's a reason she's not at Neely's, thought Mallory, *and it isn't because it's a school night*. Meredith stayed over at Neely's and got the limo ride to school a couple of times a month. How unlike Meredith to keep anything from her twin—to be *able* to keep anything from her twin, who was trying to pick the lock on her thoughts and getting nowhere with it. Because of the deliberate muddle of multiplication tables and lines of poetry that she could "hear" in Merry's head, all Mallory knew was that Merry was hiding something.

Suddenly, her sister's thoughts came through to her loud and clear— the way they hardly ever did since the twins were in the fire, the way they had when the girls were little.

And Mallory knew what the something was.

TO BE? OR NOT TO BE?

TO BE? OR NOT TO BE?

"You're meeting Ben tonight," Mallory said. Merry didn't confirm or deny. "You're sneaking out! Mer, be careful."

"There's nothing to be careful of! We're just going to a movie on the kitty bus." They both laughed at Owen's words. "I just have to sneak out because it's the eleven o'clock show. We're even going to the Belles Artes Theatre for a cultural experience."

Mallory had to smile. "Don't do anything stupid."

"Nothing I do would be stupid," Merry said softly.

"You know what I mean."

"I know what you mean, and nothing we do would be stupid."

"Look, what I think about Ben . . . you know," Mally said again. "And we'll find out tomorrow."

"He is someone I already know that I care about, Mal," Merry said. "Nothing about tomorrow will change that."

"I'll be awake when you get back," Mallory said. "So no funny stuff." She sounded like her mother. Later that night, she fell asleep instantly.

Mallory dreamed of Sasha, her hair pulled back severely and pinned, an old-fashioned nurse's cap on her head above a starched white uniform— the kind of thing that even Campbell's professors didn't wear anymore when they were in college, the kind of thing you saw in museum cases. She was filling little cups with liquid and, into the last cup, injecting a syringe of something she kept capped in her pocket. Owen, Mallory thought! But Sasha knelt and offered each of the three doses to a lady with a sweet, unlined face, who smiled briefly before turning her face to the wall. It was the lady with the hippie jeans from so long ago. Her long blond hair was now almost entirely gray, but she was still beautiful. The woman held a book in veined hands. As Mallory watched, the book slid off the comforter and hit the floor. Sasha picked it up and quickly stacked the three plastic cups, one inside the other. Reaching up, she touched the lady's neck, then with her index and middle fingers, she closed her eyes. The boy Mallory now knew was Ben came into the room. He shouted at Sasha, who turned her back on him. Still wearing the brown leather jacket, he kneeled at the foot of the lady's bed and clutched the comforter to his face, crying. But though he held the quilt tightly in his hands, his hands made no wrinkle in it. It lay flat, tucked firmly under the mattress.

Mally woke, hungry and nauseated at the same time.

A pool of moonlight centered on the floor between the beds like a gigantic coin.

Slowly, she got out of bed to creep downstairs for something to eat and to try to think. She didn't want to wake Meredith.

But Meredith's bed was still empty.

On impulse, Mallory got out her cell phone and jammed in a text message.

• • •

"I'm not a detective," Drew said, his hair sticking up. He wouldn't admit to having been asleep, but he had, for hours. "I don't even want to be. I'm happy you wanted to go out and drive down to cemetery grove with me."

"We're not going for that. And I don't care what you did there with anyone else. All I want to know is, you saw Sasha coming out of a house when you went out with your beer buddies. Was it the Highlands' house? Did you see her go back in?"

"No. She got into a car with somebody."

"Sawyer Brownlee?"

"I didn't see. It was a truck. Big new black truck."

"Be quiet now. We're going to have to find a place to park where she won't see us but we can see her," Mallory said.

"Why should we be quiet? It's winter. It's March. Do you think they'll have all their windows open? We'll pull into the excavated place. Back behind where we go."

"Okay," Mally said.

They drove past Sasha's beat-up Malibu. It was the Highlands' house. Mally was *pretty* sure that it was the Highlands' house, anyway. Why did she even have to do this tonight? Tomorrow, she could ask her parents. It was also really wicked cold.

"How long are we going to sit here?" Drew whispered. The house was two hundred feet away. "Can't we warm up a little?" He reached for Mallory. "I mean, since we can't run the engine?"

"Number one, no we can't, and number two, I don't know," Mally said. "Not long. This is one of my stupider ideas. We know where she lives now. I just want to see. I don't even know why I care. It's mixed up in my head with something else. I'm sorry."

Just then, Sasha came out of the house.

And she was wearing the nurse's uniform Mallory had seen in her vision, including white tights and nurse's white clogs. Carrying a brown bag with handles. She jumped into her car. But then she got out again and took out a cell phone. Mallory rolled the window down, over Drew's whispered protests, motioning for him to be silent.

Sasha said into the phone, "Honey, I can't even hear you! Keep your pants on. I'll be there in two shakes. Well, she has that damn funeral tomorrow so she's all crazy. They've had to put it off twice 'cause she just can't bear it. Yeah. Poor old thing. I gave her something to make her sleep good. Real good." Sasha leaned against the hood of the truck and examined her nails. She seemed to be listening to a long recitation on the phone. Occasionally, she threw back her head and laughed. The light went on briefly inside the truck's cab as Sasha reached inside and popped open a can of beer. "One beer honey! Don't y'all start being an old lady on me now. I got enough of that right here." She laughed again and took a long pull on the can of beer. "I'll never be too tired for that," she said, snapping the phone shut. Then, humming an old song, she finished the beer, stepped hard on the can and kicked it across the street into the verge of the cemetery.

It was Drew who, when Sasha's taillights disappeared, said, "That didn't sound like Sasha at all."

Mallory said, "Maybe it does and we don't know all the ways she sounds. Why's she wearing an old-fashioned nurse's uniform?"

"Why am I out in the middle of the night spying on a girl who only wants to help out an old lady because my girlfriend is paranoid? So what if she had a beer? So what if she littered? And, might I add, why am I out with my girl on the same night her sister slid down the maple tree too? Sasha's wearing an old-fashioned nurse's uniform because it probably comforts old Mrs. Highland to think Sasha Avery is a real nurse instead of a kid. Everybody has an off day. What's so bad about that?"

"What if she says she's a real nurse? That's not true."

"What's it to you? If it makes Mrs. Highland happy? Brynn, frankly, I usually go along with crazy stuff because of affection, but this is a little off the tracks even for you."

"Fine, Drew. Be that way. But first, pull closer to that mailbox and make sure it really says 'Highland.'"

It really did.

All the way home, they didn't say anything.

When Mally crept back into her room, Merry was still missing.

When she opened her eyes again, Meredith was back—fully dressed, lying on top of the quilt in her best dark skirt and sweater, asleep. But the sun was up and the sounds of breakfast were going on in the kitchen.

When had Merry come home?

IN THINGS UNSEEN

There had been nowhere for Meredith and Ben to go after the movie— no car, no house, no place to be alone. They walked up and down the block of shops outside the Belle Artes, stopping for a coffee so Meredith could warm her hands and feet. But finally, even the coffee shop closed.

Then Meredith remembered that Father Gahagan still held on to the old Catholic tradition of leaving the church doors open twenty-four hours a day. He was public about it—that the church should remain a haven to the weary and the lonely, as it had been since medieval times. People in Ridgeline held their breaths, thinking that there would be spray paint all over the ancient stained glass and the rich carvings in arms of the cherry-wood pew, each depicting an individual saint. But to everyone's surprise, there had been remarkably few incidents of vandalism, and those few had been minor, one of them an attack of Silly String draped on the priests' entrance to the church, which caught Father Gahagan in the face like a spider web when he entered to say early Mass. Later in the day, he revealed the incident and said that if it were a message from Sunday-school students, he had actually rather enjoyed it and that it had gotten his heart rate up.

Like thieves feeling that they'd be observed, Merry and Ben walked the block from the theater to the church and skipped up the steps. Inside, they felt the hush of the sacred space close around them and were comforted by the warmth of the flickering candles and the gentle glow of the Madonna's lit-up face.

Together, they sat down in a middle aisle.

"Should I sit on the groom's side?" Ben asked. "No, I'll stand up here. And you walk toward me."

Laughing, Merry ran up the aisle and out into the vestibule. She fluffed her hair and tweaked her lip gloss.

"Okay, your father is offering you his arm," Ben said. Slowly, Merry glided down the aisle, the low lights shining on her black hair.

"It will by my mother and my father," said Merry. "One on each side. And my twin sister."

"And now here you are," Ben said, as she turned to face him across the flickering of the votive candles. "Do girls think about their wedding day?"

"I do. Yeah, we all do. Not my sister Mallory but everyone else does. We know all the words."

"So?" Ben said.

"Well, I, Meredith, take you, Benjamin, to be my husband, to have and to hold, to love and to cherish, in sickness and in health, for as long as we both shall live."

"Not to obey?"

"Not me," Merry laughed.

"You'll be a beautiful bride. I wish I could see you." His smile leaked away from his face, and the mournful look replaced it.

So here it was, between them, the thing that had to be talked about. They could no longer put it off with old movies or by playing pretend or telling each other how wonderful it felt to be together. The funeral was in the morning. Merry had to ask the questions she dreaded about Ben—the Ben beside her, real and warm. The Ben in her dreams. The Ben who wasn't the same but had to be.

If only there was a chance, still a chance, that there was some confusion.

"Why won't you be here?" she asked. "When I'm a bride?"

Ben sat down beside Mallory, his arms along the back of the pew. "I just know I won't. I'm confused. I'm really tormented, to tell you the truth. I know that this funeral is tomorrow."

"Are you sad because you never met him?" Merry asked. "The Ben in your family who served in Vietnam? The one who's being buried tomorrow."

"Never met who? What do you mean, baby?"

"The boy who died. That was your uncle, right?" *Please, she thought. Please say yes; you're here for the funeral, but you have to go back and finish a job or enroll in school. I can wait for you. . . .* Ben dropped his head between his knees and held on to the back of his skull, as if trying to squeeze something in or out.

"Merry, you don't get it. And I don't entirely get it either." Meredith began to cry, which only increased Ben's obvious pain. "It's . . . it's a family problem. I . . . I'll stay as long as I can."

"Stay as long as you can? Ben, tell me everything. Now. Were you going to leave without telling me? But would you come back? Ever?" Ben gave Merry the look she had begun to think of as belonging to her, the lovely heartbroken sideways smile. "That's my answer! If you knew you would be back, you'd say so!"

"I know I'll see you again," Ben said, and he lifted his hand gently, sending a shiver down Meredith's spine, like a tiny electrical shock. "Do you know how much you look like your mom?" Mallory shook her head.

"I look like my aunt Karin and my grandma, not my mom."

"Oh, maybe that is who I'm thinking of. The Brynn girls and women I used to know. Older than me."

"Ben is your . . . uncle, right? The one who's being buried."

"No, I'm the only Ben."

"I don't know what we're talking about anymore," Meredith said dully.

"Baby, cut it out," Ben said. "Let's just stop talking. It's making you crazy."

You're the one who's crazy! How can this be happening to me? I'm the only one who can see you. And yet, you're not a ghost, not like the others. Why?

Why?

"If you were a little older, we could go on this road together," Ben said.

"Not this road," Merry said and began to cry harder. "Ben, I don't understand why this is happening to us. When I saw you, I felt instantly like I knew you."

"Me, too."

"And the girl isn't supposed to say this, but I wanted to be with you."

"Me, too. I was never hit so hard by a girl. When I'm away from you, all I think about is you. I think about what we could do in our lives. I think about how you'll be when you're a woman. I think about a place we could be together, where no one could keep us apart."

They shifted uncomfortably on the bench. Merry had never wanted anything so badly that it literally physically hurt. She understood all the words to all the songs now—about aching, hearts breaking, and the pain deep down inside. It was as if Ben had a hold of her soul and was pulling her toward him, holding it in his hand.

"But there's something keeping us apart. My sister says it's showing up in her dreams. I have to tell you about us, Ben. Mallory and me. We're not just twins. We see things in dreams. Mallory saw the funeral tomorrow."

Ben got up and began to pace. He walked up toward the altar and then back toward the bench where the two of them sat. Finally, he threw himself down on the seat, far from Merry, unable to look at her.

"I can't talk about that, baby. I can't talk about that. When I think about that, it's like cymbals clashing in my head," Ben said. "Maybe there's a way for us. Maybe. I've never met a girl like you. Back when I was in school, they all were so beautiful, but foolish.

All they cared about were clothes and shoes and who got on the pom-pom squad."

Like me, Merry thought. *Like me, before you.*

"I'm a cheerleader, Ben. I'm not a deep thinker."

"I know that. But you take it as a sport. You have this look in your eye like steel. Like you're going to nail it no matter what. And when I talk to you, it's not all about you."

"I want to know about *you*," Merry said. "Now, before it's too late. Where were you before?"

"I was always here. But I think I must have had a head injury, Merry. I know that sounds like a soap opera. I think I actually forgot some period of time in my life. Because suddenly, there I was, looking up at you on that bus. And I remember other things, but they all sank away from me. Your face was like a light."

Merry thought of the poem, of Bess, the landlord's black-eyed daughter.

"When I go into my house and hang out in my room, I remember being a kid. There's something in between though. Something bad. I think of my little mom and all that she went through. She's so sick now. It's about this memorial."

"But who is this Ben to you?"

"I'm not sure," Ben said. "It's like I'm looking at the world I used to know instead of being in it." He shrugged off his leather jacket. The dim light from the electric candles on the altar made hollows under his cheeks, as though Ben were an old photo. "Mallory, if I told you that I love you, and that I'll always love you, would you believe me? Will you stay here with me tonight?"

"In the church?"

"Yes, right here in front of God. We'll just lie down beside each other and go to sleep for a while. I won't lay a hand on you. I just want to see you sleeping. I want to see what would have been."

Meredith felt safe and protected and alarmed and distressed all at the same moment. Ben wanted to watch her sleep. He would watch over her. What did he mean by . . . what would have been? Whatever it was, whatever they had to face, they would face together. Softly, with a low face, Ben began to sing an old song her father sometimes sang. "Imagine me and you. I do . . ."

Eventually, Merry slept.

A PROMISE GIVEN

A PROMISE GIVEN

Before dawn, when he came into church from the rectory to get ready to say Mass, Father Gahagan found Meredith asleep in the second pew. Gently, he touched her shoulder and asked why she was here. Merry simply shook her head: How could she explain? Father sat down beside her. He asked if she had anything she wanted to talk over, if she was considering running away from home, or if there might be a spiritual need he could help her face. Merry sat up and touched her eyes, surprised at how tender they were, as though she had cried in her sleep. She rubbed her eyes with the heels of her hands. She wanted to cry out, "I have nothing but all the spiritual questions, every one of them, wrapped up in one person! And I don't know what to do. I don't know if this life without Ben will ever feel anything but hollow."

"Is it about a boy, Merry?" Father Gahagan asked.

Meredith smiled. "It is, Father. But not in any way you'd imagine.

I haven't done anything wrong except wish I could do something wrong."

Father Gahagan laughed. "I think you share that with about 90 percent of the human race at any given time, Meredith."

"And I'm losing someone, but not because he doesn't want to stay with me," Merry said.

"Do you want to make your confession or just talk?"

Meredith didn't even know if she truly wanted to talk. She was willing to bet that she had more to say that Father Gahagan would want to hear than almost anyone who'd ever sat in his presence. But though, as a priest, evidence of the hereafter would validate his faith, he would be very hard-pressed to believe in Merry's proof.

"Father, do you believe in heaven?" Merry asked. The priest looked surprised but then smiled. It wasn't the question he had expected.

"Why absolutely. I have my doubts about hell. But I believe in the life of the world to come," Father Gahagan said gently. "I don't think I could be a priest if I didn't. That doesn't mean I don't fear death. All of us do."

"What if I don't fear death?"

"Meredith, it's not a way out of pain. Young people sometimes . . ."

"I'm not suicidal, Father. I promise. I just wonder what the life hereafter would be like."

The long creases that had been dimples when he was a boy deepened in Father Gahagan's face. "Merry, whatever pain you feel now is temporary. Death is permanent. I can see by your face that you're struggling. But stepping away from the lives we are given on

Earth doesn't solve anything. You're a long way from heaven. And you're also a long way from home. It's nearly sunrise. We can talk more about this now or we can talk about it again. But I want to talk about it."

"I'd rather wait until later, until I think it through. Do you mind?"

"Of course, Meredith. But if I trust you and keep this between us, you have to promise me one thing. And that is if you ever feel lost, you'll come here again, just like you did tonight, only press the button behind the altar that rings my house—the gray one right up there behind the curtain. And I'll come right away. You have to promise not to make any decisions about life and death before you talk to me."

"I promise. I'll do that. I don't want to die, Father. It's not that."

"Well, I'm glad to hear it," he said, studying Meredith's face. "Do your parents know where you are?" Meredith shook her head." The priest paused. "Go out and get into the car, and I will drive you home. Mrs. Peller is going out your way, and I said I'd drive her too. I'll say Mass when I come back. I'm to do a funeral at ten this morning. It was supposed to be earlier, but it had to be postponed."

I know, Meredith thought. She sat up and pulled on her coat thoughtfully.

She wasn't surprised to wake up alone on the wide oak bench.

Last night had been deep enough for both of them. Before following Father Gahagan, she knelt for a moment in silent prayer. When she sat back, she realized that she had awakened once during the night and that she hadn't seen Ben then, either. She had not even expected to see Ben. Yet she had gone back to sleep, soothed, as though he were there, and felt his comforting presence all around her.

She felt his presence even now.

Why?

"I'm still concerned, Merry," said the priest who had baptized all of the Brynn kids. Mrs. Peller the housekeeper had tucked herself into the backseat for a quick nap, smiling at Meredith before she quickly reached up and switched off her hearing aids. "Can you give me a hint?"

"Well, Father, it's about my friend," Merry began. On the way home, she told a story about a girl who might be in love with someone whom no one else understood. Father Gahagan had heard many variations of the same story and always counseled giving the passion time to even out. He also knew that Merry wasn't talking about a friend.

Within ten minutes, they were in the Brynns' driveway. The priest reiterated the vow he expected Merry to make. And again, easily, she gave her promise.

THE GOODBYE BOY

THE GOODBYE BOY

Fortunately for Meredith, although her mother was loaded for bear when Merry stepped through the door, Campbell didn't dare say a thing in front of the priest who came into the kitchen with Merry.

Father Gahagan put on his best pulpit voice and said, "Campbell, I know you must be upset and worried. But I want to say this. I found her lying in the pew as innocent as a lamb. Alone. I hope you take that into account. Young people sometimes need to sort things out in their own ways. She was safe. And we've had a long talk this morning."

Campbell said, "Thank you for bringing her home." As Father left, Merry's mother turned to her. She said simply, "I called school to let them know you'll both be late. You'll go at noon. Let's get moving. Take a nap if you can and then get dressed for the service at the cemetery."

Carla was already there, playing in the living room with Owen, and Adam had gone to school.

Several hours later, after Mallory had commented on what a late movie her sister had gone to, Tim, Campbell, and the twins drove quietly to the cemetery, where there were a dozen cars parked along the road. Among them were their grandparents' little SUV and Uncle Kevin's snazzy BMW, which he called "my only vice." Although the snow had melted (except in the shadowy crags of the ridges above) and the grass was beginning to poke through, there was still a small canopy set up and some wide flooring boards on which there were a few rows of folding chairs. Someone had also turned on a space heater with a power pack. An American flag lay over the coffin, and three young Army officers stood at attention some distance away.

When the twins walked down the path to join the others, Father Gahagan glanced at Meredith as though *he* had seen a ghost.

Then, clearing his throat, he began, "We are gathered here today to lay to rest one of our own sons, in the certainty of eternal rest and eternal peace. Our only comfort is that the ground that keeps him warm is the ground on which he played and laughed as a child. . . ."

Merry glanced down the row and was immensely relieved to see Ben sitting in one of the empty chairs beside a pale, tall, painfully thin older woman. On her other side sat old Mr. Highland, whom Merry thought she recognized, but barely. But when the woman began to cry and sway, someone stepped forward from behind one of the thick lanes of evergreens that lined the walk at Mountain Rest Cemetery.

In a thick red woolen coat that had once been Aunt Kate's, Merry recognized Sasha. Mrs. Highland turned her face into Sasha's arm.

The priest's words faded into a buzz as Merry's mind took over.

She examined the spire in the middle of the park-like grounds. It was made of some kind of smooth gray stuff—marble or granite. Merry had seen it a hundred times but never looked closely at it. Now she saw that it was a war memorial, carefully inscribed with the names of the dead soldiers of Ridgeline, back as far as the Civil War. The town names were familiar: Brent, Brynn, Carew, Everard, Massenger, Woolrich, Vaughn. There were still kids at Ridgeline with those names, and kids from Ridgeline with those names had died in every war. They were probably cousins of Drew, if not uncles or even aunts. One was Charlotte Vaughn. Drew's older sister was named Charlotte, but this Charlotte had died in the 1980s.

"Who's Charlotte Vaughn?" asked Mallory, as if reading Merry's thoughts.

"Mrs. Vaughn's cousin. She was a nurse in the Persian Gulf War," Tim said. "Be quiet now."

"You never told us."

"It never came up," Tim said.

The little Valentine tree that Mallory had seen in her dream was real and settled staunchly against the front of a small but elegantly carved marker. It read:

Benjamin Charles Highland
BELOVED SON
(1951-1969)
Smart lad, to slip betimes away
From fields where glory does not stay

"For Helene and Charles, the only comfort now is that their son lives on in his brother, in his namesake, in their hearts. As I told a young . . . parishioner of mine just this morning, there is absolutely no doubt that Ben and his parents will meet again, at the gates of glory."

There were prayers and a gentle word from the tall, blond man whom Mally and Drew had seen with her parents the other night at the game. He identified himself as David Highland. He said it had been years since he had come to Ridgeline, and he had forgotten how dear it was to him. He thanked so many of his old friends for coming here today. Growing serious, as if tackling a task that he couldn't bear, he spoke of a little brother who had been a pest when he was young "but a pest I loved. I told him to leave me alone, and then I always looked back to make sure he was following me." David Highland said he had believed all his life that if his little brother hadn't followed him to a place where he should never have gone, Ben would be here today with his own children. In a trembling voice, the man concluded by saying that Ben had lived and died with honor—that honor was the standard by which Ben lived.

The soldiers stood then and presented their rifles. As they prepared to fire a salute, the old lady, whom Mallory knew now was the young woman in jeans from her dream, aged many years, stood up.

"Don't you dare," she said, in a strong voice much younger than her more wasted appearance. With clear but forceful dignity, she said, "Don't you dare fire a gun over Benjamin's grave. If it weren't for your guns, both my sons would have spent their Christmases with me. Both my sons would have brought me their diplomas. I didn't agree with David, but David was a grown man. Ben was not a man.

He was a child." She paused and drew a deep breath. Then she said to the Army honor guard, "I don't disrespect you. You're doing what you think is right. But I want Ben to lie in peace, not with the sounds of war as the last thing his spirit hears."

And then Helene Highland fainted. Sasha and Mr. Highland held her close.

At a nod from the tall older brother, the honor guard raised their rifles and fired three sharp, impossibly loud cracks that seemed to shatter the air. Birds burst from the trees and fled in panic. Merry pressed her hands over her ears. Fighting hard against the spinning, the ground that seemed to draw her to it, the light that seemed to flood her head, using every trick she knew to stay present, Meredith fainted too.

FOR THIS ONE DAY
FOR THIS ONE DAY

"It's from an old poem, that line on the grave," Mallory told Drew. "I looked it up. His mother was an English teacher."

"Who exactly? Whose mother?"

"Ben Highland," Mallory said. It was after school on the day of the funeral, and Drew and Mallory were waiting in the hall for Meredith to finish practice. Mallory had a plan that could prove to her twin what she already knew—what she absolutely knew now to be true. She had told Drew about the sad drama at the funeral and about Meredith's reaction. It had been their grandmother, Gwenny, who told everyone not to worry, that Merry would be fine in a moment.

"What does 'betimes' mean?" Drew asked. "What does it mean, 'to slip betimes away?'"

"I would say it means before his time."

"Okay, so . . ."

"He's dead," Mallory said. "That's why I can't see him and she can. He died in a war, a long time ago. Merry's big crush is dead."

Drew sighed. "I hate it when you say that."

They were waiting for Meredith in the hall at school. It was five in the evening and practice was over. But now, as March began to give way to April, the sky at evening went a silvery, metallic gray with a band of faded blue-jean blue. In Ridgeline, people looked up that day from their desks or their digging, from shaking out their rugs or shaking out bags of recycled paper, and thought, *summer*. Summer will come after all. Somehow, just the sight of the sun fighting to stay above the horizon lifted Mally's spirits.

But then Mallory saw Merry approaching. Merry had chosen to go to practice despite the fact that she'd fainted at the funeral. Anything was better than facing their mother.

Mallory felt a moment of pity. It was going to be a rough day for her twin.

After the service, Campbell had said to Aunt Karin that Merry had fainted because she skipped breakfast. None too gently, she helped Meredith to the car, murmuring things about low blood sugar. Once inside their car, Campbell had given Merry a glance of double fury, which Meredith thought was impossibly unfair. Okay! There was going to be a reckoning about staying out all night. But how could you get mad at a person for fainting accidentally? Still, Mallory set her chin. She was determined to sort this Ben business out, here and now.

Watching her, Drew thought over Mallory's plan, about which he had his own opinions. He tried to consider what he would do if

Meredith were his own sister. It might be kinder not to force the issue—to just let be what would be. But he had to trust his girl. For him, Mallory was as dear to him as a sibling and also the most adorable girl on Earth. If he thought about a future with Mallory, and it occasionally crossed his mind, he knew he would have to come to grips not only with her stubbornness but with knowing the person he was with was the closest thing he would ever know to . . . a witch. He would have to recognize that there would be things about Mally that only Meredith would ever know.

The future . . . this was why people didn't like thinking about it.

Now Mallory was on a mission. She'd sketched it in for him earlier and now was about to put it into practice. Although Drew didn't want to know the details, Mallory insisted on telling him. That didn't mean he wanted to witness Meredith's pain. Thick as she could be sometimes, he cared for Merry, too.

"She has to see," Mallory had told Drew when she caught up with him that day after lunch. "Here's what I think. The school has all those basketball and football pictures in those little wooden frames going back to before my dad went to Ridgeline. If he really is from here, and he really ran cross-country, he'll be in one of them."

"I don't want to know about it," Drew had told Mally the previous night.

"And then she'll have to face it."

"What do you not get about the phrase 'I don't want to know'? I'm not interested in trying to convince your sister her boyfriend is dead."

"They only meet at night."

"Maybe he's undead," Drew suggested.

"Oh, you're making this sound ridiculous! Everybody knows there are no . . . *undead* dead people. That's an entirely different thing from ghosts, Drew!"

"Pardon my mortal error. I'm only human. And this would be why I don't want to know any more about it, Mall-or-y."

"You never call me Mallory. You always call me Brynn."

"I'm trying to get your attention."

Mally said he never cooperated with her. But later, she texted an apology. It occurred to her what Drew had to put up with—what he had, in a sense, always had to put up with, from her. In a rush, the thought of Drew going away, and that it would be before another leaf on the ridge turned scarlet and fell, took root in Mallory and grew. It grew larger and it grew real. Suddenly, Mallory didn't want to give up a second with the guy she'd seen every day of her life but had learned to love, it seemed, only yesterday. He was always there for her. And soon, he wouldn't be. Who would pull her hair and call her Brynn?

"What are we doing?" Merry asked as she came up beside Drew and Mallory in the hall outside the locker rooms and gyms. "Why did you wait for me? I'll have to tell Neely. She's outside."

"I told her. She already left. So you could ride home with us," Mallory said. "Merry, look. There's something you have to see."

Slowly, following Mallory's finger, Merry began to scan the walls where the team pictures hung, gradually leading Meredith to the right place. Even in the seventies, the track outfits looked bizarre compared to now. The only uniforms that hadn't changed were the wrestlers, and they looked bizarre anyhow.

There.

There was the section devoted to cross-country. The grave said 1969, the year he died. Unless he died in school, in a car accident or something, he would have graduated at seventeen or eighteen that year. Mallory searched for 1968. There he was, his curly blond hair falling forward, down on one knee in front.

Ben Highland.

"'Ster," said Mallory. "Look."

Meredith stood on her toes. She grabbed the edge of the frame and pulled herself closer.

Then she whirled and took one running step before Mallory caught her.

"It's his uncle or something," Merry said.

"No it isn't his uncle or something!" Mally said.

"But Ben was there too! How could he be there if it was him being buried? Well, prayed over anyhow?" Merry's fury mounted. "Why are you spying on him and me? Maybe the old Highlands are his grandparents. They're old, old-old. Probably older than Grandma and Grandpa Brynn," Merry stopped. "He does look just like him. But you have to admit it's possible. Fathers and sons and nephews and cousins can look a lot alike when they're young. And I would know, Mallory. I've seen . . . you know what. And he isn't one of them."

"This is where I go get a juice," said Drew.

"Okay. Okay," Mallory agreed. "But that's not what's in my dreams. It's the Ben you know. It's his jacket, the one you described to me. I've seen him in that and in those old-fashioned tight jeans." Meredith seemed to shrink right before her twin's eyes into a small, crumpled being.

"Mallory, don't. That could be his dad's jacket. Handed down."

"It could be," Mally said. "But you know it isn't."

"So okay, say I do know. What if I want to be with him just until there is no more time?"

"Shhhh," Mallory said. "I'm thinking. If he lied about his age and got in the Army . . . people used to do that. Let me think."

"I'm sick of your thinking. Listen to what I'm feeling, Mally. You always assume I'm nuts."

"Oh, please. I don't assume that anymore than you assume precisely the same thing about me, half the time when anything like this happens. Okay . . . introduce me to him. Call Ben. Text him," Mally challenged her twin.

Merry slid down the wall and sat on the floor. When Drew came back with two glass bottles of juice, she gratefully accepted one and took a long drink. Her thoughts were drumming, and what she needed to admit was the last thing she wanted to say. Finally, she said, "I can't."

"Why?"

Mallory knelt down next to her sister. As much as she wanted to clue her twin into the reality of her obsession, she could still feel the nearly physical pain that Meredith gave off, like a heat or a scent. It affected Mallory, too, deep in her stomach, where she felt something tender like a bruise. *How can I go on with this?* she thought. They were still only in school—the nauseous yellow walls and absurd bright-green scuffed lockers, the smell and press of love and fear and anxiety and socks. Why should Merry have to feel anything beyond the general horribleness of adolescence, which was already a rollercoaster of highs and lows, even for Mallory herself, who didn't have Merry's penchant for extremes?

"Why, Mer?" Mally asked again, more gently.

"He doesn't have a cell phone."

"What does he do all day?"

"I don't know."

"Merry . . . this is what I mean. What seventeen-year-old guy doesn't have a cell phone?"

Meredith couldn't answer. At the movies the other night, before they went to the church, she noticed how people didn't stare at Ben, cute as he was. They looked right through him. There was something strange. It wasn't like the girl in the attic or the man with the accent. But it was "off." Merry didn't want to push him by asking why. He was already miserable. Was it really because she didn't want to hurt him? Or because she didn't want to know? If this was denial, she wanted to live there.

When she was with him, everything seemed to fall into place. It was entirely right and true and meant to be. When she wasn't with him, doubts whirled around her stomach as though she were locked in a carnival ride and strapped in darkness. Love was supposed to make you joyous. But look at Romeo and Juliet . . . one day of happiness.

But finally she said, "Mallory, Ben doesn't seem to want to hang around with my friends. He avoids people I know. But I have to tell you that it wouldn't matter to me what he is or isn't. Did you hate Eden after you found out that she had a double life? She was your best friend. Did you reject her?"

"That's different, Mer. Eden was there. Eden was a part of my life and your life. There was a chance to save her. You can't save somebody who's already gone."

"Ben isn't gone!"

"He might already be gone, but maybe he doesn't know it, Meredith. Does that happen with ghosts? Do they forget to cross over or whatever?"

"I guess," Meredith said. "I never met one who hadn't crossed over. Mostly they come back to do what they were doing when they died. At least I think that."

"Maybe that's why he feels real to you. Maybe he doesn't know how to pass over. How does it feel to kiss him?"

"We never have," Meredith said softly. "He's never even held my hand." Mallory reached out and hugged her twin.

"I'm so sorry," she said. "Do you believe me?"

"Yes. But it doesn't change anything. Mally, you have me confused with you. I might still want to be with him. No matter what he is." They stood for a moment as the light in the hall darkened with the spring twilight.

Mallory said, "No. That's enough, Merry."

Merry said, "Don't push me." Mallory stepped back, her eyes widening. Nothing that her twin had ever said had so fully excluded her, so entirely stepped outside the boundaries of their two-ness. It frightened Mallory into silence. Finally, Meredith said, "I know who would know. And I'm going to find out. By myself."

Mallory didn't say a word.

By the time Drew dropped them off, it was completely dark

outside, and every light was on in the kitchen. The porch lights and even the leftover Christmas lights were blazing.

Her mother was waiting for Merry inside.

She was blazing too.

A MATTER OF TRUST

A MATTER OF TRUST

ampbell said, "I'm not even going to discuss it. In other words, you don't have a side in this. You're grounded for four weeks. No, I'm going too far. For two weeks. But Meredith Arness Brynn, I want to know right now, this second, if you were out all night with a boy."

Campbell went back to folding laundry, but Merry could see her mother covertly glance at her out of the corner of her eye. Abruptly, Campbell set the second laundry basket in front of Merry and nodded at it. Merry began to search for the mates of at least forty pairs of athletic socks.

"I'm waiting," Campbell said.

"I thought you didn't want me to discuss it," Meredith said. "I thought I didn't have a side in this."

Deliberately, she folded a dozen of Adam's socks, all of which were marked with an "A" in permanent marker, now that Adam's feet were as large as the twins'. The silence lengthened.

"I'll tell you when I don't want you to discuss it," Campbell said, flustered. "So were you?"

"Yes."

"What do I have to worry about here? Other than my daughter's dishonesty and deceit?"

"You don't even have to worry about that, Mom," Merry said. "We didn't do anything wrong except for my being out after curfew."

"Meredith, dawn is hardly after curfew. Ten is curfew on a school night."

"Okay. And there was a reason for that that has nothing to do with the way I feel about him. Have you ever known me to do anything without a good reason?"

"You're kidding, right?" Campbell said. "Merry heart, I love you. But when it comes to level heads, yours is a sphere!"

Well, yeah. Merry had to agree this line of reasoning wasn't going to work.

"Well, I was wrong. But I have nothing to lie about. I was wrong, but I wasn't bad. I'm sorry that I worried you. But I'm not at all sorry I did it."

Visibly shocked, Campbell sat down hard in her rocking chair. This was clearly not the reaction she was expecting. She had been thinking Merry would fly into a storm of tears and contrition. Campbell finally got up and stood looking out over the backyard up at the ridge where the Brynn family camp was, a collection of old cabins where they'd spent several weeks together each summer. "It should be against my better judgment to believe you," she said. "But

I know my daughter. You may not have the best common sense I've ever encountered, but you're not a liar. You're looking me straight in the eye. I don't have any choice but to believe you."

Merry began to cry—not sobbing, but with tears rolling silently down her cheeks. *I wish you knew how much I have to lie. I wish you knew.*

"Mom, I want to tell you. Don't ask me more. I promise it's not a horrible thing that's going to ruin my future. It's not a secret. It's just private. For now. And I don't think it will be for . . . very long."

"Is this boy going away?"

"I don't know. I think yes, he is."

"Just like Eden and her brother. What's with you two?"

"Unlucky in love, I guess," said Merry. "At least you don't have to worry about us getting engaged in high school like Kari Walter did." She added, "Mom, I don't feel well. I don't feel like eating dinner. Let me go upstairs. You can chain me to a post later on."

"Meredith, I just don't know what to say," Campbell told her.

Merry lifted her hand in a limp wave and headed for the stairs. She had had headaches before, but the way she felt now was as though a brute hand was fitted over her head like a cap, squeezing every nerve ending. She rummaged for aspirin and fell crossways on her bed.

With dreams, without pictures, Merry slept until morning. When she woke, even the dawn hurt her eyes.

Her first thought was, *I will find out the truth, as soon as I can.*

Her second thought was, *Where is Ben? And how can I live for two weeks without seeing him?*

FOR LOVE OF BEN

FOR LOVE OF BEN

It took two weeks for the tests to come back from the hospital in New York. They were negative for everything. Owen was, for all intents and purposes, a healthy baby boy. None of the specialists had any idea what had caused the episodes of vomiting. The pediatric allergist Tim Brynn spoke to said to be glad the incidents were over for now and to watch Owen closely. Funny things sometimes happened to kids in infancy, and for no good reason anyone could ever tell, they just outgrew them. If there were any other events, the doctor said, it would be time to call in a specialist in gastroenterology, who would examine Owen's digestion.

Meredith was home from school after practice almost every day of the two weeks, as her mother dictated. But on the day when her parents went to New York with Owen to discuss the results with the allergist, she could contain her curiosity no longer.

Mallory and Drew were out with Adam. Merry was alone.

Her parents wouldn't be home until evening.

She would do it. She would take a walk with her thoughts. Throwing on her jean jacket and stuffing her hat and single glove into her pocket, she began to walk.

Merry walked all the way to Pumpkin Hollow Road, through the mellow afternoon settling down, past Aunt Kate's house, past the Aldridges', down to the last house on the street. The Highland house. The house where the woman had screamed at Meredith for riding her bike over the corner of the lawn. Why had Mrs. Highland shouted, back those five years ago? The lawn was a mess, just patches of dry brown grass with a few tufts of green scattered throughout. The house was a nice old Victorian, built just like Uncle Kevin and Aunt Kate's, but somehow, it seemed to sag, from the jagged gap in the porch gingerbread edging to the raw board nailed over a hole in one of the steps. The clapboard had been gray and the shutters dark green, but wind and sun and snow and more wind seemed to have erased its charm. Merry could see a shutter that had come loose and hung at an angle like a broken wing. Underneath was the bold gray-blue color that all the boards had once been. The whole place, from the tangled, overgrown wild rosebushes and weedy thickets with long woody arms of buds to the faded cream curtains in the windows, felt like a house out of breath.

Holding her own breath, Meredith walked up the four steps and knocked on the door.

No one answered.

To her shock, Merry was relieved.

She waited for a long time and then knocked again.

No one came.

Meredith hadn't brought her backpack. She had no pen or anything to write on, no way to leave a message. And what message would she leave anyhow? What could she possibly say in writing? She wasn't sure she could say anything in person, much less on a scribbled note. In fact, it seemed like a good idea to use the four quarters in her pocket to grab the bus and go home, this having been more of an impulse than a plan.

Then she looked up.

The door was open. But it was only a dark square. No one was there.

"Hello?" Meredith called. She jumped when a tall, straight-backed man—a sterner version of her own grandfather—stepped from behind the open inner door. "You're Mr. Highland," she said.

He said gruffly, "We're not buying anything."

"I'm not selling anything," Meredith said. "I'm just looking for someone."

"Most kids who come, it's for the band or athletics," said the man, with the smallest whisper of a smile. "How can I help you then?" He seemed to relax. Merry saw that he wore the same kind of cardigan her grandpa seemed to have in every color. Mr. Highland's was butter yellow as he stepped forward from the gloom behind him.

"I'm looking for Ben," Merry said, biting her lip, knowing that what she said must sound either cruel or insane.

"What?"

"I'm looking for Ben Highland. I'm a friend of his. Please tell him that Meredith Brynn is here."

"What kind of nonsense is this?" Mr. Highland said. He took a step back, looking into the invisible space behind him and half-closing the door. "My wife is a sick woman. We just buried our son. Is this some kind of prank?"

Meredith cringed and turned away, turning up her collar against a breeze that suddenly felt cold. She wanted to turn and run down the steps, but she forced herself to speak up. "It's not a prank. Ben. Your son or . . . your grandson. Ben. He lives here. . . ."

"Who put you up to this? I saw you at our son's memorial service two weeks ago. You were the girl who fainted."

"Yes, I'm that girl, Mr. Highland. You won't believe me, but I know Ben. I just thought, since I didn't have his phone number . . . I have to know the truth about him. I can explain."

There was a creaking sound and a glimpse of white behind the man. A soft, sweet voice, like a low piping, asked a question Merry couldn't understand.

"It's okay darling," the man said to someone behind him. "No, it's too early for Sasha. It's no one." The man pulled the door closed behind him and leaned out. "My only son is David. He lives in California."

"I mean Ben. Your son Ben. I know him."

"My son Ben is dead."

Merry's mind shrieked and then settled, like a bird from a long flight, into a mournful peace.

She said, "I know Ben, Mr. Highland. He's blond with long hair in front, and he wears a leather jacket. A bomber jacket. He wears tight jeans with cowboy boots."

"You need to stop this, no matter what you think you're doing."

"I know what you mean, but I can't stop. Can you at least try to understand?" Merry pleaded. She had not realized that her hands were out of her pockets, but she had put them together in front of her, as though she were praying.

"Ben . . . died in Vietnam, the second week in the country. He gave up a fine scholarship he won in an essay contest to go do what his country asked of him. He dropped out of high school. We begged him not to go. He felt . . . go away please. Go away now." The old man huddled in his sweater as though a winter's chill had struck him through the April sunshine. His lined face seemed to sag further and his eyes faded. Merry winced. There was the tiniest aspect of Ben around those eyes. She wanted to comfort Mr. Highland and had no idea how she could do that.

"Please," Merry said. "Let me apologize. I didn't come here to hurt you."

"I . . . don't know why you came here. You are describing our son. But we have to put this behind us now. You could have seen a picture. Our questions are answered. Leave now, please. I'm not angry. But, child, a person never forgets. A father doesn't forget. Do you think you forget?"

"No," Merry said softly. "I'm sorry." From the corner of her eye, she saw the ByWay bus coming to a stop at the corner of Pumpkin Hollow and Redfern, five blocks away. If she ran, she might be able to catch it. She didn't feel like walking all those miles back to her house. She turned and leaped down the steps and began to run. Suddenly, she heard someone from behind her.

"Girl!" Mr. Highland shouted. Meredith glanced back. "Come back."

Merry stopped, then took a few steps in his direction. "Don't be afraid. I know who you are. You're Arthur Brynn's granddaughter, the girl who was in the fire down the block. My wife, Helene, would like to talk to you."

When Merry reached the front steps, Mr. Highland had opened the battered screen door. He led her into a hall that was so old-fashioned it was almost retro. "Come into the living room. It's cold in here, as beautiful as it's getting outdoors these days. I'm going to make some cocoa. Call home so your folks don't worry, please." Merry sent a brief text to Mallory, who was with Drew in Pioneer Park kicking some balls with Adam, who started soccer next week.

• • •

Mally felt the buzz against her chest and opened the phone. "M tlking to Mr. and Mrs. Highland. WILL TK bus home. M OK."

"She's at the Highlands' house," Mallory told Drew. "Do you think we should go get her?"

"Do you think those old people are serial killers?" Drew asked.

"No. I'm afraid of what she'll find out."

"Mallory, this is what you wanted," Drew said.

"You should have talked me out of it," Mallory told him.

"Adam! Play D," Drew called out in a tone that said everything without saying anything at all. He took off down the slightly muddy field. "Please remind me to interfere next time you tell me not to interfere."

THE LOVE BEFORE MY LIFE

THE LOVE BEFORE MY LIFE

Back in the warm, actually stiflingly hot living room on Pumpkin Hollow Road, the woman who asked to take Merry's coat was as white as her soft robe. Her long blond and silver hair was drawn up in an elaborate braid, and she had an unlined face that never saw sunlight, white soft hands, and the same seawater blue eyes and sad smile Merry had come to love in her son. This was Ben's legacy. This was undoubtedly the person from whom Ben had received his blue eyes—but more than that, his gentleness. Above the mantel in the living room where she led Meredith were oil paintings made from photographs. One pictured a short-haired guy with those same eyes, his mother's eyes, and his father's square chin.

The other was Ben.

Merry put her hands on her knees and began to cry. Mr. Highland had come into the room with a tray. Setting it down, he handed her a large pocket square that smelled of bleach and sunshine. It came away covered with mascara, and Merry felt further miserable.

"Tell me," said Helene Highland, sitting down on a small red sofa across from Merry. "Tell me what you said about Ben. I won't be angry."

"You won't believe me," Merry said, accepting her cocoa with a nod. This room was too hot for cocoa. She longed for a glass of water, but the sting of the hot liquid on her tongue restored reality to the whole moment.

"I may not. But please, you've come all this way with something to say. And it must be important. People don't faint at a memorial for no reason."

"What I want is to know about Ben. Tell me about Ben first. And then I'll tell you what I know. Let me catch my breath," Merry said.

And so Mrs. Highland did.

First, she told Meredith about David, her first son, a man's boy, all athletics and rambunctious spirit, who now, surprisingly, did exactly as his mother had done and taught English at UC Santa Barbara. David had five sons and daughters—two in college, the youngest Adam's age.

Ben, said Mrs. Highland, worshipped David, but he was so different from his older brother. Dreamy and thoughtful, shy, a mother's boy, he had helped Mrs. Highland plant the orchard of trees from which she made apple pies and peach jam, with the young Ben at her side. Those same trees were still there and still bearing fruit.

Although Ben always had his nose in a book and excelled at English and writing, he wanted to please his father as well. So he took up sports that were individual. David had played basketball and baseball. Ben ran track and played tennis. At cross-country, he was very good indeed. Mrs. Highland said that Ben went all the way to state and, with his team, placed third junior year. Running, he told his mother, helped him arrange his thoughts.

"And that would be how he put it, even when he was ten or eleven," said Mrs. Highland. "He would say he needed time to arrange his thoughts." So shy was Ben as a young child that the Highlands worried when he barely talked at all. They'd considered taking him to a speech therapist. But Ben, she went on, was simply waiting to have something to say. In junior year, he wrote a prize-winning essay about how being a teenager was the time for the illusions of childhood to end: Most people didn't become astronauts or movie stars or wildlife photographers or archaeologists. They didn't even own the horses or cars they loved when they were children. Being a teenager wasn't a time for dreams but for making the best of what life really had to offer and trying to find a single strand of the childhood dream within it. People who couldn't become astronauts could gaze at the stars from the mountaintops they hiked. People could help save wildlife. But dreams lost their glory when life came true.

"That's sad but I hear everywhere that it's true," Merry said. "It's almost as if Ben knew . . ."

"I often thought that later," said Helene Highland. "I often thought that he was speaking out of some foreknowledge of what his future held." She went on to explain how she had dreamed of being a writer and a poet but grew to love teaching the words that made her so happy. "I loved teaching them to Ben, and I thought he might, just might, be a writer someday."

They had been, she added, a family of pacificists with deep doubts about the war in Vietnam. When David enlisted, his parents were terribly troubled. For David, it had not been so much a matter of principle as of camaraderie with old friends. David, said Mrs. Highland, could never resist a challenge, no matter how foolhardy. But he ended up a journalist and never saw any action. His letters home to Ben made Ben restless, said his mother, and Mrs. Highland watched as David, without intending to, seemed to issue a challenge to Ben.

When Ben dropped out and enlisted a month before graduation, his parents were horrified. Not only did Ben have no college experience that would keep him from being anything but cannon fodder, he was sent to one of the most ferocious battles of the war.

"It was called Hamburger Hill," said Mr. Highland. "The reasons they called it that were . . . obvious. Even now, I can't bear to say it. Ben was nothing but a foot soldier. In his first and last letter, he said he hoped we would be proud of him, that he was a man like David."

"It tore me apart," said Mrs. Highland. "I'm afraid I almost lost my reason. I was angry at the whole world. I kept the poems he wrote when he was younger. We called him and implored him to try to get a medical discharge. No one was less suited to military life than our Ben. But he didn't want to be different from anyone else. I think he was afraid that he was a coward and that he would never know . . ."

"No one ever said that," Mr. Highland broke in. "Ben was never bullied. He was a well-liked boy. He was happy at home and never showed any interest in violence. We still believe it was some sort of test of manhood that went terribly wrong."

Not long after the two-week battle ended, a dreaded black car pulled up in front of the Highlands' house. Two young officers got out and knocked at the door. They handed the Highlands a letter. Ben was missing, believed to be captured. The young soldiers said Ben was trying to save the life of a friend who was pinned down by a sniper.

And I thought it was a game. Some kind of rough and dirty game like paintball! A rugby game! Merry leaned forward, her cup and saucer shaking in her hand.

"Ben would never harm anyone," Mrs. Highland went on. "In fact, just last month we learned that he was buried where he fell, and the company that he was with had to fall back."

The long years of waiting and wondering had begun after Ben was declared missing. At first, David begged his parents to leave Ridgeline and join him and his family in California. But though they did visit, they could never feel at peace away from the home where Ben grew up—and the slim chance he would return.

Merry listened as Helene Highland described her walks deep in her yard, more than three acres of land, among the apple trees. They went on growing, but Ben would never go on. She talked to him, shouted at him, scolded him, begged him to come home. She said, "I would almost see him up in those branches, reading, throwing the apples down to me, teasing me. It seemed like yesterday. I would hug the trees and cry out at the sky. For years, I hated everyone whose children were healthy and alive. For years, I was just a bitter, bitter woman. I think that's what finally affected my heart. Ben's death broke my heart and I could never let him go. Sometimes I see him still. Before he left, David gave him his old brown leather jacket that he'd outgrown. Ben wore it and said he felt like David, the older brother who got all the girls. He took that jacket with him everywhere, though of course, not overseas. There have been times since I've been ill, that I believe I see him, standing in the doorway of my room in that jacket."

"I have to tell you something," said Merry. "I need to. You need to know and I need to say it." Merry took one last sip of cocoa. Her mouth had gone dry. "Are you sure you want to hear?"

"Tell the truth," said Mrs. Highland.

"I . . . I know Ben. I met Ben a month or so ago, but it seems like I've known him all my life. I saw Ben as clearly as I'm seeing you. We talked every day. When did they . . . I hate to ask this . . . when did they bring his body home?"

What little color there was in Mrs. Highland's thin, sculpted face drained away. Meredith could not have believed it could get paler. She seemed about to rise and then sat back down, her blue eyes unblinking. Mr. Highland got up and laid his head against the fireplace mantel.

"Helene, this is impossible," he said. "It's chicanery. You need to go back upstairs. Sasha will be here soon."

"Wait, Charles," said Mrs. Highland. Slowly, she said, "It was just before . . ."

"Valentine's Day," Merry said. "Is that right?"

"Yes," Mrs. Highland said.

"She could know that any number of ways. It was in the newspaper for heaven's sake."

"I'm just a kid, Mr. Highland," Merry said. "I don't read the Ridgeline newspaper. And frankly, I just thought of Mrs. Highland as somebody who once yelled at me for riding my bike over her lawn until now. I don't even care if you believe me. But I'm telling the truth. I respect myself and Ben too much to joke about something like this."

Now that she had said what she needed to say, Merry straightened her back and gave herself permission to relax, just a little. Intensely, she tried to drink in the details of the room and what little she could see of the hall and kitchen behind her. That was where Ben had eaten his favorite food— peanut-butter toast, or so he'd told her. The yard in front was where he and his father and brother would have a catch when Mr. Highland got home from work as a pharmacist. The dark stairs in the hall, across from the bookshelves, would lead up to Ben's room. Merry felt again that almost physical pull. It was the first room on the right at the top of the stairs.

"What do you talk about?" Mrs. Highland finally asked.

"Us. I would say we . . . care for each other. He's never without that brown leather jacket. Sasha Avery works at our house too in her work-study program, but she never told me she worked here. Ben told me you were ill. He was there at the service two weeks ago."

"When you say you saw Ben . . ." Mrs. Highland began.

"I mean I believe I see him. And, of course, it's impossible," Merry said. "But it's not out of the question that I could have seen him or someone like him."

"Do you believe that there is a life after this one?" asked Mrs. Highland.

"Don't get upset, dear," her husband cautioned her.

"I do," Meredith told her. "I can't say I'm sure. I know it's what I believe."

"Lately, since I've been unwell, Ben seems so close."

"He loves you very much. The main thing he was worried about, when it came to the memorial service was you. He called you his little mom."

"No!" Mrs. Highland said. "Charles, was that in the newspaper? No one ever knew that except Ben and me. Meredith, you're right. What you're saying is beyond belief. But if I knew it was true, that I might see Ben one day, maybe I could actually heal."

"I don't think I can prove it to you, Mrs. Highland. And I haven't seen Ben since the memorial service. I think he may be gone. Then again, I've been grounded for sitting all night in church talking to Ben. I'd never snuck out of the house before."

"If you should have any more of these dreams or visions, will you tell me?" Mrs. Highland said. Meredith nodded. "Do you promise?"

"I have to go now. My mother needs me at home. My little brother has been sick."

Mr. Highland said, "Sasha told us that. She's very upset about it. Would you like to see Ben's old room before you go?"

"Very much."

It was a shrine. A Yankees poster was tacked over the bed and a battered backpack hung over the back of the desk chair. There were books of poetry and biographies, mostly of Arctic expeditions and real-life adventures, stacked between two geodes that served as bookends. Around the ceiling ran a train track with an old Lionel train sitting on it. "He loved his train, and it never embarrassed him to have it there. The switch is right on his desk. It still works," said Mr. Highland. "Do you want to . . . I'm afraid I don't understand all this. But do you want to sit here alone for a moment?"

"I don't understand it either. But yes, I do."

When Mr. Highland closed the door, Merry ran her fingers over the edges of the books. She took out a marbled black-and white notebook that fell open to a poem Ben had apparently been struggling with. The paper was old. This had been written a long time ago, before Ben ever knew that there was a Meredith Brynn.

> She is only a woman like any other
> A girl
> SO ~~light~~ slight
> And bright
> My eye's delight
> I would not ~~not~~ ~~trade have~~ seek another
> The touch of her hand
> Black hair
> Gray gaze
> All these are mine
> There is no other

It did not shock her to see that, forty years ago, before her parents had met, Ben had been writing about her. Were there whorls of time that intersected in ways no one understood? Did time and destiny loop back and forward on themselves, and if

what was meant to be was not, did they collide? Merry opened
Ben's closet. There hung his pairs of faded jeans and a single blue
Oxford cloth shirt, a few summer short-sleeve plaid things and to
one side, there . . . his leather jacket. As if to touch him, she reached
into the pocket.

She found her missing glove.

The room seemed to rock. Merry lay down on the bed. She
closed her eyes and must have slept because there was a sense of
waking when she opened them. Ben lay beside her, his eyes and
piney-cinnamon scent as real as if he held her close.

"You wanted that glove back so much?" he asked her.

"Ben, why are you here?" Merry asked.

"I could ask you the same thing," he said lightly.

"I don't mean in this house."

"I do, Merry. And I don't know. All I know is, I'd give anything to
kiss you. I want to know how your cheek really feels. But I can't."

"Try," Meredith said. "Try. I'm not afraid."

Ben reached for her and at that moment, a silver light, expanding
outward, like a force throwing them back, hurtled down like
lightning contained. Merry couldn't see Ben's face, only his outline
beside her. After a moment, she couldn't see him at all.

What was this? Campbell liked to joke about lightning striking
sinners, but how could a simple kiss be a sin? Were there rules about
people on different planes being in love? What if Meredith wanted to
be with Ben, even if it meant that, like him, she never got the chance
to grow up? Would Campbell think *this* was "just biology"?

Meredith was sitting on the side of the bed suddenly, properly zipped into her coat, her glove in her hand, when Sasha opened the door, flooding the room with musty yellow light.

"Mrs. Highland is a wreck. I don't know what you're up to Merry, but she's had to have a sedative. Time to go home."

"Why are you dressed up like that Sasha?" Merry asked, shakily getting to her feet. "And why are you talking to me like that? You're talking to me like I'm a stranger or a brat."

"It makes her feel better. That's all. I'm the one who should be asking questions. Why were you here about their son?" Sasha said. "You're acting like a brat. This is my *job*, Meredith. I have to protect Mrs. Highland."

"History," said Merry. "History class. I'm leaving now. Can I say goodbye?"

"He's doing his crossword and she's asleep. Just go. It's almost seven o'clock. I can't believe you did this because you were studying it! That's so unkind, Merry. Well, you didn't mean it, I guess." She messed up Merry's hair. "I work too hard and I get too involved. I'm sorry, Mer. I feel like I'm old already because I have all the same responsibilities I'd have if I were grown up."

"I know, Sasha. It was probably stupid to come here. I'm going to just slip out."

As she rushed to catch the last red bus, Merry turned to look back at the house. She thought for a moment she saw Ben, sitting on his steps. But it was only a trick of the fading light.

In that moment, she thought, *I'll never see him again.*

THE PERFECT GIRL
THE PERFECT GIRL

Sasha showed up early, just as the twins were leaving. Campbell followed them out the door. The extensive tests had revealed nothing, and Sasha was buttoning Owen into his red dinosaur jacket for a walk to the schoolyard in his stroller. He loved to try to pick Adam out from among the other boys at recess.

Sasha was headed down the street as the twins got into Drew's car. He waved madly at them. Sasha waved too.

"Look how great he looks," Drew said. "Little kids really are like miracle healers."

That afternoon, the twins each got a text from their mother.

Owen was back in the hospital.

Mallory called her mother, who'd left class early, risking failing an advanced course.

"I don't care about school," Campbell said. "We have to get to the bottom of this. We've had New York doctors and small-town doctors and they're all saying the same thing. They're saying, 'Who knows what it is?' I'm tired of that."

"Do you want us to come?"

"Act like any other day, Mallory. If you don't have practice after school, I'd appreciate you coming. I could use a little moral support. Sasha's here," Campbell said. "But Dad has to work because Rick's on vacation. And frankly, Sasha is not my daughter."

Mallory, in fact, did have practice. But her coach entirely understood.

"Family first," he said when Mallory told him about Owen's most recent hospitalization. "You guys have had a time of it the last couple months, huh, Mal?"

"Can only get better," Mallory told him, trotting off to catch up with Drew.

In the pediatric intensive care unit, which felt by now like their living room, Sasha was talking to Campbell and Dr. Staats as if she too were a professional.

"What do you think?" Sasha said. "Are you going to do an endoscopy?"

With a slight double take at Sasha, Dr. Staats said, "Actually, that is what I was thinking. Now, I think we're dealing with more than an allergy or a virus. I can't tell. A parasite? Maybe a bowel obstruction of some sort. You're saying he became listless and all he had was his bottle?"

"That's all he'd take this morning," Campbell said. "I tried a spoonful of pears and he wasn't interested."

"Then I came, and Campbell and the girls left," Sasha said. "So we took our walk and he fell asleep in the stroller. When we got home, he started to wake up, so I just rocked him. All of a sudden the whole thing started all over again. I stopped giving him the bottle of course, but he didn't stop throwing up. And finally he was woozy. I called 911."

The doctor asked everyone but Campbell to leave the room so that she could get a better look at Owen, limp and pale and tiny on the bed. As they slowly left, the girls heard Dr. Staats say, "He's thinner, Campbell. Is he eating normally other than these incidents? He's lost a pound since his last checkup."

"He is every time I see him. But I work either all day or all night depending on when I have classes. When I'm home, I've never had an issue. Carla and Sasha both say he eats well. But you know Carla Quinn. Just the facts, ma'am. My mother-in-law has never had a single problem. Actually, he's gotten sick when Sasha was there and when Carla was there and when Luna, who's a high school girl who helps out on the weekends, when all three of them have been there. Sasha has really been the most helpful. She even went in late to her other job last night so Tim and I could have an early dinner out. When we got home, he was asleep, which is strange for him because he tends to like to stay up until seven or eight, but he's been tired lately."

"The sitter is . . . your intern? Sasha? Well, she seems steady."

"They all are. And the routine is never different."

Outside, Mallory whispered, "Oh Sasha! I can see why my mom is frustrated. Rick's away fishing! What a great time for him to be gone." Rick Domini was their father's partner at Domino Sporting

Goods. "Dad can't leave unless he closes the store, and he hates to when people are buying their sporting goods for summer."

"It will be okay. Maybe they'll find out what's going on, finally," Sasha said. "Then we can all rest easier. I'm starting to feel like I work at the ER myself. I can't believe this goes on and on!"

Campbell came out into the waiting room. Her eye makeup was smudged, and she looked older than Mally had ever seen her. Although Campbell was a champ at putting on the cheerfulness, she didn't even try this time. Her voice was monotone as she said, "They're going to admit Owen so they can test for parasites. Babies can pick up the funniest things, and maybe it's a matter of getting rid of some kind of intestinal bug. If nothing shows up in his diaper, they'll have to do an MRI tomorrow. I'll have Grandma stay with you tonight."

"We're fine, Mom," Mally said. "Really fine. You don't have to have Grandma come. It's no different than the other time."

"You don't need me this afternoon?" Sasha asked.

"Of course I do need you, Sasha. Between my baby being in here and my regular patients, I need you more than ever," Campbell said. "But not today. My girls are my rocks, aren't you Mallory? Adam is scared out of his tree. I know it's something simple but we just haven't found it. Mally, take him to the movies or something. Reassure him. Do something fun with him."

"Absolutely," Mallory said. On a whim, she opened her phone and texted Luna.

"I'll bet you're having vibes all over the place," she said when Luna called her.

Luna seemed to fumble with the telephone. "Who is this?" she asked.

"Mallory. And I have a question to ask you, Luna. My parents still think this is some kind of natural illness Owen's having."

"Is Owen sick again?" Luna asked.

"I thought you could tell," Mallory said.

"I was asleep," Luna said. She explained she'd been out late, that there was an "event" she'd had to attend. *In the grove*, Mallory thought. Could it be possible? Could Luna, who came off as a harmless goof, really be involved in something wicked that involved a little child? "Luna, if you can truly see things, why don't you see what's really happening to Owen? I'm starting to have my doubts. I think someone's trying to hurt Owen or our family. You said you could see things. Do you see that?"

"I didn't hear the ambulance call this time," said Luna. "My mom has the radio in her salon. But Mallory, I do think there's somebody out to get your family. I even know who."

"Who? And why were you burning a baby's hair in the bonfire?"

"Spy," Luna hissed and disconnected the line.

On her way out the door, Mallory ran into her twin. Although technically she was still grounded, everything that resembled a normal routine at home would collapse now, both girls knew. Campbell had told Merry to go ahead to practice, and so Merry's hair was plastered back into a sweaty, hasty ponytail. For Merry, Owen's illness was like a symphony against which her own little problems sounded like a piccolo playing the wrong tune.

"Did you see him?" she asked Mallory urgently.

"It's the same thing, 'Ster. The same thing and nobody knows why. The poor baby's going to have to stay at the hospital overnight again. Dad's not here yet, so we'll have to grab a bus," Mally said.

"I want to go up," Meredith said.

Gently, Mallory tried to explain her sense that, much as their mother loved them, the three older kids were an obstruction in her line of vision right now. Campbell was fed up and ready to do battle, and the best thing they could do was be at the home front.

"I think we should just go home. There'll be a bus in half an hour or less," Mally said. Reluctantly, Merry agreed and they sat down on the wide red brick wall that surrounded the hospital's rock garden, where a riot of daffodils bloomed.

"I'll take you," a rough voice spoke up behind them. It was Carla. "I just got off a double shift. Going home to hit the hay. But I don't mind dropping you off."

"You sure?" Merry asked.

"My daughter's all excited you're going to show her how to cheer," Carla said.

"I'm . . . going to . . . ?" Merry began and Mallory elbowed her in the ribs. "Well, of course. That's great. She can come to practice on Monday. Thanks for giving us a lift."

"I don't mind," Big Carla said. "Word was the baby was sick again. You think he's going to make it? Your little brother?"

"Of course," Mallory said.

"I've seen kids go quick. Meningitis and that. I guess he'll be fine." Carla piloted her big car out of the parking lot. Meredith couldn't stop herself from looking for Ben everywhere. There were moments when she thought she glimpsed his unmistakable walk or the dull sheen of his old jacket. She was ashamed for wondering about something like Ben when even Carla thought that Owen was weakening, that he might die. She put her head against the back seat headrest, confused and perturbed and immediately . . .

There was Sasha.

She was tending to a little child. Merry could see the child's bare feet wiggling and the fat boxy shape of infant feet. Like a series of moving snapshots without sounds, she saw Sasha mix and give the child, a little blond girl perhaps a year older than Owen, a tiny cup of juice. The child lay back, exhausted, and then as Sasha watched, her little arms and legs went rigid and began to jerk. . . . Sasha running into a hospital, her hair a wreck, her mascara streaked, the little girl in her arms, surrounded by doctors and nurses in blue scrubs . . . Sasha throwing herself across a white coffin, in which the little girl lay silent, in jonquil yellow silk, her chubby arms around a teddy bear.

As Sasha bent her head, the little girl's eyes snapped open. She sat up in her casket.

She stared at Sasha as though Sasha were a snake.

"Her!" Merry cried.

"What?" Mallory said, twisting around in the front seat. They had just pulled into their own driveway.

"Whoo! I must be more tired than I thought! I fell asleep. I'm sorry if I scared you, Mrs. Quinn."

"Are you okay?" Mallory asked, with meaning laid down, like layers of paint, between her words.

"I'm fine. I have a lot of studying tonight. I have a quiz in abnormal psychology."

"You don't. . . ."

"Yes I do," Merry insisted. "They just told us. It's very interesting stuff."

"What?"

"It's about how you don't really know people you think you know. Did Sasha go home, 'Ster?"

"She stayed with Mom," said Mallory.

"That's great," Merry said and tumbled out of Carla's car, running for the door.

LOVED TO DEATH

LOVED TO DEATH

As soon as they were inside, Meredith whirled on her sister. "Forget about Ben for a moment. Forget everything else that's happened in the past few months except with Owen. There's something about Sasha."

As Merry knew she would, Mally asked, "What about Sasha?"

"Something she's doing that's connected with Owen being sick. I know it. I saw her in a dream, just now, making another little girl sick, and that child died! She didn't look different. It couldn't have been so long ago."

It was Mallory's turn to argue with her twin's point of view. Perhaps Sasha, who, of everyone around Owen, was the most like them and the kindest, not to mention the coolest, had been trying to help the little girl. Sasha treated Owen like a little sibling of her own.

"I talked to her once in pre-calc," Mallory said. Though Mallory was only a sophomore and Sasha a senior, they had the class together because, Sasha said, she was a math idiot and Mallory a math whiz. "I asked her if she had any other brothers and sisters besides her older sister."

"What did she say?" Merry said.

"She didn't really answer me, but she told me about this little girl she loved like a sister."

Sasha had taken care of this little girl back in Texas, a preschooler, born with a heart defect, who'd been on seven kinds of medicine since the day she was born. The little girl's single mom was entirely worn out; the money was gone and so was the husband. As it turned out, the child lived only to the age of four, and Sasha didn't know how she made it that far.

"She was so broken up about that child that it was one of the reasons she left Texas and moved up here," Mallory said. "And she told me that was part of why she felt so strongly about Owen and so worried for him."

"I saw that little girl just now. I saw her in my vision, Mallory. I dreamed right now in the car. I saw her."

"How?"

"I saw her in her coffin." Mallory got up and nervously looked out the window, murmuring about how she hoped Adam's coach would give him a ride home. "Are you listening to me?" Merry said. "I knew she died. I saw her with Sasha."

"That doesn't mean anything. Sasha was close to that family. In fact, she said the little girl died in her arms, and she just held her a long time because she couldn't bear to wake her mama. She said the poor woman was just completely exhausted and that having a sick kid was like nothing else in the world."

"This was all last year? When Sasha was just a high school junior?" Merry concluded. "Why do people get sick around Sasha so much?"

"Tell me again," Mallory said. "My head is spinning. First it's this guy and then Sasha. Are you sure you didn't see her with an old woman? I saw that was *going* to happen."

"That would have been Mrs. Highland. Mrs. Highland isn't any better either," Merry said. "What did you dream?"

"I dreamed she was giving medicine to an old woman. It looked like the old woman died. Maybe she just fell asleep. Sasha was wearing an old-fashioned nurse uniform. When Drew and I well, we basically spied on the Highlands, for your sake, we figured out that the old woman was Mrs. Highland. Ben's mother. And then Drew and I saw Sasha in an old-fashioned nurse's uniform. You could be totally right." Mallory took a long sip of apple juice from the refrigerator. Her face was flushed. "I'd have been sure if anyone did that, it would be Carla because her own little boy died . . . but who does that? What kind of person makes a kid sick? Or an old lady?"

"Since when did Carla have a little boy?" Merry asked. "I only know the little redheaded cheer wannabe."

Mallory told Merry about the night of the game, when she and Drew had picked Big Carla up and seen the room decorated for the little brother who would have been three by now. Merry thought it over and murmured, "I've seen stuff like that on TV. The parent makes the kid sick to get attention. Or they pretend they're sick. There's a name for it. They throw themselves down stairs so they can go to the emergency room." She paused. "And Carla's so dark and dreary. But it was definitely, definitely Sasha with the little girl. Don't let it scare you Mally, but . . . the little girl was dead. And then she wasn't. She looked at me. I know she wanted me to know something."

Mally did something she never did. She began to chew on her fingernail. "But those people on TV are parents! Not high school kids," Mallory said. "Older, needy people."

"Let's see what the MRI shows. Maybe nobody's making Owen sick," Merry said. "Maybe, please, I'm hallucinating!"

But she knew she hadn't been. And she definitely knew that her sister hadn't been, either.

BEHIND THE MASK

BEHIND THE MASK

On Wednesday, Owen was sedated because it was impossible to tell a baby his age to lie still going through something that looked like a great green and silver tunnel.

The MRI images showed his little plumbing fixtures were all right and properly in place with nothing blocking them. The Brynns brought Owen home, but they were exhausted, asleep before the kids were asleep.

Finally, as Merry did everything except chew on her nails from nervousness, first Adam and finally Mallory—this time without suspicion—fell asleep.

When Meredith thought of what Campbell would do if she sneaked out of the house again, she felt physically nauseated. But there she was, pulling on layers, tights under a pair of thermal pants, a turtleneck and wrist warmers under her parka. Slowly, she eased her bike down off its rack and out the side door of the garage.

The way to Pumpkin Hollow Road was familiar to her by then.

With any luck, she'd be back in an hour. It was eleven o'clock at night. Thankfully, it was not two a.m. She had no idea if Ben would be home, but she knew she had to say something if he were.

By the time she reached the corner of Redfern and Pumpkin Hollow, Merry had unwound her scarf and unzipped her coat. A damp halo of curls had collected on her forehead and cheeks. And she was ravenous. What could she eat that was silent, once she got back home? Even the refrigerator whirred and made a vacuum-like sound when it opened. It was better to go easy on carbs at night, anyhow. She'd drink tons of water and wait. She'd lost three pounds in the past month as it was, just from not having her usual and considerable appetite, and didn't like the hollows appearing under her cheekbones.

As Merry began to walk her bike for the last block, she suddenly caught a glimpse of Sasha, a flash of white in her old-fashioned uniform, running down the Highlands' front steps and jumping into a car. It wasn't exactly a wreck but was too beat-up for anyone like Sawyer Brownlee to drive. And it wasn't Sasha's. She kissed whoever was driving, only a shadow to Merry at that distance. Merry paused. There were too many pieces in her head. None of them seemed to fit. Was this what her sister and Drew had seen when they made their own undercover visit to the Highlands'? No, Mally said that Sasha had been driving her own car. No, a truck! She'd been driving a truck. *This* was Sasha's car—Merry recognized it now—but someone else was driving. Who? It wasn't as though Sasha and Sawyer were some big romance, but she hadn't said anything about being close enough to somebody that she'd give him her car.

As the car pulled past her, Merry moved behind an evergreen to watch. She saw Sasha pull off the old nurse's hat and shake her hair loose, cuddling close to the guy who was driving. Confused, Merry pushed her bike forward, right into a tree limb. It clattered to the ground. Merry glanced around her and then righted the back and began to turn it inward, toward the dark sidewalk. When she lifted her head, she found herself looking up—at Ben.

"I've seen people fall off their bikes but never fall over walking one," he said, his arms reaching out for her. "Are you okay?"

"I'm fine, but Sasha . . . Ben, I have to tell you something."

"What, baby?"

"Do you like Sasha?" Merry asked.

"I told you once I didn't. Is there a reason I shouldn't?"

"She is giving your mom medicine she shouldn't be having. I saw it. Your mom isn't as weak as she seems, Ben. You know about my sister and me. Don't ask questions. It's something I just know."

"What makes you able to see things like that?"

"A birth defect," Merry said, with a sad smile.

"Be serious."

"I am serious. It's how I told your parents. About you and me. They believe me, Ben. They believe I know you and that I care about you."

"What? This is unbelievable."

"You remember when you said to me that night at the church, that it was a family thing? This is, too. Brynn girls have seen in their dreams back for generations. Most of the time, it's like something I wouldn't wish on my worst enemy. But right now, I'm grateful. It's the road that brought me to you." Ben held out his arms and Merry tried to lean into his embrace. "I can't do anything for us. Not now. But it's possible that I could help your mom. Everyone thinks of her as cranky, but I realize now she's just . . . sad. She's not really getting sicker from her heart. It's something else," Meredith said. "I think Sasha is doing something to my little brother, too."

"That's just insane!" Ben said. "I know my mother is sad. Lately more than ever. She keeps saying she wants 'proof.' She tells my dad that every day. And I believe you," he said. "I don't trust Sasha either. She's phony. But my mother . . . she doesn't hear me. It's like she's deaf."

Merry pulled off her glove and put it in Ben's palm.

"Keep this for me," she said. "You wanted it so much."

This wasn't the time to try to explain everything that weighed heavily, unanswered, between them. Her own quandary was the same as Ben's. She couldn't march up to Ben's door and tell his father that Sasha was administering the wrong medicines. She couldn't ask her mother to make a house call on a near-total stranger—especially about Sasha, her right hand. But she could, she realized, write a note. Plenty of people didn't bring their mail in every day. There was a good chance the Highlands' mail was still in there. Laying her bike down on the walk in front of Ben's house, she opened the Highlands' mailbox. There was a stack of white envelopes. "I don't have a pen," she told Ben. "But I'm going to tell your parents for you."

"There's one in my father's woodshop in the garage," he said, taking off silently at a run.

Using her left hand for purposes of concealment, Merry—who,

unlike her sister, was right-handed—wrote: PLEASE HAVE
HELENE'S MEDICINES CHECKED BY HER REGULAR
DOCTOR. THERE IS A DANGER. THIS IS REAL.

"I have to go home now," Merry then said to Ben.

"Not now. Come in. My father's asleep. I'm sorry if I frightened
you before."

"You didn't frighten me. I wanted to lie close to you," Merry said.
"I'm not going to get that chance, though. Not in this life. We can't.
I won't be able to walk down the aisle to you. I won't be able to make
love to you."

"That's not why I love you, Merry. I can wait until you're older."

If only you could. "I just never felt real love before."

"You love me?" Merry asked.

"Don't you know?"

"I know how I feel. You've never said that. You said if I said I loved
you . . ."

"I do love you, Merry. I want to be with you always," Ben said.

"I want that, too," Merry replied, her heart literally knotting, then
tearing, as though someone were wrenching it in two. What could she
say? What should she do?

"My parents think you're the sweetest thing in the world. They
talked about you all night the other night. Just like I wasn't there."

Merry couldn't breathe.

"I'll come in. If you're sure we won't wake anyone."

"I promise," Ben said.

"And I can only stay an hour," Merry told him. "Promise."

"I do." Ben put up his palm and Merry laid her small hand near his.

Then they ran up the fire escape and gently opened Ben's window.

When Merry climbed back on her bike, her body ached with a glorious unfulfilled longing. Ben had told her what he wanted to be—a bat biologist, to help the good and helpless creatures so many feared, to restore the places they could fly free. She had told Ben every secret of her life, including every detail of "the gift" except that it included her sister. That was Mallory's truth, and Merry had no right to share it. She had extracted his promise to meet her tomorrow after practice, outside school. The sky was gray and it was four a.m.; far more time had passed than the promised hour.

Merry had just an hour to sleep, and then she had promised to go with her grandmother to church. When she got downstairs, her mother was just hanging up the phone.

"That was Sasha. Her day off and poor Mrs. Highland has had a heart attack," Campbell said. "She was rushed to the hospital this morning. Sasha decided to stay there with Mr. Highland."

"Is she dead? Is Mrs. Highland dead?" Merry asked.

"No, Merry. Why so urgent?"

"I feel very sorry for her since the thing with her son," Merry said quickly. "I used to think that she was mean. But she helped me with some history about the Vietnam War. She's actually very nice. I guess she has a bad reputation for not liking very many people. She was kind to me, though. Maybe I'll go see her tomorrow."

"That would be very nice of you." Campbell hugged Meredith. "You look very pretty."

"Don't worry," said Meredith, thinking how massive her mother's regret might be if Merry chose to . . . be with Ben forever. She could think it and even say it. But she couldn't imagine choosing to cross over with Ben. "Will Mrs. Highland be okay?"

"They got there in time to give her drugs to stop much of the damage, I think, thanks to Sasha," Campbell said. "We have her to thank too. Think if she hadn't been here the times Owen got sick."

But she never was, Merry thought. *Somebody else always was. But Sasha was there first.*

THE GHOST WHO LOVED ME

THE GHOST WHO LOVED ME

"Mal, can you skip going home with Drew tonight? Can we ask Dad to pick us up?" Merry asked after school the next day.

"Why?" Mallory asked. The shadows were growing longer; spring was putting out its tender secrets. In just a few weeks, prom would come and a week after it, graduation. An aimless, endless summer stretched ahead. But for once, Mally knew it would indeed end. And she had long since begun guarding her every moment with Drew, even as he tried to turn his face toward college.

"I want you to meet Ben," Meredith asked. "I want you to see that he's real. Even if he isn't real, he's human."

"It's some kind of existential matter, I guess," Mally answered. "But I'll wait," she said, texting Drew that she'd catch a ride home and explain later.

"If I do anything, I want you to know why," Meredith said softly.

"Do anything?" Mallory asked. "When you said 'do anything,' for a moment, I thought you meant . . . dying. Actually dying. But you didn't." Mallory paused. "Did you, 'Ster?"

"Do you think that's what would happen? Do you think I'd have to drink poison like Juliet? To be with Ben?"

"It was a dagger and Meredith! This is the most bizarre discussion I've ever had in my life with you or anyone else. Are you actually seriously even for a second considering killing yourself to be with Ben? Did he ask you to?"

"I don't know. I don't think so. I go back and forth." She imagined the steely light that intruded between her and Ben whenever they tried to touch. What if she simply stepped through it, instead of falling back? What if she went into that bright light?

"If you take one more step in that direction, I'm telling Mom, and she can have you hospitalized on a seventy-two-hour hold."

"You wouldn't do that." Meredith stood quietly into the hazy sun.

"Watch me," Mallory said.

"If you loved someone, would you want him to pass over alone? Would you want Drew to pass over alone?"

Mallory got up and began stretching and twisting, warming up her calves and shoulders as she did before a soccer game. "Merry, if there is an other side, do you really think he'd be the only one there? Heaven is supposed to be better. I hate to sound vulgar, but there are a lot more dead people than living people. Cute girls, too."

Meredith hadn't thought of that. It wasn't exactly soothing. But she recognized that what she felt was beyond common sense, beyond considerations of wisdom or foolishness. She didn't want to die. She wasn't the dying-over-a-guy type, like the little heartbroken girl in the attic. For that girl, she knew the boy who left her behind was the only one. Something had happened between them that made the future impossible.

Meredith's future was wide and bright, even without Ben. She relaxed. Perhaps there was an order to things.

"When will he show up?" Mallory asked. "I've never met a ghost. You do accept that he's a ghost now, right?" Merry nodded. "Does he come out in the daytime?"

"Mallory! Most of the ghosts I've seen have been around in the daytime. We only prefer the night for the same reasons you and Drew prefer it. It's private."

"You'd look like you were talking to yourself otherwise."

"How can you be so unkind?" Merry asked.

Mallory stopped. "I'm sorry. Giggy," she added, the twin language for "I love you."

"Do you think they walk around dragging chains at midnight?"

"I have no idea. But I really am sorry." Mally did a quick check to make sure that no one passing could hear them.

"I'll meet him, and then I'll go. But as for doing anything, just rule that out, Merry. 'Ster, please. Think twice. Then think twice again." To Merry's surprise, Mallory's eyes, in the fading sunlight, filled with tears. "I don't think this situation has a lot of previous data. But I know I can't do without you."

Just then, Meredith began to run. She threw open her arms and was lifted off her feet in ways that she could easily do, cheering. But not without trying. Someone had lifted Merry. It was someone that Mallory couldn't see.

She strived, with every filament of her ability, to do that. But the rules of "the gift" stood between her and . . . and Ben, like an impenetrable shield. She could see only the future. Ben belonged to the past.

There was no doubt anymore.

Merry turned to her sister, her face a beacon of joy. She looked like an angel already. *No*, thought Mallory. *No, I will not let her go—not for Ben, not for anyone.*

This ends here. Here and now.

"Mallory," Merry said. "This is Ben Highland."

Mallory didn't know what she would say. She did know that she would, however, give Ben the grace of speaking to him, as though he were there, which she believed that he was in some way, in some sense, in some form.

"Ben, hi. He . . . he can hear me. Can't he?" Mally asked.

"He can hear you. He says he saw you kicking balls with Adam at the lagoon. He thought it was me. He didn't know I was a twin before then." At the thought of being seen by someone who wasn't visible—and Ben could hardly be the only one around—Mallory felt a quaking in her spine.

She gathered her nerves then and said, "Ben, I'm not only a twin. Maybe Merry has told you about us."

"I have," Merry said. "About me at least."

"Well, what she says goes for both of us. Except that she can see the past, but I can only see the future. Which is why I can't see you.

I . . . very much wish I could see my sister's first love. I know what it's like to feel you could fly. I felt that way once. But it had to end because life got in the way of it. Life wouldn't allow it."

"Don't," Merry warned her. "Don't try to decide for me, Mally."

"Ben, my sister would give everything for you. Love makes you that way. It's bigger than the sky. My best friend gave everything for love—for love of my friendship and for the man she loved. It ruined her life. But when they say love is blind . . ." Mallory had to stop, unsure of what she really meant but sure she had to make every word count. "I don't think they mean it makes you blind to other people's faults. I think it means it makes you blind to everything else. Meredith has a family who loves her like your family loves you. Friends who are crazy about her. She has little brothers who need her." Mallory took a step forward. There was a sense in the air, a difference in the quality of light she could almost see. She turned toward it and continued, "And, Ben, she has me. You don't know what it's like to be a twin. If you take Merry from us, if you let Merry make that choice, and it's a horrible choice, you'll kill half of me, too. I know. My grandmother has lived for sixty-six years without her twin sister. And she's a happy person but not like she would have been . . ."

"Mallory, this isn't your choice," Merry said. "Of course, I will let her finish, Ben," she said, as if in answer to someone else's comment. "I'm not discounting what she says. But I have my own mind, too." She added, "Mallory, he doesn't know why he's here. Or still here."

Then he has to, Mallory thought. *He has to because this is going too far and Merry shouldn't have to bear all the grief.*

"Just let me finish, Mer, and then you can say whatever you need to say to Ben. My grandma tells me openly that she was never the same after her twin died. If my own twin died on purpose, and I had that to live with for the rest of my own life, I don't know if I could go on. So if you really love Merry, let her go. She can tell you why."

"How could you, Mallory? Now I have to say this."

"How could you not say it, Merry? Don't you think he deserves that much?"

Meredith turned to Ben—grateful to Mallory, hating Mallory. She reached up and put her hands on his shoulders. She began, "Ben, what did you do after high school?"

"I never finished school," Ben said, with a kind of terror in his eyes. Merry could smell under his piney-cinnamon scent the coppery tang of fear.

"Did I want to be a solider? I only wanted to be what David was. My older brother. I wanted to be brave. I didn't think it was fair to skip out and just go to college and write poetry."

"What happened to you?" Merry asked gently.

Ben leaned against the flagpole and looked, achingly, the way he had the moment Meredith first saw him. "I . . . I went to boot camp, and I realized that I hated it. I hated all of it. I hated it to the bottom of my soul. Every minute. I could never kill anybody. But I couldn't back out. Other guys pretended they were crazy. They took pills to make their hearts beat too fast. But I couldn't do that. And then, and then . . ."

"You went to Southeast Asia," said Mallory. "Tell him that."

"He's remembering. You don't have to coach him," Merry said. *It was Ben's life. It was Ben's death.*

He told Meredith, "We were told to find the enemy. But out in that jungle, you couldn't see anyone. They were in the trees and hidden in the grass." Merry stood closer as Ben sat down on the black iron fence that enclosed the school's flagpole and capstone. Merry could feel something stirring, Ben's warm breath against her hair. "I remember the dirt and the smoke and the heat and never being able to sleep, always being afraid. Guys went crazy. Guys shot themselves, Merry. They shot themselves in the legs so they'd be disabled and sent home. And a few, they shot themselves dead because they went crazy. And I kept swearing I would just live through it. I wouldn't be a hero. I would just live through it. Just a year."

"But then . . ." Merry prompted him.

"But then, I hadn't been there two weeks when there was a battle. We had to fight our way up a hill. It was suicide. I had a friend. From boot camp. His name was Ian. And he came from a family like mine. Who didn't want us there. So we hung around together. We traded books. We looked out for each other because there were guys who were crazy. There were guys who would kill a kid." Ben began to cry, and Merry tried not to notice, even as his hot tears fell somehow—marks like raindrops on the dry ground.

Merry said, "Tell me about Ian."

Ben got up and began to pace back and forth between Mallory and Merry, who couldn't move. Ben said, "We were trying again one morning, crawling up the hill in the darkness before sunrise.

They were firing. All around us. From every direction at once. Pings and explosions. And Ian was shot in the back. He said for me to run and leave him. But I couldn't run and leave him, Merry. I couldn't. He was scared. He was so scared."

"So you helped him."

"What's he saying?" Mallory asked.

"He's telling me about being shot at."

"Oh, no. Merry."

Ben went on, "I pulled him behind some logs and rocks. And then all I remember is the pain. Like my body was on fire. Burning in my neck and my legs. Little fires. Then . . . I remembered, it was graduation day. May 20. My graduation day. And then . . ."

"Then, what, Ben?" Merry asked.

"Then I was home. I was sitting on my porch." Merry got up and put her hand out. Ben lifted his, and the familiar electricity passed between. "Why can't your twin sister see me? Why can't she hear me?"

"Ben, you know why."

"No, Merry. I'm seventeen, Merry. I'm just seventeen. I won't be eighteen until May."

Graduation day. No. On his graduation day.

Merry pushed forward, "Ben, how old were your parents when you went away?"

"I don't think of them as any age. Maybe they were . . . forty?"

"And now . . ."

"Merry . . ." Ben got up and stared at Meredith as though she were some creature from another planet.

"It's okay," she said, knowing it wasn't okay and it could never be okay.

"You mean, I came home but I didn't come home! That's what you're saying. Mom and Dad are old now. I'm still a boy who dropped out in April, senior year. That night with Ian. I died there! And I never thought about that. I never thought about how much I wanted to live because I was home. I was safe. Until I saw you. Merry!"

"How is he supposed to stand this?" Meredith asked, whirling toward Mallory. "How would you like to be told you died more than forty years ago? It's spring. He's in love for the first time in his life." Mallory shook her head. She could feel her own eyes spill over.

Ben said softly, "Mallory's right. You can't. I love you and you . . . shouldn't."

"You can't forbid me, Ben," Merry said. Sizzles and rockets were exploding in her head. A headache had come on, predatory and pounding. She wanted to pull her own hair until her scalp loosened. Nothing was right. Nothing was clear.

"Can't I just stay this way? Can't we be together this way?" Ben asked.

Meredith tried to think. She knew what her grandmother would say, that Ben was stuck in the passage that all human beings must make—from this life to the next. And yet, why couldn't he stay this way? The answer came to her before she could bolster her own arguments: He would hold back everyone who loved him. Merry damned her gift.

Tonight, before the game, she and Neely would pile into the back of the big, black car, two giggly girls in their varsity uniforms. But one of them would be trying to decide how she could spend her life loving someone who died before she was born.

Mallory watched, fascinated, as the conversation between two people, perhaps the most intense conversation Merry had ever had in her life, took place with Merry doing all the talking, but also listening to words that made tears course down her face and drop into the dust from her chin.

The enormity of it made Mallory dizzy, made her feel as though the world was beginning to spin, and just before she dropped to her knees, she realized that it wasn't the confusion, but something else. Mallory's hands hit the ground. Her arms buckled. "Meredith . . ." she said and crumpled on the hard ground.

Somehow, in the twilight between awake and asleep, she not only saw the lights and sounds and flurry of a hospital room far away but felt strong, tender arms lift her to her feet. *Oh, poor Merry*, she thought. *I torture my sister as a part-time job. I forget how much I love her and how deep her feelings go. Poor Ben. One moment, he awakes from a long dream; he's young and in love. And then, the dream is a nightmare. He has to face it all at once. And he's only a kid, like us. He is real. He is here.*

And I have to tell him what I just saw, Mallory thought. *I can't run home. I can barely get to the bottom of the hill. I have to call Drew. He has to come for me. And these two have to get to Ridgeline Hospital.*

"Ben," Mallory said. "Your mother is dying."

WATCH FOR ME
BY MOONLIGHT

D rew was there in what seemed like less than a minute, having run every stop sign between Pilgrim Street and Mallory's distress call. "I'm going to sit in the front," Mallory said. "And Meredith is going to sit in the back."

"What?" Drew said. "What's that got to do with the price of rice? I didn't think she was going to sit on the roof."

"She's going to sit in the back."

"There's nowhere else she can sit, Brynn," Drew told her, not realizing that the comment was not intended for his ears and was an invitation to get across town quickly, to the hospital. Mallory had no idea how ghosts covered ground. Meredith got into the back and slid over behind the driver's seat. They raced through the early afternoon sunlight to the doors of the hospital.

Mallory said, "Sasha's with Mrs. Highland. I saw her there."

"Ben's mother had a heart attack last night. I guess she'll be in the hospital for a while, but Sasha called Mom and said she was there in time to make sure that at least Mrs. Highland would survive. And that she was going to go to the hospital to be with her."

"Sasha's a wonder girl," Mallory said. *Wonder what she brought with her*, she thought, hard, to her sister and could hear Merry catch the thought.

"Except maybe not," said Merry. "I think that Mrs. Highland was given something. I don't think it was something that would kill her."

"What about the note?" Ben asked. "My father found it."

"I guess he didn't believe it," Merry said.

"Who didn't?" Drew asked.

"Or maybe what she gave your mom *would* have killed her if Sasha hadn't been there to save her. Mally didn't say she did. She said your mother passed out."

"Whose mother?" Drew asked.

"What if she does both? Kills people and saves them? What if she does it too much?" Mallory asked. "What about that little girl?"

"I'm not going to ask which little girl. I'm just the chauffeur," Drew said sullenly.

"What if that's what she's doing to Owen? And that's why no one can find out why he throws up all the time?"

"That would have to mean Sasha was with him every time it happened and she wasn't," Merry said. "But she was there right before. She prepared things he had before she left. She could have done the same thing with Mrs. Highland, and even more freely. Medicines. Things in her food. Think of all the times she's cooked for Owen."

"I can't bear to," said Mallory.

• • •

On the floor the receptionist gave them the room number for Mrs. Helene Highland, cardiac care. They found Sasha in the waiting room.

"I came to see Mrs. Highland," Merry said. "It's important."

"They're trying to figure out what's going on with her now. She was coming along and now she isn't. But they stopped the crisis, so far. Her husband is in there with the doctors. I don't think they'll let you in."

"I'm going to try anyhow," Merry said. "Come on."

"I'm supposed to stay out here," Sasha said.

"Right," Merry said with a nod. "You stay right there. Mally and Drew will stay here too."

The sweet-sick smell of medicines and cleaning fluid and the kind of food that seemed to curse only hospitals swelled up and caught Merry like a blow. She had to swallow back a wave of nausea. The anxiety didn't help either. Mrs. Highland was only the immediate crisis. From all the doors came pleading or moaning or silences even more ominous than the moans and the pleas. Before she even attempted to open the door, she could hear the doctor saying how glad he was that Mr. Highland had brought the full range of medicines his wife was taking every day and that he had no idea how she had gotten hold of or been given a lethal drug Meredith could not pronounce or understand. As she listened, the physician said that it was essential that whoever cared for Mrs. Highland's know exactly what she need and make sure that she had exercise and fresh air.

Exactly what she hasn't had, Merry thought. She turned a grieving mother who found comfort in the trees into an invalid.

"She's out there. The young woman, the nurse," said Mr. Highland. "She . . . I didn't know everything that Helene took. But I know she's become weaker this fall. Progressively weaker and weaker."

"Can you introduce me to this woman?" the doctor asked.

"Of course," Mr. Highland said. The two men came out of the room and Mr. Highland saw Meredith. "Hello honey," he said. "What brings you here? We had a bad scare a few minutes ago. Apparently, Helene's medicine was reacting to something else Sasha gave her. But she's resting now."

"Mr. Highland, is it all right if I see her? I really need to," Meredith said. The doctor looked unsure, then nodded.

"We trust this young woman. She is a friend of our family's," said Mr. Highland.

"Just for a moment," the doctor said and stepped away to consult the chart in his hand. Soon, he was busily making notes.

"Mr. Highland, try to believe why I need to see her," said Merry in a low voice. Mr. Highland's eyes opened wide and he bit his lips. Softly he said, "My boy," and added, "I think she would like that, Meredith."

Through the door, Merry could see Mrs. Highland propped in bed, her long, thick hair loose around her shoulders, her hands busily kneading the coverlet. Her graceful hands were bruised and taped to hold down the lines pushing fluids into her body, and she wrinkled her nose against the intrusion of the oxygen prongs.

She noticed the two men as they began to glance around for Sasha, so that the cardiac specialist could speak to her. Meredith heard Mallory say that Sasha had just gone to the restroom and would be back in a moment.

Mally offered to go and look for her.

And so Ben and Meredith slipped into the room with Mr. Highland. Helene Highland turned a composed and curious face toward the door.

"Mrs. Highland," Meredith said.

"Meredith! Hello! How did you hear about my being in the hospital?" asked Mrs. Highland. It crossed Meredith's mind to say that her mother had let her know because, strictly, this was true. But she had little time, and she knew she had to do what it was she had come to do.

To Ben, she said, "I'll speak for you," and to Mrs. Highland, she said, "I know that you remember that night, when I came to your house. How I knew about Ben?" Mrs. Highland nodded. "I don't know what you believe in your life, Mrs. Highland. I don't know what I believe. But you said you've felt Ben closer in the past couple of weeks." Again, the woman in the bed nodded. "He has been closer. He's here now." Mrs. Highland gasped and her husband started forward, but she waved him away. "If you get sick, I have to leave. Please just take a deep breath. And see if this really seems so strange to you."

"I'm calm," Mrs. Highland said then, in a strong voice. "I can't see him. I can't see my boy."

"But I can. And I'm not a liar. I love Ben. Ben wants to talk to you, but he has to talk through me." To Ben, Merry said, "Say something that will let her know it's you."

"Little Mama," Ben said, and Mallory repeated it. Mrs. Highland didn't flinch. But first one, then another tear rolled down her face. "Little Mama, I know now what happened to me. Merry told me. Don't be angry. She had to tell me. And I suppose I never knew because I didn't want to leave you. I never wanted to leave you. Do you believe me when I say so?" Mrs. Highland nodded. "I was wrong. I was a fool. But . . . you're my best girl, right?" Mrs. Highland nodded. "And you want what's best for me? I think that you have to let me go now, Little Mom. David needs you. David's kids need their grandmother. You don't pay enough attention to them because you think of me all the time. And Dad needs you. So I won't be there, in the house."

"Benjamin, no. Wait."

"In the house," Merry said, repeating after Ben. "But I'll see you and I'll hear you, right? I'll hear what you say when you walk in the garden under your tree. I'll be there. Not so much in the . . . in the cemetery. I know now that all those times that I was supposed to walk down the path, I didn't go because I was afraid to leave you. But I think I kept you from living all the way, Mama. Just like if I stayed with Merry, as much as I love Merry, it would keep her from living all the way."

Mrs. Highland was crying freely, and her husband had removed his glasses and was wiping his own eyes with another huge starched handkerchief. Ben went on, with Meredith's voice, "You have to live all the way in this life, Mama. And in the next life, your boy will be there waiting for you. Not too soon though. Okay? Not too soon."

Ben tried to look every inch the strong guy and the soldier, but his face was falling apart. It was clear to Merry that she and Mrs. Highland weren't the only ones having trouble letting go. Ben's lip quivered as it must have done when he was a young boy—or as his little boy would have done, had he lived long enough to have a child. Merry bit her own lip and dug her nails into her palms so that she wouldn't fall apart. For this moment, she needed to be strong for Ben. She knew there wasn't much time. Ben said, "I'm going to kiss you goodbye." Merry leaned over and kissed Mrs. Highland's soft, seamless cheek. Ben held Mrs. Highland's hand and kissed it; Merry saw the older woman glance down at her hand.

"Did you feel that?" Meredith asked.

"Like a spark? An electric spark?"

"That was Ben. He kissed your hand."

"Meredith," said Mrs. Highland. "Don't let him leave! Oh, please don't!"

"She's gone," the doctor said, entering the room suddenly. "This young woman called Sasha Avery is gone, and I need to talk to her urgently."

"It's all right for now," Mrs. Highland said. "We don't need Sasha anymore. I don't think she'll go far."

Charles Highland said, "I swear . . . Merry? Is this what you meant about Ben? This feeling? In the room? I can almost smell that pine and spice stuff he liked so much."

"I'll explain," said Mrs. Highland. "And don't worry about me crying. It's good for me. I haven't cried this way in forty years. I know something I never knew." Meredith turned to slip out of the room, leaving Ben with his parents. "Meredith, thank you."

Ben turned to look longingly at Merry. "I should spend these last days with my parents, now that they know."

Her heart echoing, Merry said, "Of course you should. The night after graduation. Two weeks from today."

"Fourteen little days. How will they know I'm there?" Ben asked.

"I think they do," Merry said, her own cheeks wet.

"How will they know when I'm gone?"

"It will be like before, but better. At least I think so."

"Watch for me by moonlight," Ben said. "You know where."

"Though hell should bar the way. Is that okay?" Meredith told him.

"You're my girl," Ben said.

RESCUE

RESCUE

The following Saturday at three, Merry arrived with the squad for the statewide meet in Westchester County.

Bonnie Jellico, Mrs. Chaplin, and Coach Everson were sponsoring, and the girls had a bank of hotel rooms at a Hampton Inn. They were planning some good mayhem. Even though they weren't favored to win this year, and even though her family couldn't be there because of Owen, Meredith was determined to be in a good mood for the last formal meet of the year.

They went over to the gym at Trafalgar County High School for a quick warm-up before dinner. It felt good to Merry to have her pyramid under her again, good to finally actually listen to the gossip instead of only hear it. Being with Ben had been like being married, and as much as she loved him, Merry knew that she wasn't ready to give up all the beloved foolishness of being one of many instead of only two. Neely was officially going out with Pearson. Kimmie, who had grown another inch over the winter and was now 5'9", had a crush on Dallas Jameson, a freshman, who was also three inches shorter than she was.

Rumors immediately began to circulate about Sasha, and Meredith wisely kept quiet, even though the seniors and her close friends asked her repeatedly what she knew. Sasha apparently *had* called Coach Everson the night before, saying her aunt was elaborately ill, which only confirmed the twins' beliefs. As the girls chattered, Meredith texted Mally and let her know what was going on. Mallory already knew and added that the police were now interested in talking with Sasha, along with the doctors.

That night, after the cheerleaders had spent the night flirting until one a.m. at the pool with some cute golfers from New Jersey, one of whom disappeared briefly with Erika, the girls ordered massive pizzas and asked about Owen.

For some reason, they could routinely stay up until four a.m. and cheer like demons five hours later.

"He's so much better," Merry said. "Whatever it was, it's over now."

"How can you be so sure?" Kim asked.

"We think we found the cause of it," Merry said. In fact, their mother would only find out about Mrs. Highland when she went in to work, but Campbell wasn't stupid. She would connect the dots. The twins were hoping that Sasha still trusted Campbell and would show up for work on Monday—feeling safe in the assumption that if Mrs. Highland were better, whatever she had done would go undetected.

"That's great about Owie! But where have you been?" Allie

demanded. "I mean, I know when your brother's that sick, it's totally understandable. But text much? Come on! I've sent you forty-two text messages, and you never answer."

"That's just it. Once practice is over, there's just so much I have to deal with," Merry said. "My mom's in school. We have to constantly be taking care of the baby or Adam or worrying about them. I hope it's over now. I could use some rest."

"I like this kind of rest," Kimmie said, waving from their window to the boys who were batting a volleyball around in the pool.

The next day, they were second after the cheer portion, far higher than they thought they would go without Sasha's amazing tumbling run, when they ran out onto the floor for their dance, choreographed to "Bella Bella You."

As they all ran out onto the floor, the captain, Trista Novak, said, "Get this. Sasha isn't here, and she's not at work. I called the old lady's house where she works, and the old man there said they fired her. Do you know why?"

"I guess the lady is getting better, I heard," Meredith said. "Maybe they don't need a live-in anymore."

"Would she go to your house then?" Erika asked.

"Not on a Saturday," said Meredith, but she nearly stumbled and not for any kind of psychic reason. Sasha! Gone from the hospital! She wouldn't go back to the Highlands' house now, except maybe to collect her things. Where else would she go? Off with the guy in the almost-crummy car? Meredith grinned and flirted with the crowd, doing her best to make every step crisp, every landing slam-picture-perfect—all while worrying her brains out.

When they ran off the floor, the scoreboard said they were tied for first, and her teammates were going crazy. Merry slapped hands but slipped away from her place to kneel at the end of the row, as they were taught, to wait for the performances of the final teams. It could take hours to finish, and they were more than two hours from home. Meredith ran into the locker room to call Mallory. No answer. She tried home.

To her relief, Campbell said, "Hello?"

"Mom . . ."

"I'm just walking out the door, Mer. Make it snappy."

"Where's Mallory?"

"She's sick. It's weird. She came into the kitchen this morning and ate some oatmeal I had for Owen, and she's been sick as a dog ever since," said Campbell. "Maybe we have . . . environmental toxins here. When Sasha showed up, I made Mallory go to bed. I was glad she stopped by. Mrs. Highland is in the hospital after all, but she seems to be doing better."

Merry felt the sweat run like a cold river down her chest. No. No! She would throw it to Mallory. She would say Mallory came across something from reading for her psychology class about people who get attention by making people sick. Did Campbell know that neither of them even had a psychology class?

"You haven't been to work yet?" Merry asked.

"No."

"You haven't heard about Sasha and Mrs. Highland?"

"No. Is she worse?"

"Well, I went to see her, the way I said I would and . . . I heard that someone apparently messed with her medicine and has been messing with her medicine for a long time."

"I'll look in on her."

"No, Mom! Listen! The person who gives Mrs. Highland her medicine and was with her when she had this heart attack was with her when she got sick again, right in the hospital."

"Meredith, make sense! You're blabbering."

"It was Sasha, Mom. It was Sasha. And when the doctor wanted to talk to Sasha, all of a sudden she got up to go to the bathroom, but she never came back."

Campbell said, "Mother of God. Get off the line, Meredith."

"Mom, listen!"

"I am listening, Merry. Get off the line. Sasha left about half an hour ago to do some errands for me."

"So she isn't there, thank goodness. Do you think she actually made Mally sick?"

"Get off the phone," Campbell said. "Sasha took Owen to the shopping center with her. I'm calling the police."

Meredith wanted to scream, but she couldn't. She didn't know if she could move. And then, since she didn't know what to do, she let her body take over its familiar routines. She ran back to her place. It was torture to watch the routine by the home team, the Westchester Warrior Princesses, who eventually won. Even as they were handing out the trophies, Meredith heard the ripple through the crowd of Ridgeline parents and fans. Kimmie was finally able to pass it down the line of girls waiting in ranks for their own trophy. The gossip was that some chick their age hit a tree with a baby in the back seat and they were on their way to the hospital now.

Meredith threw down her pom poms and ran for the exit.

But where would she go? How would she get anywhere?

She ran back.

Suddenly, she noticed Trista chasing her to the exit.

Trista's father, Mr. Novak, Meredith remembered, was a cop, one of Ridgeline's twelve finest. "Merry," Trista said. "My car is the old blue Volvo. Let's run for it."

"Is it . . .?"

"Yeah, it is. My dad called. Let's go."

THE TRUTH ABOUT PERFECT

THE TRUTH ABOUT PERFECT

The emergency room was crowded with the usual Saturday night screwups, slings, and swollen eyes. Trista and Meredith pushed through to the desk and asked for Campbell Brynn.

"Campbell is busy with critical care," said the receptionist. "Oh, Meredith? I didn't see you back there. Don't be afraid, though. Owen is fine. He has a cut on his head, and it's bleeding like crazy. But he was in his car seat, and he's just fine. Crying his head off."

Meredith hugged Trista Novak and pushed through the double doors.

"What's wrong with the cheerleader?" some guy who'd had one or eight too many yelled. "I've been sitting here for two hours with excruciating pain in every bone in my body!"

"Mister, you sit here every Saturday night and give me an excruciating pain in my rear end," said the receptionist.

It took Meredith only seconds to spot first her sister, then her mother. Mallory was standing upright, but looked almost green under her freckles. "Now I know how Owen felt," Mallory told Merry. "Whatever she put in my food packed a wallop." Weakly, Mallory found a place on a hard green plastic seat.

Campbell was a pro; she would never attempt to work on Owen or even be in the room herself. Bonnie Jellico handed instruments to the doctor, a man Merry didn't know, as he cleansed and numbed Owen's head wound before suturing. Bonnie said to the girls, "Your dad is on his way. Owen's going to need six tiny stitches, and they will come out in a week or so, knowing how fast these little guys heal. We already rushed an X-ray, and there's not a thing broken. Thank God for car seats. She did that much."

"Who?"

"Sasha Avery."

"She took Owen to the shopping center," said Merry. "I don't know how we got here so fast, except we went ninety. Trista's dad got us a police escort from some town, and we whammed it all the way in."

"I need you here now, Bonnie," the doctor said.

The girls huddled outside the drawn curtain, listening to Owen's wails. With tears in his eyes, Tim rushed through the curtain with Adam. "How did you get here so fast, Meredith?

"Magic," said Meredith, who grabbed her dad and hugged him. "I can't believe all he got was a little cut on his head."

"Isn't even that too much?" Tim asked. "How much did he have to go through before we got it through our heads, the poor little mite? Frank Novak said that the car hit the tree going thirty miles an hour. She slowed down to get on the exit a few blocks from here. The highway headed east, and that's when she almost hit some guy in the road. Swerved and hit the tree instead." Tim then asked, "How's Sasha?"

Neither girl had thought to ask.

Merry slumped on the green sofa next to Mallory. Her body had begun to cool, and she began to shiver. One of Bonnie and Campbell's friends thoughtfully draped a light hospital blanket around each of the twins' shoulders. "Siow," Merry said. "Fizzit ter." *It will get better.*

"Poor Owen, I've never felt cramps in my stomach like this," Mally said.

Moments later, Campbell emerged from an ER cubicle a few doors down. She said, "Sasha's conscious, but she's in a bad way. Collapsed lung, six broken ribs. Broken arm and they don't know about her spleen. If her spleen is okay, we can deal with the rest. She's on her way upstairs to the OR."

"You took care of her, Mom?" Meredith asked.

"Why wouldn't she take care of her?" Mallory said.

"Of course, I'd take care of her," Campbell said. "I don't know if Sasha did anything wrong. I do know that she was going the wrong way to be headed for Pilgrim Square." Campbell sighed. "Right now, she's a really sick girl, and I'm not going to make any judgments. It's a long story, and it's going to get a lot longer after she comes out of surgery. But the gist of it is, Mallory, she was headed out of town with Owen when she went around a curve right before the entrance to the highway. Supposedly, a guy stepped out into the road, and Sasha swerved to avoid running him over. And she hit a tree."

"A man stepped out in front of her?" Mallory asked.

"Some kid. Some guy your age. She said he was, well, her words weren't pretty. She said he just stood there in front of her with both hands up."

Tim said, "That's what Frank Novak told me, too. But nobody found any sign of him." Merry's eyes filled with tears. *I wonder who that was, she thought? I wonder why he had nothing to lose?* She disappeared for a moment into the washroom. When she'd splashed some water on her face, she came out and nearly collided with Carla Quinn.

"I kept praying," Carla said "Is the little boy okay?"

"He's good, Carla," Merry said, hugging the big woman spontaneously.

"He stole my heart," Carla said, and Meredith felt pelted with a riot of emotion—shame for how she'd felt about Carla, pity for the little boy that Carla would never again hold close and rock the way she rocked Owen. Then Meredith went back to the room where Campbell had worked on Sasha. When Campbell was finished cleaning up, Merry asked, "How could you take care of her, with what you know?"

"Do you think I want her to die before I can ask her what the hell she's been up to?" Campbell said. "Forgive me for that. I don't wish anything bad to happen to Sasha. I just need some answers. Dr. Renfrew, the cardiologist, needs some answers too. And Sasha is the only one who can give us those answers."

Merry went out into the waiting room and snuggled back down beside Mally on the sofa. Mallory looked to be half asleep.

A few moments later, the elevator doors opened, and Luna Verdgris emerged in all her black-and-silver glory, her eyes and lips animated with purple glitter in a slash.

"Don't," Merry said, "Tell me you intuited this."

"Nope," Luna said. "I heard it on my mom's scanner, and I had to see what the action is." Luna blinked. "What's wrong with you, Mallory? For your information, Sara Solokow's older sister is a hairstylist. She was going to get some floor sweepings for our next moonlight . . . thing. We never even got them because her sister said it was against state law to take human whatevers. Now I know Corey Gilberston told you. I have to kill her."

"Don't even say that for a joke, Luna. Mallory saw it in a vision. It hasn't even happened yet. My sister can see the future."

"Why do you do this? I don't make fun of cheerleaders. It's my extra-curricular activity."

"I'm not making fun," Merry said. "Honest, honest. I'm not. Just teasing a little." Gently, she patted Luna's arm, and Luna, after a moment, relaxed.

"How's the little guy and sweet Sasha?" she said.

"He's fine. She's not so fine."

Luna said, "Good."

A STOLEN LIFE

To the delight of the Mountain Beanery, the dry cleaner, the Picket Fence B&B Inn, and Pizza Papa, national press descended for days on Ridgeline. They dutifully wrote headlines that screamed a strange story, with such headlines as "Fake Teen a Feral Misfit?" Sasha Avery, a.k.a. Sandra Avery Hammond, was a nurse—in fact, she was a registered nurse. She was also thirty years old. The exam at the hospital showed that she'd given birth to a child.

But they never heard the story that Officer Novak told the Brynns, all alone one evening at their kitchen table.

Trista's father visited all the Brynns on the first night that Owen was home. Sasha was still in the hospital, recovering from surgery. The girls didn't know Trista's father well. But he played on one of Tim's softball teams, and he said he had information he needed the Brynns, every one of them, to know. With care for what the Brynns had already endured, Officer Novak came over to their home in his own car—which would not attract the attention of reporters who cruised the house periodically—hoping to catch a glimpse of one of the Brynns.

"She is from Texas," said Frank Novak. "And she's been a heckuva cheerleader and a very good nurse. That's all that's true. And there are other things I wish I didn't know."

The girls glanced at Adam. Frank Novak nodded and cast his eyes to the corner of the room.

"Go upstairs now," Campbell said. "Watch anything you want. You know how bad Sasha was, but we don't want you imagining you see her outside the window when you're trying to sleep. Your imagination is probably going wild, Adam. But I swear to you she will never come near this house again. She'd have to come through me or Daddy. No one will ever take care of you or Owen except Grandma."

"Or Carla," Adam said. "Carla's a good person. Her daughter's in my grade."

"She had a crush on you, Ant," Mallory said. Adam whirled and raced for the stairs, startlingly lacking in curiosity about the woman whose acts had ruled their lives for so long and nearly ruined them.

When Adam was out of earshot, Frank said, "Sasha Avery has never been charged with a crime. But she's what we call a person of interest in the deaths of three people." Even Campbell gasped and held Owen closer.

"Deaths?" she said softly. "Deaths?"

"It's worse than that, Campbell. One of them was her own daughter, a little girl named Monique," Frank said, shaking his head and staring down at his shoes. Married at twenty and divorced at twenty-five but still involved with her drifter ex-husband, Sasha had a chronically ill three-year-old who died two years before Sasha came to Ridgeline. "But that kid's hospital folder is as thick as a dictionary. She was sick. She was born with a heart abnormality. But she was always getting infections that had nothing to do with the heart thing."

The infections weren't all that Monique suffered in her short life. She was also prone to chronic vomiting and seizures that gradually weakened her and finally led to a fatal heart attack. Although it was never proven, police and doctors suspected that Sasha gave her daughter syrup of Ipecac, a medicine closely guarded by pharmacists because it was used by girls who wanted to get thin by throwing up their food. It was actually made to give in an emergency to little children—or even adults—so they would throw up things they ate that could injure them.

There was a brown bottle of Ipecac syrup in the Brynns' medicine cabinet, high out of reach of anyone except Campbell using a stool or Tim on his tiptoes. Campbell gave Owen to Tim and reached for the bottle, using her oven mitten. She had never opened it. But when she handed it to Frank, a third of it was missing. Frank Novak would later tell the Brynns the police could find no fingerprints at all on the bottle.

"What's wrong with Sasha?" Tim asked. "Is she a cold-blooded killer? A psychopath?"

"Not really, or so far as we can tell. She actually loved her daughter very much. She was a young woman with a chronically sick kid and no mother or father of her own. The nurses got to be like her family, I guess. Nobody had ever given her the kind of approval they gave her for how well she took care of Monique. But when Monique started to get better, all those good feelings were gone."

Frank explained the report that the police had been given by a psychologist who evaluated Sasha during her involvement with the deaths of Monique and two of her young patients, both mortally ill children too young to describe what was really wrong with them. Sasha might well be a sociopath—someone who was standing behind the door when a conscience was passed out. She also had a knack for knowing exactly what people wanted almost before the people did themselves.

But what really was wrong with Sasha, Frank said, was something called Munchausen syndrome by proxy, a mental illness in which the person literally made another person sick—usually a child or older adult who couldn't speak for himself—to get the attention.

"Id a quo," Mallory whispered to Meredith, twin talk for "just what I said."

"Stop that," Campbell said, without turning her head. Even now, the girls' use of their exclusive language annoyed their mother, who had to be in on everything—or so the twins thought.

"People like this usually have medical training," Frank went on. "They love that hero role, and of course that includes rushing the person to the hospital just in time and having people trust them."

"Like we did," said Tim. "Why didn't we see it? Why were we such fools?"

"Don't beat yourself up, Tim," Frank said. "You either, Campbell. You had the best specialists in the world looking at Owen. And they didn't catch it. Mr. Highland is a pharmacist, and even though he's retired, he's a sharp guy. These people are smart. She knew just what to do."

The complication with Sasha was that Ipecac, unlike other medicines or drugs or toxic things like cleaning products, didn't stay in the system long. Traces of it were hard to find, even for crime scene investigators and medical people. The terrible thought of exhuming poor little Monique's body would do no good. Nothing in two years had changed which could prove that Sasha, probably not intentionally but with knowledge, helped kill her own child. Frank went on to say that there were plenty of ways that she could have given the syrup to Owen. A little sugar could have covered the bitter taste. Those bottles had long since been washed and sterilized. The Brynns had thrown out the baby nipples and bought only two more—just to make sure that they could keep track of them.

Officer Novak then admitted he had to ask a few questions in an official capacity.

"You mean, there's some suspicion of us?" Campbell said.

"No. No one believes that. But when a kid is chronically ill, we always have to ask the parents and give a report to the state social services. I told my chief that I was a friend but that I would do the honors anyhow. We have to look at every angle and then turn that angle over and look at it upside down."

The only suspicion, it turned out, arose from the numerous times that the parents had hauled Mallory and Merry into the hospital for this test or that, having to do with their "fainting spells"—all of which came to nothing. Once more, the girls squirmed, hating "the gift" that was now placing their innocent parents in a fix. Campbell explained that the cause of the fainting spells was exclusionary: She and Dr. Staats, the pediatrician, had determined that stress or low blood sugar (if the twins hadn't eaten) caused them.

"Then that's that," Frank said. "I'll type up a little report, and we'll go from there." He sighed. "But to tell you the truth, I don't think we're going to learn very much more than they did down there. If she was doing this years ago, she's only better at it now."

Finally, all the police could do was establish that Owen's illness took place at the same time that Mrs. Avery entered Ridgeline High and the Brynns' lives. Everything that could condemn her could also clear her name, it seemed.

Sasha did have an aunt in Deptford.

But that aunt lived in a nursing home, a victim of early-onset Alzheimer's. Like Mrs. Highland, Beatrice Avery had weakened in recent months as well.

"Wonder if that's a coincidence," Mallory said bitterly. No one knew, said Frank, if, when Sasha visited with a man who might or might not be her ex-husband, they brought more than flowers. The public record showed, however, that Sasha and her sister Serena were heirs to Beatrice Avery. Her savings and her small house— especially given the value of the land it was on—amounted to more than $300,000.

"More than enough to give anyone a really fresh start," said Tim.

"Why do people get this syndrome?" Merry asked. "And why can't you pronounce it?"

Frank had to consult the file and explained the disease was named after some ancient German baron who told all these fantastical stories about himself to get approval. People were so hungry for attention that they swallowed nails or stuck pins in their heads or injected things in their veins to cause an infection throughout their whole bodies. They had unnecessary surgeries—and liked feeling special.

"You said proxy," Mallory said.

"Well, that's when they make other people sick so that they can get attention and praise," said Frank. "A proxy is like a stand-in for somebody else." Sometimes the people were actually medically trained, like Sasha. Some of them were so brutal that they did things such as hold a pillow over a child's face until the child passed out so they could call 911. "Nobody gets more attention in the hospital than the sick kid's parents."

"Talk about get a life," Tim said.

Campbell said, "Imagine feeling so hollow you had to invent yourself over and over again."

The girls tried to feel some of their mother's heroic compassion. They failed.

SAFETY

I t wasn't as easy as the Brynns had hoped to go back to the only thing they wanted—their ordinary life.

Weird facts about Sasha flowed in from Merry's friends, who were glued to the TV and the Internet. It was *the second time* Sasha enrolled in a high school. The first time she led an Oklahoma cheerleading squad to a state championship.

"Why didn't they get her then?" Merry asked.

"She didn't do it for money or anything," Neely said. "And I guess the school was happy to have the trophy. It says . . . wait. Sasha said she was married so young she never got to live a happy young girl's life. Don't you feel sorry for her?"

Merry said, "Please."

All the attention shifted on the day Sasha was to get out of the hospital. For the first time, the twins could go to school without someone trying to take their picture or ask them a question.

Campbell's professors were more than understanding, and other nurses took her shifts. Rick volunteered to work the store alone until the uproar died down. But when the twins came home from school just over a week after the day Sasha was unmasked, Uncle Kevin and Frank Novak were at the house, with a story to share with the family.

Sasha was wheeled out of the hospital by Bonnie, who looked ashamed to touch the wheelchair handles. Sasha was smiling for the camera through her bruises, waiting for her sweetie to bring the truck, Tim later said, so she could "go off somewhere and do it all over again."

No one heard what a small, neatly dressed woman in a gray cardigan said to Sasha just before she was about to give an interview to CBS. No one, that is, except Bonnie Jellico, who recognized Gwenny Brynn, the twins' grandmother.

"I think Sasha, that you must have good in you," said Grandma Gwenny. "There were moments I saw good in you. Perhaps you can redeem your life. I hope that is the path that chooses you." Gently, she laid her hand on Gwenny's arm. "I will know. Be assured of that. And if you lay evil on another head, you will never sleep. You will see things you cannot imagine. You will see the sun go down in fear. I promise you." She stood up and smiled brightly. "Hello, Bonnie. How is the little one? Enjoy your day!"

Gwenny Brynn strode away in her cheerful way.

Sasha decided to forego the interview. Taillights were the last anyone saw of Sasha Avery.

BEYOND THIS NIGHT

BEYOND THIS NIGHT

Graduation was that morning.

Merry dressed carefully in a jersey with tights and a long, loose, and light sweater. Mallory dressed slowly in clothes she did not realize were muted, feeling more than a bit weepy. Both girls were on the way to see their senior friends get their diploma.

That long summer lay ahead, but Drew would never drive the twins to school again in the Green Beast.

This would be the last time.

The twins waited for their grandmother, whom they regarded with more than the usual respect since Bonnie's dramatic rendition of what they now referred to as "the curse of Gwenny." It was difficult, still, to laugh, difficult to celebrate, difficult not to imagine the blameless, broken life of Sasha's little girl, Monique. It was hard not to picture Owen, still and silent. There were thoughts from which the girls still had to rush away.

That bright morning, Mallory tried to think of what she would say to Drew.

And with no way of knowing if she would have a chance to say it, Meredith tried to think of what she would say to Ben.

Campbell went back to work for her first full-time day shift since the macabre circus had come to town. Grandma Gwenny was caring for Owen full-time during the days now, and Carla at night, while she studied for her RN. Even Campbell, stubborn as she was, had evident proof that Owen had a strong and stable family and that she would be wise to entrust him to their love. And while Carla might not be Mrs. Personality, she was as loyal as they came.

As soon as Grandma arrived, Meredith pulled on her black boots and took one last look in the mirror. Her face appeared dreamy— hair shining, lips rounded, almost as though Merry were a retouched photo of herself. Although she knew it was a little over-the-top, she had tied one side of her hair back with a red ribbon. She didn't have long black hair, but Ben would know what she meant when she saw him after the ceremony. If she did. If what she both feared and hoped came true.

Mallory called now, "Let's go. Neely's limo is outside."

"It's not a limo!" Merry said. Neely now had her driver's license, and along with her sixteenth birthday had come a bright red VW Jetta. ("Used," Neely told everyone. The car was one year old.) "It's just her car!"

"To me it's a limo. Closest I'll ever see to one," said Mallory.

This was not, in fact, true. When she became an adult, Mallory would have the occasion to ride in a limo often, as an author, researcher, and speaker, who would prove that communication by thought existed among high primates, such as chimpanzees and gorillas. Her books would be famous, and it would be she, not Merry, who would give birth to the next generation of Brynn twin girls. But since this was a piece of the future that was about her, she couldn't see it.

Meredith, the out-there, show-off twin, would be a homebody, living the life she had always wanted—as a teacher and cheer coach at Ridgeline and the mother of many children. She would eventually marry a young doctor named Drew Vaughn. There would be no hard feelings: She and Drew and her twin sister would remain best friends all their lives. Drew and Merry would live in the house where Merry grew up, the fifth generation of her family to do so.

Graduation day was a time for beginnings and endings, but had anyone asked the twins if they wanted to know what lay ahead, they would have said, with emphasis, "No way!"

That early afternoon, they sat on folding chairs on the football field, near Mr. and Mrs. Highland. After Drew passed across the stage, flashing his trademark goofy grin, one of the last of the graduates in line, the principal asked for a moment of silence.

"Today we wish to award a diploma to one of our own, a boy loved and missed at Ridgeline High, a fine student who would have grown up to be a fine man, who already was a fine man and did the finest thing anyone can do. He gave his life for his friend," said Mrs. Dandridge. "Recently, he has . . . come home. We'd like his parents to accept his diploma on his behalf."

The Highlands rose and walked slowly to the stage. As they did,

Ben appeared in a misty incarnation Merry had never seen—she thought, He's already going—wearing a black cap and gown just like the others. As the principal read, "Benjamin Charles Highland," and put the diploma into Helene Highland's hands, Ben leaned in to brush his mother's cheek with his own, and she raised her hand to touch. Then, suddenly, he was not there.

Merry had a brief sensation of what it would be like never to see Ben again. It was a piercing pain, but she would survive it.

EVER AFTER
EVER AFTER

Later, after the ceremony and before the parties, Drew obligingly drove the twins to Mountain Rest Cemetery. The moon was not yet up but was hovering in ghostly form, and the dusk was crisscrossed with bats and night birds.

As the twins walked down the pebbled path to Ben's grave, Mallory remembered her vision of the cemetery, of Ben asking Merry to come to him, to take his hand. Which could have meant only one thing.

She would trust. And wait.

What Mallory didn't know was that she had nothing to worry about: Merry was no longer tempted, even in the tiniest way, to leave her life. She wanted to see Owen and Adam grow up, and not through the veil of time. She wanted to see what passions of the non-romantic kind life held for her, what she might do or be. Her love for Ben was genuine, and, if he were here with her,

Merry thought she might want to be with him exclusively. Still, she couldn't promise forever. Forever could really be forever. Without her mother and father, and especially Mallory, Meredith did not think forever was possible for her to negotiate.

As Merry left Mallory, taking the last steps alone, Mallory whispered, "Giggy," twin language for "I love you."

Merry sat down on a fallen log and waited for Ben to arrive. Suddenly she heard a breath and realized he was next to her, standing, leaning against a tree—almost exactly as she had first seen him leaning against the wall at the shopping center under the old light pole. She jumped up and ran to him, holding up her face for Ben to kiss. He framed her face between his hands and, with his rainwater eyes, looked at every feature that made her Meredith.

"I'm going to have to remember you for a long time," Ben said. Meredith couldn't bear it anymore. She pulled his head to hers, feeling the electrical ecstasy of the sensation of the perfect fit, the expression of a love that fate had ordained and then denied. Standing there with Ben, Merry's resolve weakened. Her mind was a wild thing, crowded with Ben's smile, Ben's eyes, the spicy smell that, for seventy years, would remind her of Ben—pine and cinnamon. She fell into a dream. In it, they lay in tall grass, under a benign sun, her only worry being she would get freckles. Red-winged blackbirds swung on the longest stalks and, all around her, where the Haven Hills houses now stood, there were fields and the occasional sturdy upright saltbox farmhouse.

Beneath the surface of her fantasy, Merry knew that this was the scenery that they would have lived in together, and that it was gone, gone since her parents were children.

It was when he gently pulled away that she seemed to become conscious again, to fall back into her body. Merry wanted to return to the world of her dream, soaring in the heat and freedom of an extinguished summer.

Ben said, "Merry. We have to talk."

"Not now."

"Right now. Now is the only time we have."

"I know," Merry admitted.

"Merry. You were the one who told me. You were the one who showed me the path I had to walk and helped me tell my mom."

"I didn't mean it," Merry cried, getting to her feet. "I would take it back. I want you this way if I can't have you any other way. Ben! It isn't enough time. There's so much more left to say. Please don't leave me."

"Baby, I don't want to leave you. If there was any other way . . ."

"There is. You know there is."

Ben looked down at her. "Meredith, you would be the girl in my life, and you would be the woman in my life, but you're going to grow up and do something amazing. You're going to fall in love and get married and have children. You'll be so happy someday."

"Ben, I don't want all that without you," Merry said. "I don't. I don't."

"But you will. I know you will," Merry's cheeks burned and her eyes brimmed. Her longing was tempered by shame for the knowledge that Ben was right. She didn't want to make it harder for him, and it was time for both of them to let go. Holding her head back to keep the tears from spilling, Meredith looked up into a strong last ray of sun that pierced the dark fringes of the pines. The moon rocked on its back. With a huge effort, she swallowed and composed herself. Ben said, "And this thing you have, that you do. That's important. It saved my mom's life. You were meant to do that."

"Are you afraid?" she asked.

"No, Merry. I haven't been afraid since I first could talk to my mom and dad. If I'm afraid, it's of missing you. But who knows? Who knows how long it will seem to me until the time comes and you're ... there?"

Who did know what happened? Beyond? Would the fifteen-year-old Merry rise up someday from an eighty-eight-year-old body that had lived so long and well it had worn itself out? Would she run into Ben's arms, while the other woman she had been all her life held out her hand to the man she had loved for forty years or fifty years? What happened to widows? If they married again after their husbands died, whose wife would they be? What about Ben? Would he be a teenage boy offering his arm to his mother, one day? Or would he be six or eight, the boy in the apple tree, and jump into arms strong enough to lift and hold him? How hard she would hold him. Would the thought of that sustain Mrs. Highland?

Few people had proof of that kind of eternity.

Meredith could not imagine that the afterlife was a place where jealousy or first claim or mistakes had a hand in anything.

Ben said, "I know there's something that I have to do. I feel that.

I don't know what. Maybe souls come back, not this way, another way. Maybe as a baby. I don't think angels watch over people. I think angels are different from regular spirits." He smiled sadly. "But I know I'll always know about you, Meredith. I'll always know. Maybe I'm just whistling in the . . . dark. But that's what I think."

They stood up and, side by side, faced the grave. Just where the sun behind the tall peak of the memorial cast a long shadow over the grave with the black oval above it, they stopped. Merry saw something she had not noticed before, a small iron flag and cross behind the small and browning Valentine tree with its cheerful small hearts and rocking horses. Mrs. Highland still thought of Ben as her little boy.

"If I come here, will I have a stronger feeling? Of you?" Merry asked.

"I don't know," Ben said. "I hope there will be a way that I can touch your cheek or be there to brush your hair away from your face on . . . your wedding day," Ben's face crumpled. "Meredith, I love you."

"Ben," Merry said. "I wrote down something. From my father's poetry book." She read,

"How do I love thee? Let me count the ways.
I love thee to the depth and breadth and height
My soul can reach, when feeling out of sight
Smiles, tears, of all my life!—and, if God choose,
I shall but love thee better after death."

Merry closed Ben's hand around the folded paper. He folded it yet again and put it into his pocket. Merry said, "I don't know how to say goodbye. I want my life to seem like a moment so I can be with you again."

"They say it does pass like a moment if you live to be old. That's what I wanted. To write and grow old, to leave something behind. Do that for me. Don't wish your life away, Merry. Be happy every minute that you can. And don't say goodbye. Say, 'See you later, Ben.' Say, 'I'll remember you, Ben.' No one really dies who's remembered." Merry rushed toward Ben's arms and made the motion of a kiss. "Don't make it harder. There's something for you on my porch. Don't forget it. Promise."

Meredith tried to say that she promised, but she was sobbing too hard to speak. Then, just as a glow seemed to grow and pulse around Ben, as if he were lit from behind, he suddenly reached out both hands to Merry, pleading, and she nearly stepped forward to take them.

But rougher hands grabbed her around the waist and hauled her backward. She looked up as the light against the stainless sky was absorbed into the sun—up in icy altitudes where she could not go. Why did people think of heaven as up there? It was possibly right here, and hell, too. It was possible that it was never far away. Sasha was a representative of one reality and Ben another. Merry finally turned. There was Mallory, who held her twin against her shoulder, patting her as one of their parents might.

"Merry, I'm sorry. I knew you'd nearly give up at the last moment. Anyone would. And I couldn't let you go," Mallory said. "I knew there was a chance."

"I don't think he would have really taken me away."

"You were all surrounded by this glare. I almost couldn't see you."

"I think that's the deal," Merry finally said, exhausted as though she had run upstairs for hours. She said, "I feel as though I haven't breathed. Not really."

"I'm so sorry, Mer."

"Me, too. I don't know how much yet."

With Mallory's arm under her own, Merry stumbled toward Drew's truck, where he sat in the driver's seat, a Mets ball cap pulled down over his eyes. Mallory opened the door and the peppery, oniony locker-room smell of Drew's old car twined around her like the bonds of her life before Ben. She lay back as Drew put the truck in gear and turned around.

Then suddenly, she sat up.

"Stop!" she shouted at Drew. "I have to get something off the Highlands' porch. I almost forgot."

"Oh, fine," Drew said. "If it's a big gray pod that's going to crack open in the attic and devour my parents, I'll be okay with that. Nothing surprises me anymore."

With Mallory behind her, Meredith slowly climbed the Highlands' porch. At first, she could see nothing unusual. Then she spotted something in the old rocking chair at the far end of the porch. Ben's jacket. She held it to her face, rubbing its worn softness against her cheek, inhaling the soapy, piney Ben scent, wondering how long it could last, if it was already vanishing. She turned to the windows and waved at the Highlands, whether they were there or not. Even if they couldn't see her, it would not have surprised her if they knew.

Back in the car, Meredith laid the coat over her like a blanket and put her hands into the pockets. Her note on yellow paper with the lines from the poet whose name she couldn't recall, who married the man her parents tried to separate her from, was gone. But there was a scrap of paper. It was one of the last lines from Romeo and Juliet, and it said, "O, thinkst thou we shall ever meet again?"

Ben, Merry vowed in her mind, *I won't say goodbye. I'll say, "Ben, see you later." No one really dies who's remembered. The years will spin away, and I don't know what will happen in my life. But I'll remember you Ben. I'll remember you. I promise. I promise.*

Drew turned the corner toward the sun. Merry closed her eyes.

She would put the scrap of paper in her memory book, with her photos and her little-kid cheerleading certificates and . . . and the ribbon she wore today in her hair. She imagined someone finding it one day and finding it hard to believe that Mom or Grandma was ever so young—as she sometimes found it hard to believe that her own mother or grandmother had been young and barely brushed by life, as Merry was now. She would hang the coat in her closet and, she suspected, touch it every day for a year, and then forget it and someday find it like a diamond earring that had rolled away, with that much incredulous, nearly painful delight. As she pictured that, the corners of her mouth turned up in a smile.

Mallory turned to sneak small glances at her sister. She seemed to be asleep, but her hands kept exploring and stroking that old jacket.

And Meredith smiled, all the way home.

THE ANCESTORS

THE ANCESTORS

t was midsummer, at the family camp high on Crying Woman Ridge, when Meredith finally summoned the courage to tell her grandmother all about Ben.

As usual, they had their private conversation when everyone else was swimming, and Grandma had asked Meredith to help her strip corn for the pot that was already boiling on its iron hook above the fire pit. Potatoes were turning black and flaky among the coals, and soon everyone would come tromping up the steps.

No one outside Tim's family knew what Grandma Gwenny had said to Sasha that day at the hospital. But there were moments when Tim called his mother "Tiger," in reference to her willingness to battle on behalf of her own—though she slapped away his teasing with a flick of her hand. When everyone had gone for a swim, Merry seized her moment.

"Grandma, I know that most of us only thought about Owen last winter, but do you remember, before he really got sick, asking me if I was I was constipated or in love?" Merry asked, nearly smiling at a memory she thought would always make her cry. The air was punctuated with early fireflies, although, blessedly, the mosquitoes that adored Merry and Mally's necks and backs seemed to avoid them at the camp. Grandpa said it was because of the wintergreen he had planted all around the six cabins and the entrance.

Grandma's nod was somehow moody. From the town below came the sweet, mournful distant sound of a train whistle, the sound that awakened a person at night and made her yearn for something she didn't even know for sure was out there. Gwenny didn't say anything. She simply tucked her feet up under her on the bench and kept carefully stripping the leaves and silk from the corn. Merry wondered how many women Grandma's age could curl up in a chair like a teenager; clearly the yoga Grandma took every Sunday after church at the community center was doing her good.

Finally, Merry said, "Well, I was in love. I think I still am."

Grandma said, "Yes. That's clear."

"There's a big problem, though," Merry began and told Grandma everything, including how much she had wanted, on some level, to join Ben in the beyond. She told her grandmother about the light that exploded between them when they tried to touch and the moment in the cemetery when the light was as bright as a sun on the ground.

"Well, Meredith, as a woman, I'm sorry for you that you didn't get to be with him as a lover. So far. But as a grandmother, I'm glad that fate got in the way," Gwenny said.

"Do you know the Highlands?"

"Yes. Less than some others, more than some others. I knew David and I knew Ben."

"Why was he here then, Grandma? Why did I love him and why does he love me?"

"I don't know. I can only guess that he was here because his physical body came home, although not on this plane, and because his mother was on the verge of death. Clearly, he hadn't crossed over."

"I don't think Mrs. Highland would let him."

"Maybe not."

"Grandma, I did want to be with him. If there's a life after this one, I would almost go . . ."

Grandma Gwenny got up and crossed over to the verge of the ridge, looking down on all her children as they sent bright drops into the faltering sun. As she had as a girl, as a young woman, as a mother. As Brynns would always, at least as long as Gwenny knew. Something more important than the sturdy wood of these cabins bound this family. Gwenny didn't think it was brains or beauty or even tolerance or talent. It was the loyalty that comes of appreciating the small things people have.

"Meredith," she finally said, coming back to the fire, "you have a better head on your shoulders than to even think about that. You proved it when you had the chance. And your sister was right to pull you back. That's what a twin does. But I know what the feeling is like, to want to join the other."

"Vera?"

"Yes, Vera. And someone else."

"If death is a transition to another world, better than this one . . ."

"Meredith, what would happen to you in that other world?"

"I'd be with Ben. I was supposed to be with Ben in this world."

Grandma Gwenny said slowly, "Do you think each of us has only one love?" Slowly, she slipped each ear of corn, twenty-four in all, into the huge bubbling cast-iron pot. They would use the water later to put out the fire.

Merry thought for a moment and finally said, "Yes. And no. Can you go on loving someone when you love someone else, with all your heart?" Merry asked. Her grandmother nodded. "Do you believe Ben was real?"

Grandma got up. "I have no doubt that he is." She picked up the shawl she'd been sitting on and draped it around her shoulder as the sunset brought a slight chill to the air. Then Grandma looked back at Meredith.

"You know, I loved a boy before Grandpa. I loved him my junior and senior year in high school. I loved him as I thought I could never love anyone else. Perhaps I did love him as I could never love anyone else."

"Why did you end it?" Meredith asked.

"I didn't. He died. Like your Ben."

"How?"

"He died in the Korean War, Meredith."

"I'm sorry," Merry said. "But I can't imagine you with anyone but Grandpa."

"So you see what I mean," Grandma Gwenny said. "I'm not saying I don't love Kevin still. I always will. But life had other plans for me. And for him. I'm not saying that your love wasn't real, or that there wasn't a reason for you to have loved him. I don't know what it is. I'm just saying wait and see. You are so young."

"What about Romeo and Juliet?"

"What about them?" Grandma asked. "Why is this play taught to every high school and college student as the greatest of Shakespeare's tragedies? 'For never was a story of more woe, than this of Juliet and her Romeo.' There's a reason. The real meaning is that even real love can cost a sane person her reason. And no one who's young, pardon me, Merry, really has all her reason yet."

"I've heard more poetry in the past month than in the rest of my life combined."

"Good for your memory," Grandma Gwenny said. "Does your sister know? All about this?"

"Yes. She's been with me every step, Grandma."

"Imagine how it would have been without her," Grandma said. Meredith did think. For all those months, so often she had simply wished Mallory would . . . disappear, that she could be frozen in time standing still with some sort of psychic remote control. But now, she realized that Mallory's dear, sour, earth-bound ways had saved her, kept her tethered to a real world Meredith wanted to reject. "Did you get angry with Mallory? Did you think she was trying to stand in your way?

"I don't know. I might have. I was trying to prove that Ben was here, that he was real . . ."

"Now do both you and your sister think he's here and that he's real, even though he might have passed over a long time ago?"

"Yes." Then a thought popped up. "Kevin! You named one of your children Kevin."

"I've always thought it was a good, strong name."

Meredith thought about heaven. Would this Kevin be there? Would he like Grandpa? How would they share, if they did share? Would everyone find a way to rejoice?

Thirty-five years later, Meredith would remember that night, when she was fifteen, as her firstborn son, Benjamin Brynn Vaughn, graduated from the University of Chicago Medical School.

The occasion would cause a big stir. Benjamin was the first of the grandchildren. Campbell and Tim were brimming with pride, along with their sisters and brothers and Mallory's husband, as well as all five of the twins' combined offspring—young men and women themselves. Adam was there with his wife and son and Owen with his wife and daughters, Mary and Melody, just a slight variation on the names of the older sisters he adored.

Watching and beaming, also, were Grandma Gwenny and Mrs. Highland, who had become great friends, although not, as Grandma said, on this plane. They congratulated each other and the boy's namesake, Ben, who was sometimes a young boy and sometimes the teenager who had loved Merry long ago and loved her still.

And there were other witnesses too, Brynns and Vaughns and Highlands from hundreds of hundreds of years before. They had attended every wedding, helped usher every new baby into the world, stood close to every hospital bed as human life ebbed, as the bright light dissolved and the newcomers learned that heaven was not so very different from human life—minus all the wondering.

They welcomed every family member with abundant love and joy and recognition, as ancestors always will.

ACKNOWLEDGMENTS

The author wishes to thank Dorothea, a psychic medium who spoke to me of crossing over, and Dr. Elliott P., professor emeritus of psychology, who shared with me his experiences with Munchausen syndrome. I thank also Ben Schrank, the best pal a manuscript ever had, and always, Jane Gelfman, agent best pal, and my beloved friend and coworker, Pamela English. No words can describe your influence on my words. Thanks also to you, my reader, for welcoming Merry and Mally into your hearts, and my children—Rob, Dan, Marty, Francie, Mia, Will, and Atticus—for putting up with me.

March, 2009,
Savusavu, Fiji